Gold Bars

and Jaguars

Philip L. Moore

Gold Bars and Jaguars
Philip L. Moore

Paperback Edition First Published in Great Britain
in 2015 by Defiant Publishers

eBook Edition First Published in Great Britain
in 2015 by Defiant Publishers

Disclaimer

This is a work of fiction. Names, characters, businesses, places,
events and incidents are either the products of the author's
imagination or used in a fictitious manner. Any resemblance to
actual persons, living or dead, or actual events
is purely coincidental.

ISBN: 978-1-908073-01-3
Defiant Publishers

defiantpublishers@gmail.com
http://www.philiplmoore.com

Dedication

STEF WAUTERS
31st August 1971 to 14 November 2014
"a true friend" RIP

THE HATTON GARDEN HEIST GANG "RESPECT!
HATS OFF TO THEM."

GOLD BARS AND JAGUARS IS AVAILABLE IN
SCRIPT FORMAT AS A SCREENPLAY

IF AN INDUSTRY PROFESSIONAL WISHES TO
APPLY FOR A COPY PLEASE CONTACT THE
AUTHOR/SCRIPT WRITER PHILIP L MOORE

info@philiplmoore.com
www.philiplmoore.com

SCRIPT IS AVAILABLE IN PDF FORMAT FOR £15.00
TO FIND OUT MORE FOLLOW
GOLD BARS AND JAGUARS ON FB

OTHER WORKS BY THIS AUTHOR

AMELIA'S DAUGHTER

KEZ (Every decade needs a hero)

THERAPY (A BOOK OF POEMS)

ETERNAL WISH

UTTERLY RIDICULOUS

All these books are available on Kindle download through Amazon

For paperback's please contact the author

info@philiplmoore.com
www.philiplmoore.com

Chapter One

*L*et me introduce myself, the name's Squid... "SQUID RYAN!" son of James Ryan... A lovable rogue as my mother Sylvia used to refer to him as, this meant dear old dad wasn't around as much as he should have been. As a child mum would tell me the Queen has sent him on holiday for a while. Of course, as I got older, I got to understand he was "Banged up!" So, you can probably guess my life was going one of two ways, either I follow in his footsteps or I try to change things and go down the old straight and narrow route. After seeing what my father was up too, all I ever wanted was a quiet life, to meet the right partner, have a couple of kids, one of each of course, and be in good health. "Well isn't that a cliché I hear you say!" I mean why should my dream be any different from anyone else's? Maybe that was Dads dream as well, but we all know dreams don't always go to plan.

I'm a family man. Family is everything to me, and as a father all I want is for my kids to grow up to be the best they can. "Just like any good father" I hear you saying! Well I wish I could say that's how my father thought, but he was more interested in the good life and making money quickly. We have all heard it said or had someone say to us "Life is what you make it!" Well my father's saying was "life is for the taking and you have to take as much as you can!" For me the first works best, although it's not exactly true. I can tell you that first hand, I wonder how many people reading this story can relate to what I mean, for as I mentioned, many of you will know even the best made plans have

1

hick-ups somewhere along the line. This is usually caused by other people interfering in "Our plan." One or two is expected, four or five is put down to bad luck, more than that, then you are doing something wrong, "It's your fault!" So, imagine on top of all the normal stumbling blocks life throws at you, then you're having to put up with being pursued by the criminal underworld and the police as well as a curse. "A curse!" I hear you say? Yes a curse! Now you are all thinking Mummies, tombs along with ancient scrolls, cobwebs, spiders, and ghostly figures. Sorry but no! This was a different kind of curse; nevertheless it was still a curse which regularly raised its ugly head, disrupting my plan for a normal life. Yet, I still made the best of things. Even today with all this shit behind me, the only difference being I have crossed a line I never wanted to cross. So, this is my story.

I was born Stuart Ryan, but from an early age "Squid" became my nick-name and it stuck like shit to a blanket. Remember me mentioning my dad? Well, what I forgot to mention was he was a bank robber, yes stocking or balaclava over the face and sawn off shotgun . . . that sort of bank robber. Back in the 80's my father was one of the Brinks Mat bullion robbers, and there my dear friends is your curse "The Brinks Mat Curse." Looking back on things now I am guessing dear old dad did care about me and wanted the best, it's just his idea of the best was doing a job. He did say to me once, when I was visiting him in Ford prison as a child, that being banged up was just a hick-up. And that once he was out and the right "job" comes along, one day I would have everything and would never want for nothing. Well that "Right Job" did come along, but it wasn't planned. It was a bit of a surprise for us all to be honest, it was one of those life- changing moments for everyone. So, let me take you back to 1983 when I was a spotty 16 year old kid.

It's the 25th of November 1983, and a sixteen year old boy, with red hair called "Squid" is watching 633 Squadron on TV. The theme music to 633 Squadron is heard as the film is half way through. The clock on the front room wall reads 6:33am.

Like most teenagers Squid is as skinny as hell but never seems to stop eating, so, being hungry, he gets up goes to the kitchen to raid the cupboards. His focus changes in a second from watching the film to food, yet Squid can hear the film in the back of his head playing away on video.

"That's Norway, and you can have it." Says' a voice on the telly.

Cannon fire thumps out through the tiny speaker of the large monster of a TV. Squid grabs a bowl and a packet of Corn Flakes. He tips the Corn Flakes into the bowl, then plods over to the fridge and gets out a pint of milk. This fridge was very temperamental, the seal on the door either stuck like glue or it didn't stick at all. So, every time Squid opened it, it either opened with ease or he had to pull like hell and it popped open suddenly hitting him on the head. This particular day it hit him on the head, leaving a bright red lump.

"Fucking fridge!" Squid shouted rubbing his head.

Like in many households, the fridge is covered in fridge magnets holding notes to other members of the family which have been read once and left, or just ignored. One note is tatty and worn, it was placed there by Squids mother Sylvia Ryan. It reads "Don't forget to go to Spain this year!" Spain had never happened the reminder still sits there, just one of many family jokes. The pint is un-opened and Squid can see the cream at the top. He relishes the thought of being the one to have the cream of the milk. That lovely yellowy bit sat on top of the white, which we're now told we can no longer enjoy. Squid presses his thumb into the foil removing the cap; quickly he looks around at the TV as he hears:

"Got bandits up ahead boys, got bandits up above, keep down low."

This is a good bit of the film, the music the flying, its epic! Squid tips up the milk bottle over the Corn Flakes, but nothing comes out. But there's nothing unusual in that, it often happened if the cream was a little thick, so he gives it a shake as he watches this action packed scene. Then, "PLOP" it's fucking happened all over the table and Squid's only pair of work trousers. The frigging milk had gone off, and now Squid is covered in sour cream.

"Fucking hell!" Squid shouts jumping back.

Squid starts to urge at the smell, why didn't it smell like that when he popped the top open? And why is it always bloody Corn Flakes! Just once in a while, it would have been nice for his mother to have picked up some Sugar Puffs, or Coco Pops even, but no in the Ryan house back then it was always Corn Flakes! Pissed off he grabs a tea towel and wipes himself down, trying not to vomit as he does so. Squid then walks over to the TV and turns it off, he's lost interest in the movie now, and he needs to try to lighten the stain on the front of his trousers before he sets off to work. Squid walks through the front room to the base of the stairs.

"Mum the fucking milks off." He shouts up to her.

"You sure?" replies Sylvia, Squid's mother.

"Mum it's off, it stinks, I ain't stupid I know the difference between a pint of milk and a fucking yogurt. I mean, come on this isn't rocket science is it?" Squid explains.

"Oi language, and don't be cheeky, now ask your father to check it?" she replies.

"Dad's in the crapper! Why does no-one ever listen to me? I am not some fucking idiot who doesn't know whether the milk is good, bad, or fucking ugly yogurt!" DAAADDD....... Squid shouts once more.

"What . . . Can't I have a crap in peace? I'll be down in a minute." replies James Ryan.

"The milk's off. Mum said I had to get you to check it, but it stinks and it's thick like lumps of yogurt, It's fucking off." Squid replies.

"Well what do you need me for? I can't make it un-off. Can I?" shouts James.

"I know that, I was just letting mum know we ain't got no milk, that's all." Squid replies.

"Well, have you told her?" asks James smiling to himself.

"For fuck sake yes, you must have just heard me you deaf old git." she said to tell you."

Squid is now getting very frustrated at this stupid and pointless conversation.

"Well, you sure it's off, you haven't opened a yogurt by mistake have yah?" replies James.

"Old-man, take it from me it's off."

"Mother, the fucking milks off again, have you paid the bloody milk bill?" James asks Sylvia.

"Are you sure, have you tried it?" asks Sylvia.

"Why the fuck would I want to fucking try it if it's fucking off you silly cow?" replies James.

"Don't call me a silly cow you fucking bastard, if we ain't got no milk then send Squid down the shop to get some." Sylvia shouts back not wanting to move from her nice warm bed.

"Squid, your mother said go down the shop and get some." James shouts down to Squid from his cosy thrown whilst he tries to read yesterday's paper.

Squid shakes his head, he really doesn't want to walk to the shop and back now, all he wanted to do was to simply inform his Mother and Father that they have no milk.

"I ain't got no money."

"For fuck sake, all I want to do is have a fucking crap in peace . . . shit! I'll be down in a minute." James shouts back.

"Check my purse Squid." replies Sylvia.

"OK"

Squid hunts for his mother's purse, which he finds in her bag. Down one side he spots a bunch of notes folded over. Looking over his shoulder he pulls out the wad of cash, there is over two hundred pounds, so, Squid pulls out a twenty and sticks it in his pocket. Carefully putting the cash back where he found it he opens the purse as he hears the toilet flush.

James, an overweight forty year old in a string vest and white Y fronts, walks down the stairs, each step creaking as he does so.

"What the fuck is that smell, and what's that down your trousers? You got excited son?" mocked James when, he saw the state of his son's trousers.

"The milk's off? Is that what that smell is?" Sylvia shouts down.

"That's what I have been trying to tell you both, for the last ten minutes, . . . for fuck sake!"

The stairs creak slightly again as Sylvia comes down to join them.

"Oi watch your fucking language." she says as she slaps Squid around the side of the head.

"I stink; I am going to get changed. Dad you got some cash for the milk then, mums purse is empty?"

"Oh there's a surprise!" says Sylvia with sarcasm.

James walks over to the radio and switches it on ignoring Squid's request; The Flying Pickets are playing 'Only You'.

James grabs Sylvia and has a little dance with her. Sylvia, an attractive woman in her late thirties, still quite petite, with bleached blonde hair shrugs him off.

"Get off you daft bastard."

"Who needs money when we have love, my sweet?" replied James with a smile.

As James swirls Sylvia around the room he catches a glimpse of his series three Jaguar through the curtains sitting on the drive waiting for him to put some more fuel in it. He smiles as if he has all he needs.

As Squid leaves the room to get changed, he smiles at the two shaking his head. He sees his father smiling at the Jag, it was his pride and joy.

"I need some dinner money as well." he shouts climbing the stairs.

"Ask your mother son I'm skint." James replies.

"All I wanted was some fucking cereal." Squid mumbles under his breath.

"Maybe if your mother will lend me a few quid to get some fuel, I could run you to the shop, save you putting on your bike gear?" James replies hopefully.

Sylvia pushes him away and walks to the kitchen to put the kettle on.

Time for a cupper I think, says Sylvia as she enters the kitchen.

There's no milk sweetheart replies James with a slight snigger.

"FUCK IT!" Sylvia storms out of the kitchen and heads back up to bed.

There was a lot of fucking going on in them days and none of it was in the bedroom. Vocabulary was not my parents' strong point. So that's what every morning was like. I was used to the old man being a bit dodgy, he was often away on holiday at Her Majesty's pleasure, but at 6.33 am on 26th November 1983, everything would change forever! A "curse", as they called it, would be created that day. A curse which would follow me through my life until such I time when I am forced to deal with it.

Inside a warehouse close to Heathrow airport, was James Ryan, known to his friends as (Mustaffa) because of his wandering eye. James was on a job, a bank job, with five of his mates. There was "The Colonel" who, as you can guess, always wanted to be in charge. Then there was "Avalon." Again, his real name sounded like a member of Roxy Music, a band from the seventies, so it stuck. Just like the nickname Squid, all the gang member had picked up strange names over the years, this was no different for the other members of the gang. One was referred to as "The Mule" or just Mule. This had something to do with a 1950's film "Francis..123rd Mule Detachment...[serial number] M52519."And the fact he always wore a donkey jacket! We are then left with "Mad Mickey", whose name says it all, and "Bullyboy." Bullyboy was the nastiest member of the gang, and if the truth was known, they were all scared of him. He was very unpredictable. This gang was a bunch of small time crooks, who had been in and out of court or prison most of their teenage and adult life.

Together they pulled off the Brinks Mat Heist, a robbery that would change the way the criminal underworld operated forever. The gang gained entry to the warehouse by one of their mates who worked there as a security guard. He was known as "The Black Widow." James thought his gang were going to steal three million in cash, as that is what "The Black Widow " had told them was in the safe. But, what they failed to notice when entering the warehouse was three million quid sat on a pallet right in front of them. Admittedly it was covered over with a sheet, but they could have been in and out in minutes if only one of them had noticed it. But, the Black Widow had stated it was in a safe, so it was to the safe they all went. They soon had the other guards incapacitated, leaving them free to claim their reward. However, once inside they had a problem. With a pair of Sylvia's tights pulled over his face, James looked quite comical as one of the legs dangled down from his left ear.

"Fuck it, there's a safe!" said James as he looked at a huge set of doors, both had a combination lock on each door.

"Well of course there's a fucking safe, what did you think? There was going to be three million quid sat in the middle of the warehouse? There's always a safe, we're bank robbers Mustafa, with bank robbers come safes." replied Avalon.

"Yes I know about safes Avalon, but look at the fucker . . . it's the size of the Queen bloody Mary!" explained James.

The others promptly looked round at the two huge doors which had been behind the roller shutter James had just lifted up. The Colonel looked at his distorted reflection in the stainless steel doors, lowering his arm which held a crowbar. He then preceded forward a few steps and as he loosened his grip, the tool dropped to the floor. They all turned to The Black Widow as the noise of the crowbar hitting the floor echoed around the warehouse.

"When you said a fucking safe, I thought you meant a fucking safe, one I could jimmy open. Not a fucking fortress, my names not fucking Oddball you know, I haven't got a bloody Tiger tank outside to blow the bloody doors in." said The Colonel.

"Well it is a safe, just a bit of a bigger safe." explained The Black Widow.

Bullyboy bent down and picked up the crowbar.

"I am going to shove this up your jacksy and rip out your intestines, fool, bloody fool." shouted Bullyboy as he moved towards The Black Widow.

James moved in and stopped him.

"We're buggered boys, we should get the hell out of here!" replied Avalon as he stood staring at the safe doors.

"Buggered . . . buggered, buggered means to be done up the arse, to have a penis inserted up your bottom. Do you feel like you have a penis up you bottom right now Avalon? Because I am thinking larger, much larger, more like a full on anal assault with that forklift over there! That's how buggered we are." explained Bullyboy.

"Why would they have a forklift in here Mustafa?" asked Mule.

"Because it's a warehouse Mule, and in warehouses they have forklifts OK?" replied James.

"Have you ever seen three million in cash? It don't fit in a suitcase Mule, it's probably on a pallet." explains Mad Mickey.

"Now what do we do?" asked Avalon

"I tell you what we do, we stop with the negative waves as oddball would say and work out a solution." replied Bullyboy.

Suddenly there was the sound of a forklift revving up. They turn to see Mad Mickey speeding towards the doors.

"I'll get the fuckers open. I am going to ram the bastards!" Screamed Mad Mickey as the forklift sped towards the doors.

"Well this is going to hurt!" announced The Colonel, looking at the other four.

The forklift made contact at around 30 miles an hour stopping dead and throwing Mad Mickey into the safe doors knocking him out cold.

"Now I know why they call him Mad Mickey." explained James.

"Mule go to the Jag and get out my Glock!" Mustafa said pointing to the door.

"What you going to do?" Asked Avalon.

"Put a bullet in one of these guard's brains if they don't hurry up and tell us the combination!" Mustafa explained.

Bully Boy started to ruff up one of the tied up guards, but he wasn't talking. Mule soon returned holding the clock out of the Jag.

"What the fuck is that Mule?" asked Bully Boy.

"It's the clock out of Mustafa's Jag, he told me to go get it." Mule replied.

"I said Glock you moron! GLOCK!!" Mustafa shouted.

"You could tell him the time as you hit him over the head with it." said Avalon, laughing as he took the clock from Mule and threw it to Mustafa.

"You better not have made a hole in my dash Mule, you know how much I love that Jag." Mustafa said as he threw the clock back to Mule.

"Errrr, well, I'll just go put it back and get the gun. A Glock you say, and it's in the dash?" Mule repeated to himself as he headed back to the door.

"Don't bother Mule, I have had enough of this shit." replied Bully Boy and he walked out of the door towards the small van they had parked outside. He soon returned with a can of petrol in his hand, walking over to one of the guards who was still tide up, he covered the man in petrol.

"Now one of you bastards knows the combination, now is the time to tell me!" screamed Bully Boy in the man's face.

"Hey we said, just in and out, no violence remember?" said James.

"So why did we bring shotguns, and why tell me to get the Glock?" asked Mule looking confused.

"It was a bluff, I was bluffing . . . ok?" Mustafa replied as he scratched his head where the tights were irritating him.

James stood between Bully Boy and the guard, who was now wriggling and screaming under his gaffer taped mouth, trying to get away. Bully Boy stood back slightly and pulling out a box of matches lit one.

"Damn it man no! I don't want murder on my conscious; I don't want any part of this, let's just leave it and go!" screamed James, trying to keep Bully Boy away from the guard.

"Come on Bully Boy, Mustafa is right, I doubt these guys even know the combination." replied Avalon.

But, Bully Boy was having none of it. Knocking James to the ground he drops the match in the struggle , James immediately rolls on it putting out the flame, before it could do any harm to the guard. Bully Boy stood back laughing.

"I mean it you fuckers, this time I will do it!" he screamed totally out of control.

The guard's eyes widened then quickly he started to nod his head letting Bully Boy know he would co- operate. Pulling off the tape from the guard's mouth, Bully Boy looked at the man straight in the eyes.

"Now Sonny Jim, you had better get this right first time. Now what's the numbers, or do I need to light another match?"

Within minutes Mad Mickey was awake and the doors to the safe opened. As they pulled the big doors back there was total silence and you could hear a pin drop in the room.

"What's all those brass bars doing under the cash Mustafa?" asked Mule.

"That's not brass Mule . . . That's GOLD!" James replied.

What followed was one of those thirty second celebratory moments that happens in your head but not in reality, you know corks popping out of Champagne bottles, streamers, balloons, grown men cuddling and jumping around in circles like a bunch of ten year old school girls. Like I said, but not in reality. From what the old man told me, they just stood there gawping at it, too stunned for words. You could hear a feather settle on the floor. They had stumbled on, by accident, three tonnes of gold bullion, over 7000.00 ingots, three million in cash, and 6 million in cut and un-cut diamonds. The total heist was well over £26 million pounds Stirling.

"How're we going to get that in the back of Mad Mickey's Astra van and Mustafa's Jag?" asked Mule.

"We don't, come on lads we need to act fast; Mustafa, Avalon and Mule go find the keys to the security vans parked outside, Mad Mickey you best try to get that forklift going again. Then, we'll load up and it's each man for himself." replied The Colonel, taking charge and organising everyone.

As Mad Mickey reverses the fork lift he hits a pallet sat on the floor of the warehouse which is covered over with a sheet, as the two make contact with one another, bundles of cash fall all over the floor. Three million in cash, it had been there right under their noses all the time. Now it seemed to have little value as the gold and the other cash was loaded in the vans.

"Just grab what you can and leave the rest, we need to get going." said Mustafa, as he threw a few more bundles in the van.

Moments later, well two and a half hours later, three Brinks Mat Transit security vans scream down the road past Heathrow airport with two occupants inside each one. James is with Mad Mickey, as they come to a crossroad and each van speeds off in a different direction.

This South London gang of six armed robbers, headed by my dear old dad James Ryan, had just pulled off one of the biggest heists in history....by accident. I really must re-affirm what they had just accomplished as it changed the cause of history. They were expecting to make off with about 3 million in cash. They left with over 26 million pounds worth of Gold Bullion weighing 3 tons in 76 boxes, over 7000.00 gold ingots, plus two boxes of Diamonds and an undisclosed amount of new cash! Using three security vans, they were then able to steal the lot and get away undetected. Hats off to the old man, it had been a Swift operation. But a fluke.

"We fucking done it, we've only fucking done it!" screamed James

"Yeeeerrrrrrhhhhhooooooo, no-one's going to stop us now." screamed Mad Mickey

"We need to get hold of Charlie, he's working on that new road, and he might know where we can hide this lot for a day or two." said James.

"There is a phone box by Denham Airfield we can call him before he leaves for work." replied Mad Mickey.

Keeping the conversation brief, as they knew there was a good chance someone at the telephone exchange might be listening, the two men arranged to meet up with Charlie. James then heads over to the airfield where he has a workshop space in one of the hangars. Mad Mickey looks at his watch, it's 9:15 am and no sign of any police.

Now whilst all this is going on, I'm at work in the scrap metal yard thinking about the best way to try to get into the pants of my sweetheart Jenny Davison. She was a laugh but she was from a better class than me, she was what we called a Posh girl. She went to the high school, but we had been friends now for about six months, walking to and from her school together hand in hand . . . it was nice. We even hung out together after school sometimes and met up at the local café. Jenny had even started to come and visit me on afternoons and Saturdays at my place of work in the breakers yard. It was nice, she made me feel like we could do anything together. I guess this was normal life for a sixteen year old boy whose hormones were going through the roof.

At 11:15am James kept looking at his watch. A splash of white paint on it, cheesed him off a little and he sat there wiping it with his thumb.

"Wouldn't worry about that old thing, will be able to buy a Rolex now." said Mad Mickey who was sat there watching him.

"Yeah, never thought of that, where we heading?" asked James.

"Andover" replied Mad Mickey.

"How much further is it? I can't believe we have seen no coppers." said James.

"Just a few miles to go and I doubt the pigs even know yet. Charlie said he is going to meet us on the edge of that new stretch of road." replied Mad Mickey.

The two men glance over their shoulders at all the gold, cash and diamonds. James picks up a gold bar and kisses it with such passion. This was the heist of heists, all their worries are now over.

"Brilliant. Squid my boy, you'll never want for anything ever from now on . . . it's the easy life for us all!" screams James excitedly.

"Yes dad. The easy life! Thanks for that!"

The two men drive on until they reach the road works.

"You are late! Thought the cops may have got you, as you said, it's something dodgy." explained Charlie who was a slim chap who stood over six foot three.

"Mate you are not going to believe this, we hit the jackpot. Turns out there was far more there than any of us knew about." replies an excited Mad Mickey who was slightly shorter at just five foot four.

"How much more?" asks Charlie.

James, who was the largest of the three weighing around eighteen stone jumps out of van, walks to back of it and opens rear doors.

"This much more." replies James "And this is just a third of the haul, the others have the rest in their vans."

"Wow, shit this is big. Fuck what the hell we going to do with all this? There was no mention of gold and diamonds. Cash you said when we spoke the other day, a cash only job, in and out. It was supposed to be an easy haul remember, used notes only. This is shit man, real shit. I trust I get a decent cut if I help you out? I mean this is far bigger than we discussed over the phone. When the pigs find out about this, it's going to be mayhem. Fuck man fuck, there must be millions here?" said Charlie.

"We're going to have to sit on this for quite some time." explained Mad Mickey.

"You sure you haven't been followed? I bet the shit's hit the fan by now. You need to make sure there's no sort of tracking devise on this van? You know how clever these security people are these days?" replies Charlie in a bit of a panic.

"Charlie calm down, it's all cool no one knows yet, they're not even looking for us." Replies James as he smiles and pats Charlie on the back. James throws Mickey and Charlie some bundles of cash,

"Just smell it lovely ain't it!" James said with the smile of a Cheshire cat. Between them they put it into sacks and bags.

"Look we take this for now. This will tide us over until the heat disappears. We are going to have to play it by ear as to when we can touch it. Can we take your car Charlie? You can get a lift home with one of the lads. Just make sure this is well hidden and don't tell a sole, no one else needs to know about this." explained James.

"Yes, listen I know this guy down in Kent "Noye" he might be able to help, but I am telling you now this man is mean, mean and ruthless no one crosses him. I will grab a lift with my mate Tony, here are the keys." replied Charlie throwing a set of keys to James.

"This Noye might be able help with the gold, not sure about the diamonds though James? I mean where the hell does one get rid of this shit? From the way the others were talking there must be over twelve million here. We're not geared up for this. It was supposed to be cash only." asked Mad Mickey starting to stress.

"I know, I know, look I don't have the answers, for now we can live like kings on this cash. We can just have some fun for now, but don't get caught. Charlie lets load up your car, we need to get home so things don't look out of the norm. Mickey you can drop me in Salisbury road, that's where Mule was dropping off my Jag. I've heard of this chap Kenny, I believe his name is, let's hope he can help." said James.

Back at home in Croydon, Sylvia is cooking tea, and it is late afternoon by the time James gets home. He walks in happy slaps Sylvia on her arse, and then heads to the bathroom for bath, where he lies there soaking with the biggest smile on his face a man could have.

None of us were any the wiser that day, Dad just seemed a little happier than normal, well you would be wouldn't you?

27th November 1983 Day after the robbery.

Squid picks up a bowl, grabs the cereal, and then goes back and gets the milk from the fridge which opens with ease. Sitting down he watches once again 633 Squadron, mimicking the words as the pilot is talking where he has seen the movie so many times. As he does so he tips up the packet of Corn Flakes and then goes to pour the milk over them.

"Fuck me, Mum . . . mum . . . " shouted Squid.

"What is it now Squid? If the fucking milks off again I am going to kill that stupid fucking milk man." Sylvia replied.

"I think I won that prize they put into the cereal packets every so often!" shouted Squid up the stairs.

"What crap are you on about now?" Sylvia shouted back.

"You gotta see this, my cereal packets full of cash!" Squid shouted back excitedly.

Squid nudges the wads of cash with his spoon in bowl. James who was still very sleepy suddenly sat bolt upright next to Sylvia.

"My cash, fuck. I hid that there in case the pigs came round."

"Wanker, he always has cereal for breakfast, next time try the sauce pans he never uses them." replied Sylvia as she slaps James round the head.

"Leave it out woman, I've only just fucking woke up." said James as he rubbed his head.

"Anyway where did you get a load of cash? Do a job last night did we?" she asked her eyes wide.

"Ah that's the point. I was here all night with you, wasn't I? So, I couldn't have done anything could I? But, should anyone come asking, like the pigs or anyone else come to that, I was out decorating a place with Chris yesterday and here all night. Ok?" James explained with a smile.

"OK come out wiv it, what you done? You still pissed, because you look like the cat that got the bloody cream. So come on out wiv it what you done?" once more Sylvia slaps James around the head trying to get him to answer.

"Princess, sweetheart I can't say much but we're rich, rich beyond our wildest dreams!" James replied.

"OK now I know you are pissed, or on something. Look me in the eyes let me see your pupils." said Sylvia as she pulled at his eyes with both hands.

"Will you stop it woman. What's up wiv you? Most women would be content at being millionaires." James explained pushing away her hands from his face.

"Millionaires!" replied Sylvia.

"Yes, that's what we are fucking millionaires. We just can't touch it for a day or two. So if anyone asks where I was and you can't remember, just say we were making love." James replied.

"Well now I know you are on something, it's that funny weed of your Chris's isn't it? If you haven't fucking noticed, we live on a rundown council estate in frigging Croydon, and it's not even the nice side of Croydon. The last time we stayed up all night making love was . . . well . . . fucking never, we haven't . . . ever!"

Sylvia got up from the bed and slapped James once more.

"Will you cut it out woman, honest my sweet, just except were fucking rich. Now go down and see what Squid's up to wiv that cash. Then later I will take you out and buy you something nice." James replied.

Whilst Squid listened to the arguing upstairs he promptly preceded to stuff cash anywhere he could before his mother came down. In his socks down his pants, all his pockets, he stuck bundles where ever he could. Suddenly Sylvia grabs him by ear.

"No you don't sunshine it ain't fucking Christmas yet, give that cash here."

"It's only my dinner money mum." Squid replied.

"Dinner money, fucking dinner money!" since when did Duke Smith start taking you to the Fucking Ritz for lunch? You must have a bloody monkey there boy, now hand it over before I call your father and he comes down those apple and pears to sort you out. Keep a pony to cover what's owed on your wages I borrowed last week but, you make sure that's it, no nicking any, don't want another thief in the family." Sylvia explained.

Handing back some of the cash, Squid can't wait to get out of the house before it's discovered he has more hidden away. Swiftly he grabs his work bag and leaves the house shouting goodbye to his parents as he shuts the door. He jumps on his Yamaha FS1E and scoots off down the road, once he is well out of sight, Squid pulls in and hides behind a hedge. He looks around making sure no one is around to see him, the last thing he wants is to get mugged. Pulling all the cash out he starts to count it, with the bundles of notes in his jacket pocket and a large grin on his face he carries on past the gates to Duke Smiths scrap yard and goes in to town and parks up his bike. Talking to himself whilst walking, Squid count's more of the cash. Squid is extremely pleased with his quick thinking.

"Fooled you both, a monkey! There's well over five hundred quid here, in the thousands I would say. Take a Pony she says. Where the hells twenty five quid going to go in this day and age. That's another Pony, got a score here . . . "

But back at home, Sylvia's mind is already working overtime wondering where all this money has come from. She sits down with a cuppa and turns on the TV. As she sits listening to the telly Sylvia slurps on her cup of tea. She counts the piles of cash in front of her. Sylvia's concentration is broken by a news flash. *"Brinks Mat bullion robbery"*, she looks down at a holdall by the side of her which contains more cash and sees Brinks Mat wrappers round notes.

"Oh my fucking god! . . . James, what the fuck you done now?"

James walks into front room, his hand is down his Y Fronts and he's scratching his balls, he farts then yawns.

"Nice! Morning to you too! Look James you are on telly. Well not you but the job you did" replied Sylvia.

"Fuck, what they said about the robbery babes?" asked James as he catches the news report.

"They're saying you got away with 36 million in gold bars and £100,000 of cut and uncut diamonds and £600,000 in used notes, three million in new notes and travellers cheques. So you weren't fucking about then, we really are loaded? You will be able to get Yoda off your back." said Sylvia.

"Well you have to remember sweet, it's not all mine, we had to split it up, and the bastards are bullshitting the amount for insurance purposes, there wasn't that much, but don't worry there's enough to live the rest of our lives in absolute luxury and Yoda's already sorted. But keep it quiet, not a word to anyone, and remember we can't touch it for a while."

"What's awhile?" she asks.

"A year maybe two, but I got enough to see us by babes." James explained.

Sylvia's eyes widen as up on the screen a reward is offered. It doesn't take her long to figure out that the reward money is legal and can be spent straight away. On a hit like this she would probably get a new identity and moved to a warmer country. She soon comes up with a plan of her own. Knowing full well with a hearty breakfast inside him James would probably go back to bed or fall asleep on the sofa. Sylvia headed to the kitchen and cooked him a Full English. Once that chore was taken care of she quietly left the house and headed for a phone box. Sylvia had to test the water on their reaction before she could head to a police station.

"I want to talk to your top bloke, the one in charge, the one who does the deals." Sylvia announced down the phone.

It didn't take long before she was being taken seriously. She only stayed on the line for a few minutes at a time, moving from phone box to phone box. At this point she had to be careful not to have her call traced. At one stage her heart nearly stopped as a police car came tearing past with it's two's and blues going. Luckily for Sylvia it was on its way to a road traffic accident further down the road.

Two hours later Sylvia walked into a police station.

It was at this define moment in time the Brinks Mat curse was born for me, and from what I found out later from a certain CID officer, called Morris, the first time the words "Fools Gold" were murmured.

Sylvia stood at the reception desk.

"My name's Jane Smith, I have been talking to a couple of your CID officers this morning. Could you let them know I am here?" Sylvia explained to the young constable behind the desk.

"Sorry, you are who?" asked the copper.

"Jane Smith! His birthday and Christmas present all in one love, just give him this." Sylvia replied.

Sylvia hands the Policeman a Brinks Mat wrapper that was originally around one of the bundles and had a serial number typed on it, confirming it was from the raid. The young Policeman's eyes widen.

After a day of spending in the shops in town and playing pinball in his favourite café, Squid met up with the love of his life Jenny Davison, a 14 year old petite posh girl, with long dark hair and green eyes. Over the last few weeks they had been getting closer and closer. Jenny went to Croydon High, a private girls school she came from a classier side of town. As they leave the school gates they walk towards her home holding hands.

"Here, I got you something." announced Squid as they walked along the road. He put his hand in his pocket and pulled out a bag, in the bag was a small case containing a gold watch.

"Oh my god Squid, it lovely, it's the one I've been looking at, you remembered, but how? And I see you have spent on yourself, new shoes, watch, chain, ring. You seem very flush today, I would say you got your wages from the breakers yard, but that wouldn't cover this lot. Robbed a bank have you?" Jenny mocked.

"Sort of, long story will tell you some time, but got enough to treat you. How do you fancy eating out tonight, I'll take you somewhere nice?"

"Well Ok, Mum and Dad are away for a couple of days, so stay the night if you like, but no funny stuff. You can finger me if you like, but that's it! I am saving myself, you know till I get married." Jenny explained.

You can't imagine how I felt at that moment, not only was I going to get in the girl of my dreams knickers, but I would spend the night with her and I had loads of cash.

"OK, better stop at a phone box and call mum to let her know I won't be in, mind you doubt they would notice anyway." explained Squid.

"So don't go thinking you are going to pop your cherry with me tonight, because it's not happening!" said Jenny, as she play-fully poked Squid in the ribs.

"No, I wouldn't, I respect you, you know that. But I tell you what, would love you to suck it, like you did last time, I liked that." Squid whispered in her ear as he put his arm around her waist.

"Maybe, only if you buy me something nice, I am a classy girl Squid, if you want to keep me then you have to look after me." Jenny replied.

"I just got you a gold watch Jen, do you know what that cost me?" Squid replied feeling a little hurt by Jenny's banter.

"No how much . . . come on tell me please I want to know?" replied Jenny as price was very important to her.

"Let's put it this way it was over five hundred and under eight hundred. Do you know how long I would have to work in the breakers yard to be able to buy you that?" Squid joked

"No, I know it would be a long time, but you didn't earn the money you bought this with, did you? You nicked it!" Jenny replied.

Squid was reluctant to divulge too much info to Jenny and despite her persistent requests he made her understand she was better off not knowing as even Squid didn't know what the implications of his actions were yet. Normally when he nicked some cash off his mother, he was able to blame it on his father as normally James was always dipping into Sylvia's purse.

It was now two days after the robbery, 28th of November 1983. A frustrated Squid walked with Jenny. He had hoped to see her naked at least, but last night she had been a tease and Squid had settled for a handful of tit and a smelly finger. But, they walked to Squids home together hand in hand, his plan of shagging Jenny put on hold till another opportunity arose. At the family home there didn't seem anything any different from when Squid had walked out the door the day before, but much had happened. Walking in doors Squid throws his bag down on the sofa.

"Take a seat Jenny, will see where the oldies are." said Squid as he called his mother and father. There was no answer so he then checked their bedroom.

"Mum-Dad I am home, I got Jenny with me." He shouted but still there was no reply.

Now, Jenny being nosey, like she always has been, was already wandering about downstairs opening cupboards and looking in the pantry to see what was worth lifting. She may have been a posh bird, but she had a wild side to her and often took unnecessary risks.

"Sounds like no-one is home." she shouted stating the obvious.

"You think?" Squid replied in sarcasm.

As Jenny wanders around she sees a note sat on the draining board by the sink.

"Squid you got a note, it says . . . read note on fridge." shouts Jenny as Squid walks into the kitchen.

"That will be my mother, she always leaves me notes telling me there's a note somewhere else in case I don't see it." Squid explained as he walked over to the fridge and reads the note: *"Squid, yer old-man's banged up, paid the rent up to the end of the year, left you some cash in the fridge. Don't worry about me I'll be fine, starting a new life abroad, sure you can take care of yourself, take care mum x"*

"The Bitch!" replied Squid as he screwed up the note and threw it on the floor.

"What is it?" Jenny asked looking a little concerned at Squids mood change.

"It's me mum, the bitch must have grassed the old-man up and she's done a bunk, she isn't coming back." Squid replied.

Squid runs to the window and looks out onto the drive and road, his father's Jag's gone the pigs must have it he thought.

"What do you mean grassed him up, for what?" Jenny asked.

"He did a job the other night, you know that Brinks Mat bullion thing everyone is on about. Twat! Bet he's going to get life for that." said Squid as he dropped to the floor, crouching against the work unit. He let his head fall into his hands and ran his fingers through his red hair.

"No shit! Don't worry, no more rules. You can do your own thing now. How you going to manage for food and stuff?" said Jenny.

"The bitch has left me some cash in the fridge." replied Squid as he kicked out his leg at the fridge door. Walking to the fridge Jenny tries to open the door but it is stuck again, Squid gets up and pulls hard on the door which flies open hitting him on the head again.

"Fucking fridge, I hate fucking fridges!" He moaned as he sat back against a kitchen unit rubbing his head. Jenny looks in and sees lots of money, both shelves and the freezer section had cash on them, on top of the cash on the bottom shelf was yet another note for Squid saying: "For you sweetie, have fun."

"Don't worry about your head Squid, looks like she's left you a little present. Party time or what!" screamed Jenny as she grabbed a pile and throws it in the air. As it floated down over the kitchen floor, Squid smiled to himself, this was his chance to do his own thing and why not, like Jenny said-Party time.

Jenny sticks a few twenty pound notes down her top whilst Squids not looking, she then waves a wad under his nose.

"Bloody hell Jen, how much do you recon there is?"

"Not sure looks like loads, over ten grand, guess this is why you were so flush the other day. With what you robbed off you old man, I think you are well and truly loaded. Tell you what, look after me and treat me right, and you can fuck me if you want?"

Jenny raise's up the hem of her school skirt until her knickers are on view teasing Squid. He stands walks up to her and kisses her whilst his hand firmly rubs her bottom.

"You can be my first." she whispers in his ear as she rubs her body against his.

"For real, are you going to let me do it to you?" said Squid forgetting everything else in an instant.

Jenny nods, "Be gentle with me though won't you." she says blushing slightly.

Grabbing two cups and a bottle of his mother's sherry, Squid starts to lead Jenny up to the bedroom.

"You go up get ready, I just need to ring Mum and tell her I am staying wiv Julie tonight." Jenny explained.

"Ok don't be long!" Squid replied excitedly.

Five minutes later and after a few swigs of his mother's best sherry the two start to remove one another's clothes. But, it didn't take Jenny long to take the lead. Squid, clearly still a virgin, was fumbling with Jenny's bra when she pushed him back on the bed and within seconds was straddled over him totally naked. For Squid it was a very educating evening, it never for one moment entered his head to question Jenny on how experienced she was in the sack.

Straight away the curse set in and by the third day after the robbery I got a taste of what my life was going to be like.

The next day was a dull and wet November morning. Squid wakes to the sound of car screeching up on the drive. He looks around the room for Jenny but cannot see her, his head is still spinning from a night of drinking his mother's best sherry. Opening the bedroom window, Squid looks out; it is Barry the Bakers boy from in town. Jenny appears from the side of the house and runs towards the car carrying two carrier bags.

"Jenny! Where're you going?" Squid shouted.

"Sorry Squid, it wouldn't have worked, Barry's my boyfriend and he doesn't like me seeing other boys." Jenny shouted as she climbed in the car.

"But, what about last night, you said I was your first, it was special!" Squid screamed back.

"You were, that day." shouted Barry, as he hung his head out of the car window, laughing at Squid.

Barry promptly gives Squid the finger whilst yelling abuse at him from the car window.

"Squid you can't drive and Barry, well he's got a Cortina. Don't beat yourself up over it Hun, you were good, but, well you know how it is." Jenny shouted up at the window as she closed the car door.

"But he's a fucking baker and he's fat. I thought you were classy! What's with the carrier bags?" asks Squid as Barry starts to wheel spin away.

"Yes two steps up from you. Loser!" shouted Barry as the car shot off the drive and up the road.

As the Cortina spins away up the road Barry wave's a wad of cash out of the window. All Squid can see and smell is the burnt rubber smoking away from Barry's tyres. Well, that and Duran Duran's 'Is There Something I Should Know' blasting from the speakers. As first shags go this wasn't the way Squid had planned the morning after, suddenly it dawned on him.

"What the fuck, no . . . please not my cash!" For a moment time just stood still as reality thundered through his brain, a shudder of anger quivered through his body, the little boy in Squid just died.

Squid ran down the stairs, hurries to fridge, where he finds the fridge door ajar, opening it wider there was just a small stack of cash left, six hundred and thirty three pounds. Scribbled on reverse side of the note left by Squids mother, was a note from Jenny: *"Sorry Hun, But you know how it is."* Jenny had done him over good and proper.

"Bitch, you fucking bitch and no Jenny, I don't know how it fucking is, but I guess I am learning." screamed Squid, as he kicked hell out of the fridge. When the fridge door then flew closed hitting him on the side of his ribs he really was well pissed off. For the first time he felt broken, he had loved Jenny, still did, he would take her back instantly with or without the cash. Sitting with his knees up to his chest and resting once more against the kitchen unit a tear ran down his cheek. But, he wasn't going to be broken for long.

Pulling himself together his moment of self-pity had lasted about five minutes. Squid soon realised there was a brighter side, he still had some cash to see him by, the rent and bills were paid and the loss was Jenny's not his. He takes the cash from fridge and counts it £633.00. What was with the three quid he wondered. Running up stairs he opens his sock draw, undoes his socks and pulls out sixteen hundred quid, robbed from his father on morning after the heist. He still had something to see himself by for a while.

Leaving the house Squid walks to his Auntie's house in town. Across the road two plain clothed police officers in an unmarked car make note of the morning's events. The house was under surveillance.

"Radio the station let them know the boy's on the move, let's see where he leads us." said the first copper, to the second.

As Squid got close to his Aunties house he could see a police car there and quite a bit of commotion. He started to run to see what it was all about. As he reached the bottom of the path he could see police tape everywhere.

"You can't come in here son." a copper said, stopping him from crossing the tape.

"But I need to see Auntie Sandra . . . Auntie Sandra it's me Squid." he shouted through the tape as Sandra is led from the house, a blanket was placed over her shoulders. She looked pale and shattered.

"Auntie Sandra, it's me, it's me-Squid, what's happened, are you OK?." asked Squid pushing past the policeman as Auntie Sandra beckons him over, he runs into her arms.

"Oh Squid my boy you're ok, they haven't got to you like the others. I've always had a soft spot for you, I am so glad you are ok." Auntie Sandra sobbed.

"Got to me, what do you mean-got to me? Dads banged up and Mums buggered off somewhere, bloody Spain I expect. I think she done some sort of a deal. I am on my own." Squid explained.

"So am I sweetheart now, so am I. Never did like your mother, always out for herself, 'BITCH!' This is all her doing I hope she rots in hell for this. They came in and blew Uncle Joe away whilst he was on the crapper. Now I just heard they got to Chris as well, it's the Brinks Mat curse boy. They're dead all of them and everyone is dropping like flies at the moment, anyone and everyone slightly connected to the robbery they're after. You have to run Squid. Who knows who's safe. Their putting me in protective custody, if you don't want to run, come with me if you want? We'll be safe there together." sobbed Auntie Sandra.

"I can't, I need to work things out for myself." Squid gives her a big kiss then turns and runs before anyone could stop him. Squid headed to the café, he's soaking wet and needs to dry out. Staring into his large cup of hot chocolate he lifts his head up and looks out of the window and sees this raggedy man heading towards the café. Instantly he recognised the man as Duke Smith as he always reminded Squid of Steptoe out of the old TV series. Duke Smith was his boss from the breakers yard, with his fingerless gloves and old woolly hat, he was quite a character.

"Hello Mucker, thought I would find you here, missed you at work. Where the fuck you been boy?" said Duke in his common manor as he entered the café.

"Duke, God, it's nice to see a friendly face." Squid replied.

"What the fuck have you got yourself into son? Every Tom, Dick and Harry is looking for you." asked Duke, as the waitress came to the table to serve him.

"Usual Duke?" she asked.

"Please Wendy and a coke for the boy." he replied.

"It's not what I've done Duke, it's my old-man, he did the Brinks Mat bank job." Squid explained.

"Bugger, all makes sense now, you aware there's a five grand reward out on you? I figured you'd be here." Duke replies.

"Is that why you're here?" Squid replied in a sarcastic tone. Duke slaps Squid around the top of the head.

"Don't be a cheeky cocker, you know me better than that, been in some tight holes myself in my day. You can count on me as a friend, you know that. Said Duke as he then ruffles the boy's hair.

"Thanks Duke." Squid replied, grateful he had someone to count on.

"Squid, every fucker that has ever come to work for me in that yard has been a thieving bastard. In the five years you have been coming in you are the only one who has nicked nout. You haven't nicked nout aver yah, or it may change things?" joked Duke.

"No... Duke, no, I wouldn't steal off you." Squid replied.

"No, I didn't think so, you're a good un you are Squid. So come on tell what the fucks going on whilst I eat my breakfast."

The waitress puts Duke's Full English breakfast in front of him and gives Squid his coke. Squid watch's the waitress walk away, being careful in what he says. Duke wiped his nose on the back of his sleeve and sniffed as he waited for Squid to continue.

"Well, as I said the old-man does this job, then the old-dear grasses him up doing some deal with the insurance people for some cash, leaving me six grand in the fridge, whilst she buggers of to the Costa Del bloody Sol." Squid explains.

"Ha the good old Costa Del Sol, Ronnie and I had a fucking good time out there, not the best place for her to go to hide though, too many bloody criminals out there."

"Well, I am just guessing it's there, it's the place she always talked about going with the old man. You know mother and her tan. Anyway, Jenny was with me and saw the cash and well one thing led to another........" said Squid explaining the events in brief as he watched Duke ram more bacon in his mouth.

"That's that posh bird you been seeing init?" asked Duke spitting bits of bacon out over the table.

"Yes.... well she said she loved me and well......" as Squid was explaining, Duke butted in.

"You fucked her didn't you, don't tell me she got you on the old "You can be my first" line, flashed her snatch at you and you fell for the old pussy hook line and sinker. You wanker Squid, how much did she take?" Duke scratched his head moving his woolly hat from side to side frustrated with what he was hearing.

"All of it....well most of it. She fucked off with Barry the Bakers boy, that's his old-man's shop across the road, how was I to know her knickers have been up and down more times than a British Airways 747." explained Squid feeling a little stupid knowing that with the kind of upbringing he had had, he should have known better.

"Pussy Pissed! That's what you were Pussy Pissed. Must make you fucking blind now as well, Just goes to show the old saying is still relevant even now, "*A man will travel further for a fuck, than dynamite will blow him.*" So what're you figure, you going to steal it back?" asked Duke as he wiped his nose on the back of his fingerless mittens and then had a dig at a bogy.

"I dun-no! I came in here to dry out and try to get my head together." Squid replied.

"Come on man up boy. Remember this if nothing else, a woman is like a road the more curves she has the more dangerous she is." Duke explained curving his hands in the air as if drawing the outline of a woman "Slap her arse next time show her whose boss."

"I'll try to remember that Duke." Squid replied.

"And so the shit hits the fan." Duke announces, as he looks across the road.

Two cars screech up an SD1 Rover V8 and a V12 Jag. Two men jump out of each car, all in balaclavas, they run inside the bakers. A shot is fired and screaming can be heard. Seconds later they come out dragging Barry into the waiting Rover, then the Rover and the Jag speeds off up the road leaving a pile of smoke behind them.

"What the fuck. SHIT!" mumbled Squid as he took in what was happening,

"Auntie Sandra was right, whoever these people were they're after anyone connected to the Brinks Mat bullion heist." said Squid.

"Look boy, you best get out of here and go keep your head down. You got a set of keys to the yard, if you need anything or somewhere to go. Hide out there but be careful, it won't take these people long to find out you work for me, so I will try to distance myself. No doubt I will be getting a visit very soon." Duke explained shooing him away like an unwanted guest.

"Ok Duke, thanks, you are a real mate." Squid expressed his gratitude with a nod.

As the henchman disappear Squid runs over towards the bakers shop. He looks in through the window to see a woman on the floor, her shopping spread everywhere. Barry's father is on the phone giving police an account of the gun point abduction. Squid suddenly realises Jenny is probably in the same danger.

"Oh shit Jenny!" he mumbles under his breath as he runs down the alley behind the shop and heads for Jenny's house. Squid runs as fast as he can to her house but, as he reaches the bottom of Jenny's road, Barry's Cortina skids to halt hitting some dustbins. Squid can see Jenny is driving. Jenny stalls the car at the junction and Squid can hear her cranking it over trying to start it. Jenny is sobbing her eyes out. Looking up she see's Squid heading towards her, panicking she thinks Squid is after her for what she did to him. Desperately she tried to start the car but it's flooded and won't go.

"Jenny its ok, what's wrong? It's me Squid we're cool. Look I am not mad at you, let me help please." Pleads Squid as he sees how distressed the girl is. Jenny's head slumps onto the steering wheel. She starts to cry uncontrollably, Squid opens the driver's door and puts an arm around her.

"I am sorry for taking your money Squid, but Barry said he loved me. We went back to his place and after he got his own way he then told me to piss off. All he was interested in was the money not me. So, I took his car keys and nicked his Cortina along with the cash. Then two men just kicked in the front door of my house. They shot my Dad and were coming for me. But, I managed to escape out the back and take the car from where I hid it. I am scared Squid, What the hell's happening, why are they trying to kill me?" sobbed Jenny.

"I am so sorry Jen, this is my bloody mothers doing . . . It's OK Jen, I will look after you." Squid replied hugging her. At the top of the road a car screeches round the corner. Squid looks up to see a Jag hammering down towards them. Luckily for him a car was trying to park and the Jag is blowing it's horn and flashing it's lights at the driver trying to get them to move faster "It's them, we need to get the hell out of here. Barry must have squealed." cried Squid.

"Move over babes." said Squid, as he helped a still very upset Jenny out of the driver's seat. Jenny slides into the passenger's seat, still sobbing. Squid jumps in and holding the throttle open cranks the engine, the car splutters once or twice then manages to start. The Cortina spins off down the road but the Jaguar is hard on their tail. Jenny screams as the Jag tried to nudge them off the road.

"Jenny listen, I have an idea. I need you to drive again in a minute. Our only hope is to get these twats in my own back yard, that way I have a better chance of dealing with them. I need to get to the breakers yard." Squid explains.

"No way, they are trying to kill us. I can't drive as good as you, I don't want to die." she screams at Squid shaking, this wasn't fun anymore this wasn't the fun she had intended.

"I know neither do I babes, neither do I. Now listen, here's what I want you to do..." Squid explained as inside he took another leap of growing up.

The Jag chases the Cortina down several streets, the fact Barry had tuned the car up a little was helping in the chase, but the huge jack ups on the arse end were not helping in the corners and as soon as Squid could gain some distance the Jag was soon back on their tail. Squid manages to get ahead of Jag as the driver loses control on a sharp bend hitting another car. Sparks *'This Town Ain't Big Enough For The Two Of Us'* blasts out of

Barry's stereo. Squid tries to turn it off, but up ends up turning it up, Jenny lets out a giggle between her sobs.

"This is kind'a exciting in a weird way," Jenny giggled.

The V12 Jag with its four occupants was a heavy car, it wasn't great on corners either, but it's power on the straight was incredible. With it's nose lifting in the air, the Jag's 12 cylinders screamed up behind the Cortina. It was a real game of cat and mouse. Squid in the lighter Cortina was just lucky that people and other cars were getting in the Jag's way, and a dust cart backing out on the road allowed Squid to gain head way. With the breakers yard in sight, Squid smashes through the gates into the yard. Jumping out Jenny knows exactly what to do. She gets in the driver's seat ready to move.

"Now go quickly, they're nearly here." shouted Squid, as he ran towards the large tracked digger, which had an electromagnet on the end of its arm. Squid climbs in, but as he looks around at Jenny his heart sinks as she stalls the car. Does he run too her or carry on? In his heart he knew his only hope was to carry on. The Jag is tearing down the road behind her. She cranks the engine calling Squids name, but as the Jag screams through gates, it rams straight into back of the Cortina. The impact crinkled the Cortina's arse and the Jags bonnet flips up. The bump starts the Cortina's engine and Jenny is able to keep the car going. She keeps her toe down round the track in the yard, like Squid had told her, with the Jag hard on her tail chasing her, but with it's bonnet popped visibility was restricted. Squid sets too with the digger. The digger lets out a huge puff off black smoke as Squid opens up the throttle on it. The Electromagnetic plate fitted to the 360 degree digger lands firmly on the roof, but the first two attempts Squid can't hold it and it releases. On the third attempt he catches it spot on and then lifts the Jag in air. As soon as the Jag loses traction, Squid has better control.

"Fuck, fuck, fuck, fuck, fuck oh no, shit, shit, shit, shit..." cries Squid as he struggles with the car. The Jag's engine screams as the driver panics and puts his toe down.

"What the fuck, what's happening, he's got us with the magnet. Shoot the fucker, kill him quick." shouts one of the gangsters in the Jag.

The swinging arm spins round and round. As it does so, Squid lifts up the swinging arm of digger and shuts off the magnet. The Jag flies through the air, over a fence and into a river. Squid jumps from the machine and runs to Jenny.

"You ok babes?" he asks concerned for the love of his life, because that is what she is to Squid. But, the doubts of how Jenny really felt about him thumped through his head along with the adrenaline.

Jenny puts her hand behind the car seat and pulls out two carrier bags of cash feeling uncertain at how Squid was now going to be with her . . . it was her bargaining gesture.

"You did it Squid, you did it! Here these are yours. I am really sorry Squid. I didn't mean to be such a bitch. It's just, well, it's a lot of money and like I said Barry had a car." Jenny tries to explain her actions.

Squid looks around at the state of the Cortina.

"You're right about one thing, he did *have* a car!" Squid smirked

"You can shag me again if you want to make up for what I did like." she said as the tears still trickled from her eyes.

"It was never about the sex, or the money, it was about you. I love you, you silly cow, don't you realise that?" Squid explained leaning in the car and taking her in his arms.

Helping her out of the car with the two bags, the two headed for Dukes office.

"Come with me to Duke's office. I know where he keeps the office and car keys. I will find us another car then we can get the hell out of here." Squid replied.

Squid and Jenny walk towards the office, Squid puts his arm around her to give her some reassurance and comfort. She turns her head and kisses him. Entering into the office, Squid searches for keys to cars which he knew were up and running in the yard.

"God I am buzzing, it must be all the adrenaline. Fuck me now Squid, before I cum in my pants." She said as she wrapped her arms around him.

"I'm guessing you were not a virgin then? Its ok, it doesn't matter." he said turning to face her.

"Oh Squid I am so sorry, if I could change the last 24 hours I would. I didn't know if you were just using me, like the others. I like you and I thought if you knew different you wouldn't stay with me. Now I find out you love me and it's all gone to shit!"

"Stop crying Jen, Duke seems to think I am just a door mat for you to wipe your feet on as and when you feel like it. He thinks you need your arse slapping." Squid replied as he lifted her chin and looked deep into her green eyes.

Squid takes off Jenny's top, bends her over office desk, lifts her skirt, then spreads her legs apart. Jenny doesn't resist giving Squid his moment to do with her as he wishes. Taking a moment to enjoy Jenny's nice firm bottom he ran his hand over her pants, then taking his hand back he slap's her hard on both cheeks three or four times. Jenny turns her head and smiles at him as she bites on her bottom lip, this just added to the excitement of the day.

It was at this moment I knew Jenny was always going to be a handful. Sex was like a drug to her and it allowed her to manipulate men. In the end it was Jenny who was in control, not me, yet knowing this I knew she would forever have my heart. I would always be putty in her hands. You can have the strongest, hardest man, but it only takes the right woman to soften you up and make you weak, break, destroy, fuck with your head and manipulate you. Jenny for me would be my strength, yet also be my weakness. If the curse wasn't my nemesis she was.

Outside on the other side of the river two of the gangsters from the Jag climb from the river and collapse, the other two hadn't been so lucky. Ox looks at Syd "There has to be an easier way to make a living than this." Ox says shaking his head.

After their quickie, Squid runs down and closes up what is left of the gates to the yard and parks a van across so no one can drive in. He decides that whoever was after them wouldn't come looking for them in the breakers yard, they would think he would be long gone. So, it was the safest place for now. He hid Barry's Cortina behind some of the other cars so it was out of sight and then headed back to the office. As he manoeuvred his way through the maze of cars, he caught his reflection in the mirror of an old bus. He stood there a few seconds, "Skinny" he thought, as he then ran his fingers through his messy red hair, then he focused on his spots. At 5'10 he wasn't the hottest teen-ager. "I wonder what she sees in me?" He thought to himself. His heart sank, maybe a pretty girl like Jenny would always just want his money and not him. He remembered her words that day when he had bought her the watch "She was classy and if he wanted to keep her he had to look after her." He walked back to the office feeling down.

"I think we're probably safer here than anywhere tonight, so we best try to make up a bed on the settee." suggested Squid as he pulled at the bed settee Duke had in the office.

"Well, you could have done that just now instead of making me bend over the desk." Jenny said as she slapped Squid on the back. "What is it, you look sad?"

"Nothing" he replied . . . "and I like you bent over the desk." he replied smiling.

"So, are we gangsters now?" Jenny asked

"Gangsters! I guess sort of, we have some cash. I don't want to get used to this life style Jen, if it excites you, then go find one of those blokes driving the Jag. The thought of ending up like my dad scares me." Squid replied.

The next morning the two woke in each other's arms.

"You awake Squid?" Asked Jenny.

"Yes babes, I was just enjoying having you in my arms." Squid replied as the door to the office suddenly flew open.

"Morning young lovers, you two look just like Bonnie and Clyde. I hope you ain't left stains all over my best settee." said Duke with a smile.

Squid and Jenny jumped out of their skin then breathed a breath of fresh air in relief and laughed at Dukes outburst.

"No! Christ Duke you scared the life out of us." Squid replied.

"Nice to see you used the gate key, that's coming out of your wages, you know that don't you?" replied Duke sarcastically.

"Get some clothes on you two and come with me." Duke announces.

Squid notices Duke has a black eye and a couple of scuff marks on his face.

"What happened to you?" asked Squid.

Jenny looks at Dukes face.

"They found you, didn't they?" she asks.

"I got a visit, but you are both ok for now. I threw them a bone . . . in the wrong direction, but we do need to get you both away from here."

Duke grabs a pair of keys off a hook in the office and then after pulling on some clothes they follow Duke down into the yard. Duke opens the doors to a large shed, inside is a car under a tarpaulin.

"What's this?" asked Jenny.

"It was a little project for some lads over Southend way; it was going to be their getaway car. Fucking twats got themselves banged up before it was finished, so, it is surplus to requirements now." Duke explained.

Duke pulls off the cover, underneath is a ford Capri finished in black.

"Fuck......nice" Jenny screamed.

"That's one fucking hot car! It looks like something straight out of Mad Max." said Squid as he walked around it. Duke flips the lid.

"V8 on a slush box, four branch exhaust either side, with a twin choke Holley carbs, electric fan and pump, stainless steel exhaust. Roll cage....." Duke explains.

Duke opens the door and fires her up.

"Is that an RSJ running through it?" asked Squid.

"Sure is! Two in fact and I've welded an RSJ behind the front and rear bumpers, nothing is going to stop this mother fucker.

Here take her, she's all legal." said Duke turning off the engine and throwing Squid the keys.

"Are you serious?" Squid replied.

"She's got a top speed of 130 mph, she'll do 65 in reverse. When you get to where ever you are going, park it up somewhere safe and call me. I will pop down with the truck and pick it up in a few days. Behind the number plate is a hidden compartment, leave the keys in there." explained Duke.

Jenny runs round and cuddles Duke. Squid walks round and puts the key in the ignition, fires the car up and after revving it a few times, he then turns off the engine and smiles at Duke.

"You done more for me than my old man ever has, you always been there, thank you." Squid said as he got out and hugged the man.

"Get away with you, both of you, what you trying to do, make me all mamby pamby. I just want to see the back of you fuckers, now get in and fuck off before you cause me more grief." said Duke.

Jenny plants a kiss on Dukes cheek, as she turns to walk away Duke slaps her arse playfully.

"You, behave yourself young lady and look after him. And you Squid look after her. Just remember, if you go to bed with an itchy arse, you will wake up in the morning with a stinky finger." Duke smiled knowing he was giving them a fighting chance.

Duke watches them get in the car and leave the yard. As they drive away they wave at Duke.

Chapter Two

At a large house in Kent, the police were outside waiting to raid the place. Two huge rottweilers sit behind a large set of gates.

"Here Boys, come and eat the nice juicy steaks." says a plain clothed policeman. As the dogs come close he sees they are both wearing thick leather studded collars, each has a gold tag hanging from the collar, one is called '*Brinks*' the other is called '*Matt*'. They were obviously at the right address.

As the policeman throws the two juicy steaks through the gates the two dogs chase after them and gulp them down. Within fifteen minutes the dogs were fast asleep.

Inside the large mansion house Mad Mickey, who was now covered in gold jewellery, is having a good time with his wife Jacqueline.

"See Jacqueline told you I would give you everything." said Mad Mickey as he lay back against the silk pillows, with his hands behind his head. Under the silk sheets Jacqueline is giving him head, with loud music playing and joint on the side of the bed smoking away, Mad Mickey thinks he's died and gone to heaven.

"You are the best Hun!" she replies

But outside, and totally unbeknown to Mad Mickey, are the armed police, with armoured cars and guns ready to swoop on yet another member of the Brinks Mat gang.

"The dogs are sleeping Sir. We're all ready to go in, sounds like they are having a party in there. We will catch him with his trousers down for sure sir." explained Morris to his boss.

"Right everyone be alert, you know what to do, let's keep this clean and smooth, were going in." explained the senior officer.

An armoured car smashes through the gates, followed by four police cars, they skid up by house and around twenty policemen are ready to flock into the building. Two of them smash the door in, run up stairs and burst into the bedroom. Jacqueline is tied to the metal framed headboard topless. Mad Mickey is under the sheets pleasuring her orally.

"For fucks sake Mickey, what kinky fuckery you got planned now?" she screamed.

Pulling back the silk sheet Mad Mickey was stoned out of his mind oblivious to what was happening.

"Mad Mickey I am arresting you for your part in the Brinks Mat gold bullion robbery. You have the right to remain silent . . . " the copper said reading him his rights. Yet another member of the gang had been caught. It didn't take Squid and Jenny long to see it in the papers the following day.

"What we going to do now? This Brinks Mat thing is cursed for sure. Everyone's getting killed or banged up, what are we going to do Squid?" asked Jenny as she put on some music.

"I don't know, all we can do is hideout somewhere until things die down a bit. We can head down to Brighton if you like? See if we can find some work each and just keep our heads down for a while until we think it's safe to surface again." Squid suggested.

"We will have to make up different names Squid, so no one knows who we are." Jenny replied.

"Get a paper every day as well and follow the news, try to see what's happening. That way, we will know whether it's safe or not to surface. Don't worry babes; we have this cash so we can get by for a while, just trust no one, OK?" Squid explained.

Once in Brighton they leave the car somewhere safe for Duke as promised. Squid and Jenny walk the Brighton streets, both searching for work and somewhere to rent. Jenny finds work on market stall. Squid finds work distributing leaflets. The two find a shabby bedsit and for three weeks they survive well, touching little of the cash they had brought with them.

The bedsit is small and damp, they have a little stove and oven, gas and electric are all on meters. Squid had bought extra gas and electric fires in order to try to keep the place warm and dry. Jenny is trying her best to cook a romantic meal for the two of them, when the electric goes off. Squid feeds ten more 50 pence's into meter? He smiles at Jenny, but in his heart he knows she is missing her family and her old way of life. Jenny sits trying to smile and enjoying their meal. But Squid notices a tear run down her face.

"It's going to be ok Jenny I promise. Here I got you something. I was going to wait till Christmas but this is as good a moment as ever." says Squid as he gets up and gives her a hug. He hands her a wrapped present, Jenny wipes away the tear, takes the gift and opens it. Inside a solid gold bracelet, her name is inscribed on one side and on the other side 'My Girl Forever' is written.

"It's lovely, hope it's not Brinks Mat gold. Thanks Squid, here I have something for you. Sorry it's not expensive like this, but it's all I could afford." said Jenny handing him a present.

Jenny takes a small box from her pocket. Squid opens it, inside a silver necklace with silver ingot on it. On the back, it reads 'Squid.'

"Wow it's neat, thanks Jenny, I promise you next Christmas will be better." said Squid excitedly.

"It's ok, I just miss my Mum and Dad. Mum must be worried sick about me. Have you seen yesterday's paper, this robbery has got so big. They think you are the connection to the missing gold Squid." Jenny explained.

"I suppose I have my parents to thank for that, I have grown up with this shit for years, I will get through it." he replies.

Squid gives her reassuring hug, then sits back down and enjoys the dinner Jenny prepared for them both. Looking in his eyes Jenny re-assured Squid she could see he was worried for her.

"I am not the same little girl I was Squid, you aren't the same either, we've been changed by all this. But I am not going any-where, you are my life now." She explained putting her hand on his.

"Where's that come from, I am OK babes." He said shrug-ging it off.

"I know you , you're worried this is all about the money, you still don't trust me, I can see it in your eyes." Jenny looked down at the table.

"You are wrong, I just don't know what you see in me, not exactly the best catch am I." He sighed as he moved some peas around on his plate.

"Like I said we have changed, stop doubting us and stay focused, we can do this." She smiled squeezing his hand.

The next two weeks were cold and wet. Squid decided it was time he let Jenny know how special she was, so he finished work early and headed home. Walking the Brighton streets he was deep in thought as he walked, it was just after Christmas and the decorations are being taken down. Squid stops at a flower stall and decides to buy Jenny some flowers. Then he thought later he would take her out for a meal and maybe go night clubbing.

"Hi, could I have a bunch of roses, my girl she loves flowers?" Squid asked the man on the stall.

"Sure my friend, red or yellow, it's all I have left now?" the man asked.

"Red, I love her, so it has to be red." he replied.

Squid pays the man and takes the flowers, he's on cloud nine as he walks and thinks of how Jenny will love the flowers. As Squid slides the key in the door, he hears moans and groans coming from the other side. Opening the door he sees Jenny laid out on the floor, her jeans down around her knees. A big middle aged fat man is stood over her his trousers around his ankles.

"What the fuck! Jenny, leave her alone, she's just a kid you sick pedo!" he cries throwing the flowers on the floor. The fat guy looks round at Squid, laughing.

"Keep back boy or the girl gets hurt and you don't want that do you? And you bitch keep fucking still. I ain't finished yet, don't go getting all shy on me now your boyfriends home." said the man giving Squid an evil look. Jenny mumbles and cries. Squid feels helpless not knowing what to do for the best. The situation was grim he didn't want to make it worse.

"Look I don't know who you are, please just leave." Squid pleaded.

"He's my boss Squid" Jenny sobbed.

The man stops and grabbing Jenny around the throat he pulls her back towards him, then smiles at Squid as his hands go under her top and pull her bra up over her breasts.

"Whose your Daddy sweetheart who?" chanted the man enjoying every moment.

No . . . please NO!" Jenny spluttered out in tears.

"Jenny!" Squid cried, he had to act quick, this man wasn't going to stop.

"What's this Jenny shit, I thought your name was Mandy? So, you do like to play games. About time you had a man by the looks of it." The fat man whispered to her as his hand rubbed over her breasts. Jenny struggled but the fat dirty old man was able to hold her still and pulls down her jeans to her ankles. He starts slapping her arse as he turns her over on to her stomach. Squid is desperate to help her, but he knows he needs a weapon of sorts to stand any chance at all against this thug. His eyes scoured the room constantly looking around for an opportunity.

"After all you need to keep the boss happy, don't you my sweetie, I am guessing you need this job." says the man as he slaps Jenny across the arse once more.

"For Christ's sake she's only fourteen. For fuck sake leave her alone now and I won't call the pigs." Squid screamed worried for Jenny and what was about to happen to her.

"No you won't son, it's obvious you two are runaways, no doubt hiding from the Old Bill. So just go sit down over there until I've finished with her and get used to this happening on a regular basis. Let's say its perks of the job, just like when I let her bring home a bit of fruit and veg." replied the disgusting brute.

"I mean it!" shouted Squid.

"Fourteen eh! How do you fancy it up the arse too? Bet that young boy friend has no experience at all, need a bit of good old Daddy here don't you my sweets." says the man as he pulls at Jenny's pants. This was Squids one and only opportunity whilst the slob was drooling over Jenny's rear end. Squid picks up one of the electric fires, smashes it over the fat guys head. The fat guy steps back from Jenny screaming as the element burns him. Squid hits him a second time and the fire breaks electrocuting the fat guy who judders on the floor. The trip switch clicks, and the power in the flat goes off. The man is out cold. Jenny turns pulling up her pants and jeans. She bursts into tears and kicks man several times in groin.

"Bastard, fucking cunting bastard, fucking twat! That's my job gone down the fucking pan!" she cries as she kicks the man.

"Hey Jenny it's over sweetheart, it's over." Squid sobbed as he hug's her tightly.

"My job Squid, what about my job?" Then pushing away from Squid she kicks the man several more times.

"Bastard-fucking... Bastard!" she screamed as she kicked him.

"There is always a weapon somewhere in a house Jenny. Try to always remember that. We can't trust anyone. Why didn't you say he was coming on to you? You should have ditched the job, we would have managed. Get your stuff together we're getting the fuck out of here, it's not safe anymore." Squid said as he wiped his eyes.

"I thought he was just being nice to me, we needed the money Squid. Do you think he's dead?" she asked suddenly looking worried as to what they might have done. She prods him with her foot.

"No, he will live. Come on Jenny let's get the hell out of here. He's going to be fine. We don't need the money that bad sweetheart and I won't let anyone hurt you, now come on get your stuff together."

"He wasn't going to pay me and we needed the money. You do believe me don't you? I love you Squid, I love you." Jenny said panicking, thinking she might lose Squid.

"It's my fault not yours. It is just more shit I have got you into, I am sorry, so sorry." Squid said as he took Jenny in his arms. He hugged her until she had calmed down, then emptying the man's pockets of cash, he passes it to Jenny. Within minutes the two were packed and ready to leave.

"Do you think he's dead Squid, he wasn't moving much?" asked Jenny as they hurried down the street with a couple of bags.

"No he'll just have a sore head and nuts for a day or two. Probably his nuts will be worse than his damned head the way you were kicking him." Squid let out a laugh trying to lighten what had just happened.

"I thought he was going to rape me, if you hadn't of come back when you did who knows what that pervert would have done to me." replied Jenny as the realisation of what had just happened sunk in.

"This is my fault not yours. You don't have to explain or feel guilty. I am so sorry I have brought us down this low. It's all a mess, a fucking mess. I am so sorry, I do love you Jenny, but this is just all wrong. Fucked up, you deserve so much more. No matter where we go or what we do there will always be some dick head wanting a bit of you. I need to get you home. I need you safe." said Squid as he thought out loud.

"No Squid, no, they will kill us!" Jenny replied.

Squid stops in the street, he starts kicking the fuck out of a car door, Jenny sobs, she'd never seen Squid like this. They squabble briefly as she tries to stop him, until they both collapsed in tears on pavement, cuddling one another on ground. By now the car alarm screeches and it's drawing attention to the two of them. As they talk, passers-by cross the road to avoid them, thinking they are drunk or on drugs.

"I am taking you home and that's that. Then I will hand myself into the police for protection, we can't go on like this Jen. I need you safe. I can't be responsible for your life being ruined." Squid explained.

"But they will kill me, like they have my dad and everyone else involved. You, you will be killed too." Jenny sobbed as she broke down in tears once more.

"No you will be safe, once I have handed myself in, they will have no reason to come after you. It's me they want not you. I love you Jenny, I always have from the moment I set eyes on you but it's not supposed to be like this." Squid said looking deep into her green eyes.

"I love you too sweetheart. Barry was just a bit of fun, that was just sex but when I am with you it's like wow the real deal, I don't want to lose you Squid." she replied trying to dry her eyes which were now smeared with mascara.

Suddenly a window slides up and a man hangs out of the house looking down at his car.

"Hey you two fucking little shits, that's my car, I am calling the police, don't move!" he screams at them.

"Come on Squid we need to move, NOW, come on Squid lets go." Jenny screamed pulling at him. As the two run past a barber's shop "D REAMS" 'Things Can Only Get Better.' Can be heard on a radio, Squid laughs to himself as they run past heading for the station. Catching a train, within two hours they were back in Croydon. Squid searches for his house key, finding it in the bottom of his bag. After checking the place out to make sure no one had been in there, the two then settle there for the night.

Squid manages to find some food in the freezer and whilst Jenny takes a relaxing bath, Squid cooks Jenny a nice meal. After dinner and a few glasses of wine the two retire to the bedroom.

"Wouldn't it be nice if it was like this all the time?" said Jenny as the two lay naked in one another's arms.

"Maybe one day it will be, but for now, I have to know you are safe." Squid replied.

They make love several times that night knowing it will be the last they see of one another for a while. Wet, Wet, Wet 'Love Is All Around.' Plays on stereo in bedroom, the two feel the closest they ever have to one another. Jenny realises that Squid is the one she has been waiting for to make her life complete. The next morning the two sort out everything they need to and head off to Jenny's house. Squid kisses her good bye, hugs her and watches her walk up path. She opens door and calls for her Mother. But for Jenny there is an even bigger surprise, there hobbling down the hallway towards her on crutches is her father. Jenny lets out a scream of excitement and runs into his arms. She is just so shocked to see her Dad there alive, Jenny is overwhelmed.

"Daddy you're alive. Oh Daddy I thought they had killed you." Jenny loses control and bursts out in a flood of tears. Then remembering Squid outside she runs back to the door.

"Squid, it's my dad he's alive." she screams with excitement.

"I heard babes, I know, that's amazing, now go to him, I can't hang around, I have put you in enough danger." Squid replied as Jenny's father walked up behind her.

"Come here sweetheart I am fine. Come here and give your dad a big hug and a kiss." her father says taking her in his arms once more.

"Squid, stay away you are not welcome here, if you think anything of my daughter you will leave her alone." shouted Jenny's father down the path, her father was right he had to go.

Jenny looks round at Squid, she's heart broken. Squid puts up his hand, turns and leaves, there can't be any more goodbyes, no more cuddles, no more kissing, he just had to go, his heart was being ripped apart, but he knew he was doing the right thing.

"Sorry Mr Davison none of this was my doing. Jenny I love you, take care, if I can stay in touch I will." Squid said as he turned and walked away.

"Don't bother staying in touch boy, leave her alone, I'll look after her now, just go and never return." Mr Davison shouted, knowing Squid and his family were responsible for everything that had happened to them, which to be fair to the man he was right. As a father he now had to do whatever it took to protect her. Jenny screamed sobbing after Squid.

"Jen we live in each other's hearts you and I, remember that never forget it. Squid shouts back at her.

But her father takes her in his arms and shut's the door.

Squid walked back to his house, he had to make preparations for himself. So he goes into garden and buries the cash close to his mother's washing line pole. He knows there is a good chance the police will take off him whatever cash he has that is linked to the robbery, so leaving himself just twenty quid he locks up the house and catches the number 63 bus. Squid then goes to Croydon Police station and tells them everything that has happened to him. He is placed in protective custody and like his mother given a new ID.

It was days before Squid was released and taken away from Crawley, overall he was kept at four different police stations.

"Right Squid, we have a new ID. Your new name is Andrew Mathews, were moving you to a foster home in Salisbury. A real nice foster couple. He works for social services and she's a nurse, nice upstanding people, well respected in the area. It's going to be a bit different for you, but I am sure it will work if you try." explained the policeman.

"Will I be safe, will you check on Jenny as well, what will happen to the house in Croydon?" asked Squid concerned.

"You have to forget Jenny, forget Squid Ryan and the house in Croydon. It's Andrew Mathews from now on ok, no looking back, it's the only way you will survive." the copper explained.

Squid realised for now he had to focus on himself for a while.

Chapter Three

At Crawley police station six months later a police officer briefs his team.

"The criminal underworld has been a hive of activity since this heist and the nets closing in on them. If we can't get them on the gold, get them for something else. James Ryan made a very stupid mistake. He couldn't trust his wife and she couldn't leave the cash alone. Then as the noose tightened we raided Mad Mickey's house in Spain. Police found £633,000 in cash and jewellery worth £300,000. For a man who was on the dole claiming benefit he suddenly had a lot of explaining to do. In between times they're helping us out by killing off one another. Where closing the net in on Noye, it's only a matter of time. Now someone needs to speak to James Ryan's boy again and see what he knows. Now come on, I want results."

The inspector knew they had to act fast in order to recover the missing gold.

"Where is the boy Sir?" asks one of the PCs.

"63 winterbourne close, Salisbury, his foster parents are nice law abiding citizens and his life is totally different from the chaos he knew as a child. I'm guessing he follows what's going on in the papers, so doubt it won't be a surprise visit." the Inspector replied.

"Is it right there may be some bent coppers involved in the West Country Sir?" asked another policeman.

"Two days after the robbery, a couple saw a white-hot crucible operating in a garden hut at a neighbour's property near

Bath. . . . yes two days. Suspecting it may be linked to the bullion robbery, they immediately informed their local police. They arrived and were shown the hut, but they said it was just beyond their area and would pass the information on to the police responsible for that area. These people were never asked to give a statement to us. Now I smell a rat, so be open- minded when speaking to other police stations."

"What about Black Sir, is it right he's squealing on the others?" asked another PC.

"Yes, he's singing like a canary, we have 'The Colonel' we have 'Mustafa' and we have 'Mad Mickey.' So come on, read the notes in the case file, look at the faces of every suspect and their connections. Who they know, where they go, what they do and who they're sleeping with. Leave no stone unturned I want this case closed."

"What about the boy is he a suspect Sir?" asked another copper.

"Everyone's a suspect, I am sure the boy knows more than he's saying." explained the inspector before closing down the meeting.

Squid had settled in nicely, his new life was totally different to his one as a child. He had been able to catch up on school work and take his CSE's, managing to get work at McDonalds, he enjoyed being able to earn his own money. He had bought himself a moped and was happy as he could be without Jenny. Squid had also started working out in the gym and building himself up. He did a little boxing and two martial arts. Squid was determined to be able to look after himself if he should need to at any time in the future.

Then one day Squid was leaving McDonalds after his evening shift when two plain clothed police officers are waiting for him as he came out.

"Andrew... we need a word..." asked Morris.

Sitting in the police car Squid has a brief chat with them.

"What do you know of a gangland boss called Yoda?" asked Morris.

"Nothing replied Squid, I think my old man borrowed some cash off him for a while, but never met the guy." Squid explained.

Morris asks him a few more questions and then Squid gets out and walks back to his bike and rides home. The conversation with the two officers made Squid realise this still wasn't going to go away and he got the distinct feeling they thought he knew something. The next year went quickly and the Christmas of 1985 came and went. Squid passed his driving test and enrolled at college taking business studies, his next goal was to pass the last exam and save for a car. He wanted a life beyond Mc Donald's.

"Last exam today Auntie Brenda. No more collage after this. I will See you both tonight, remember I am working, so don't worry about tea, the burgers are free. Bye." shouted Squid as he left this foster home.

"Bye love. Good luck with the exam as well." Auntie Brenda shouted back.

For the first time in a long while I was beginning to feel like I could put all this behind me and make a good life for myself, however, I would learn never to get used to that comfort zone.

Squid had just finished his evening shift at Mc Donald's when two Policeman enter as he was ready to leave.

"Andrew, can we chat a moment?" asked Glen Maw a CID police officer.

"Yes sure, if you've come to ask me more questions I really can't tell you anything other than I already have." Squid replied.

"We were scheduled in for a visit to see how you were doing last week, but unfortunately there have been some complications and well I am afraid we have some bad news for you. An incident involving your father took place last night at Pentonville. You may want to take a seat. I am afraid your father died yesterday in hospital. He was attacked by one of the other prisoners." explained Glen Maw.

"Well hardly an accident then is it?" replied Squid.

"We think it was related to the Brinks Mat heist, however he left this message for you before he passed away. "Mark.633 Squadron, a 303. Love you Dad." explained Glen Maw.

"These were his last words whispered to one of the doctors before he passed. Does any of the message makes any sense to you? We think Mark is the name of the doctor, obviously 633 Squadron is a film, but what about a 303?" asked Sergeant Morris

"None, I don't know any Mark, 633 Squadron was always my favourite film growing up and I had a few old 303 bullets I collected from stands at air shows when I was little, but nothing more, I'm afraid. So, is someone getting done for murdering him then or has no one bothered because of who he is?" asked Squid as he answered the man's question.

"Could your father have left you a message or directions to the missing gold in one of these bullets or the video case do you think?" Morris replied.

"Well it's possible but as you know I was put in care and the house was returned to the council. All of my belongings were in the house. I was never given the opportunity to collect any of my stuff so god knows where any of it is now. You need to speak to whoever packed up the house." explained Squid.

"Ok, we will see if we can follow any of this up. Should you think of anything else please give me or my colleague a call, we're sorry for your loss." said Maw as the two turned to leave.

Squid rode home, he told his foster parents about his visit and the bad news.

"How do you feel about the fact your father in dead?" asked Auntie Brenda.

"Well angry to be honest, I mean all this shit he's left me in and has put me through. Now he's gone and I am left with his mess. We were never that close a family, so I don't miss him or anything, just annoyed at what he's put me through really." Squid explained.

"Well you may feel different once it has sunk in, if you want to chat about anything were both here for you." she replied.

Squid went to his room, he thought for a while about his parents, then about Jenny and he just felt angrier because due to them he had missed out on a life with the woman he loved. He had to try to find her. As soon as he had a car he would go and see her whether her father liked it or not.

Over in Spain Squid's mother, Sylvia, had not heard the news that she was now a widow, not that she would have cared that much, she rarely ever thought of Squid. As for James she hadn't thought about him since the day she grassed him up.

As she drives her car along a winding Spanish mountain road, she sings to an ABBA song that is playing on the radio.

"I work all night, I work all day, to pay the bills I have to pay, ain't it sad. And still there never seems to be a single penny left for me, that's too bad. In my dreams I have a plan . . . "

As she turns some of the sharp bends she realises the steering is getting heavy. She pulls into a lay- by to take a look and see what the problem might be.

"Damn it, now what?" she mumbles under her breath.

Sylvia gets out of the car and walks to the front and she sees the tyre is flat and kicks it. As she looks up she sees another car pull up a little way behind her in the lay-by.

"Ah, a knight in shining armour . . . hopefully." she mumbles as she walks towards the other car.

In the other car a man sits watching her approach, on the seat next to him is a pistol with a silencer attached. He pretends to read map. Seeing her get closer he hides the pistol from sight, covering it with the map.

"Excuse me you do you speak English? I have a puncture. You couldn't help me could you?" asked Sylvia in a posh voice.

"I guess it's these hot Spanish roads. Mines overheating a little, letting it cool down. Here let me help get you back on the road." replied the hit man.

He exits the car and walks with Sylvia to the boot of her car, removing the spare wheel, jack and wheel brace, he soon has the car jacked up and the flat tyre off, within five minutes the wheel was changed and the car ready to roll.

"There all done." he states rubbing his hands on a cloth.

He looks around for other traffic. The roads clear both ways, he then looks at his car considering killing her there.

"Where are you heading?" Sylvia asks.

"Torremolinos. My friend's letting me stay on his yacht down there, the name's Tom by the way."

"Sylvia . . . "

The two shake hands and smile at one another.

"That's where I am heading I have a boat in the marina there. I am having a little party tonight just off the coast, if you are at the marina by 4:00pm you could join us, you could be my guest of honour after being my hero? It's called the "Dreamy Owner" It's an anagram by the way," she said fluttering her eye lashes at him.

"Cool would love to, as Arnie would say, Hasta la vista baby..." replied the hit man.

The man coolly walks back to his car, gets in and drives off. When he reaches Torremolinos he finds a phone box and rings his client.

"I have made contact with the target and have put off our original plan, I think I can make it look like an accident, won't be as messy, will call you tomorrow." the man kept the conversation brief in case anyone was listening.

"Hello Sylvia or should I say, ahoy there! Permission to come aboard?" mocked the hit man as he got to the dockside at 4:00pm.

"Permission granted, I was unsure as to whether you would come." replied Sylvia as she beckoned him aboard. There were around twenty others on board and the Sun-seeker looked a little crowded, this was perfect for his plan.

"Come on, the chance to spend an evening with a beautiful woman on her yacht partying, I would be crazy not to except such an invitation." the hit man replied.

"We're just waiting for a few stragglers to turn up then we will be heading out of the harbour. Going to drop anchor about half a mile out, should be a lovely evening the sea's calm." Sylvia explained as she offered the man a drink.

"What's your poison?"

"Bloody Mary for me please." the hit man replied smiling to himself as he said it.

The evening developed well, everyone partied away until the early hours of the morning where all the party dwellers are falling asleep due to the excess of alcohol and a Micky Tom had slipped in the punch. The hit man and Sylvia are the only ones awake, being the hostess, she had paced herself well. Tom brought her a cocktail and the two sat on deck chatting.

"So Tom, I do hope you are not trying to get me drunk and take advantage of me." Sylvia asked.

"Why, I wouldn't dream of such a thing, there are some honourable gentlemen left in this world you know." Tom replied.

"So honourable gentleman, are you single, here on holiday or business?" Sylvia enquired.

"Business, but it's nearly completed. I had a go at your anagram by the way, not very good at them, could only work out 'Rye Mad Owner' sorry stupid I know." Tom chuckles as he says it.

"Well that's me a mad owner. When I know you better maybe I will explain it." she replied running her fingers through Tom's hair.

Tom walks to the bow and Sylvia follows with a wobble due to the cocktail kicking in.

"I say it's so lovely here at night, the waters so clear you can see the bottom." he kneels down looking through the polished chrome rail.

"I can see the bottom alright." said Sylvia as she focused on Tom's rear end.

"Now that's just naughty, I can see you are a bit of a naughty girl Sylvia." replied Tom leaning further over the side.

"Oh I am if only you knew, what on earth are you doing Tom, if you are not carful you will fall in and don't think I will come in after you, as I can't swim." Sylvia joked.

"There is something in the water glistening in the moonlight, looks like gold, hey maybe it's some of that sunken Spanish treasure, it must be reflecting off the hull." Tom said in an excited tone.

"Where let me see, I expect one of these tarts has dropped an earring more like it and if there is any gold out here it's more likely to be Brinks Mat than Spanish." Sylvia laughed at her own joke, the alcohol clearly getting the better of her now. Sylvia kneels down next to Tom. "Where is it then? Show me." she slurred.

"Look just there, see it?" Tom replied pointing. As Sylvia strained to look, Tom slides her into the water. Sylvia coughs and splutters, kicks out with her arms and legs in the water trying to save herself.

"Actually I am quite good at anagrams. I thought 'Drown Me Year' suited you better, better than 'Reward Money' any way." Tom stands there smiling as Sylvia tries to scream but her lungs are filling with water and she can't, her pupils widen with fear as it registers in her head she is about to be another victim of the Brinks Mat curse. Tom casually walks to the rear of the boat as Sylvia sinks to the bottom of the sea. He looks in on the other guests who are all still sleeping, on the table and work surfaces he leaves out some small packets of cocaine, the very substance he had spiked the cocktail with. Then walking down to the back of the boat he undoes the dingy and rows back to shore. As he reaches the shore he climbs out and pushes the boat back into the water.

Chapter Four

Two officers Sergeant Morris and Glen Maw find themselves once again returning to McDonalds. This time with more bad news for Squid.

"You two again, I only saw you two weeks ago, now what?" asked Squid.

"I am sorry to inform you that your mother has died in an accident aboard her yacht in Spain." explained Morris.

"She had a boat, wow nice, glad she was enjoying life." Squid replied showing little interest, yet the thought of his mother living it up on a boat did make him angry.

"She's left you a Bar called Goldie's, the proceeds from the sale of the boat and whatever is in her bank after expenses are deducted, you know funeral costs and that? We need you to sign for the assets so the funds can be transferred to you." Maw explained as he put the papers in front of Squid.

"I always thought something might happen to her." Squid replied sitting down and signing the papers. He isn't shocked, if anything he feels a sigh of relief, now that part of his life was clearly closed.

"Was the death of my mother an innocent accident or a hit organised by one of the many gangs now involved in all this? This Brinks Mat gold bullion robbery has become a damned legend. The amount has grown as have the stories told and past down. I don't even know what the original amount is any more do you? I guess finally I am getting my cut." Squid chuckled to himself as he thought about it.

"Not off the top of my head no, is that how you see your mother's death as you getting your payoff?" asked the policeman.

"Every treasure hunter in the world knows that James Ryan was involved and that I am the missing link to it. So please, I think I am entitled to something out of this mess and the shit they have put me through." Squid replied.

"Well we're not sure, the autopsy shows she drowned, she had alcohol and cocaine in her system but there was no evidence of foul play." Morris replied.

"We'll have the money transferred into one of the Police accounts and then transferred to you, that way it will be untraceable. But if you want to do yourself a favour just come clean tell us what you know. Once this missing gold is found, the threats gone, you can be free!" explained Maw, as he put the signed document in a case and headed back to his car. Squid watches both men leave in their unmarked police car. He couldn't help but wonder how many more visits he would have from the police. Squid headed home, his only thought now was regards to how much money he had coming and the car of his dreams.

"You ok, Andrew?" asked Auntie Brenda as Squid walked in the door.

"Yep, the dreaded Brinks Mat curse has struck again but hey ho, I am finally getting used to it now." Squid mocked.

"Oh Andrew no, what is it this time?" asked Brenda.

"My Mum's dead. We weren't that close, still I have some money to come from the sale of her assets and whatever is left after costs is mine. Makes up for being a shit mother I suppose." Squid replied.

"Well Uncle Bob and I are here if you need us, you know that." Brenda replied.

"You two have been really good foster parents and have helped me no end. You are honest and stable and that's something I wasn't used to in my life until I came here. It's nice to have someone I can really trust. I am so settled and content with my life here, I am determined to put the past behind me you know. Hopefully this Brinks Mat ordeal is in the past now and has died with them." Squid replied.

"Awe sweetheart thank you, that's so nice of you, I am just glad we have been able to make a difference and Uncle Bob and I are here should you need us."

The next two months were agony for Squid, he had found the car he wanted but was still working in McDonalds which he hated. It felt like it was taking a life time sorting out his mother's estate. Then one Monday morning a cheque arrived in the post. Squid walks to the front door and picks up the mail from the floor. He opens the one addressed to himself. Pulling out the cheque he stepped back in surprise, this was far more than he had expected. He looked again at the amount and sat on the foot of the stairs. Three hundred thousand pounds, it made Squid wonder how much she had actually sold them out for. Grabbing his helmet he walked to his bike and then headed into the bank.

"Hi, I would like to bank this cheque." Squid announced to the cashier.

"Wow that's a nice amount for a lad of your age, guess this isn't your McDonalds wages." the clerk joked.

"Wish it was be nice that, once a month. No it's my inheritance. Now I can quit my job and buy myself a decent car. I passed my test a few months ago, so going to spoil myself for a while maybe go on holiday as well." Squid explained.

"Well there's a lot of money in your account now, I see you have been saving regularly too. It may be worthwhile making an appointment to see one of our financial consultants they could advise you on ways to invest it sensibly, in a way you get a good return."

"Nah, you are OK, I want to have a think about things first." Squid replied.

If you have the money and let's face it I now did. Then in the 80's and coming from my background there was only one car to have a series three V12 Jaguar. So I bought one.

One week later and the cheque was clear in Squids account. He rode to a second hand car sales garage and asked what the guy would give him for his moped in part exchange against the beautiful series three Jaguar he'd been eying up for the last two months. It was finished in a stunning metallic red. The salesman thought Squid was playing with him until Squid got the man to phone his bank to confirm he had the money to buy the car. Three hours later the car was insured, taxed and ready to go with two full tanks of fuel.

Now I know what you are thinking, how can a 17 year old kid get insurance on a v12 Jag? Well you see, back in the day before things went all computerised, there were fiddles you could do "Legal fiddles." I bought an old 850 cc Mini, insured it fully comp, this covered me to drive anyone else's car legally, see where this is going? So the Jag was put in my foster parents name and in the dash was a little letter from them in case I got stopped saying I have their permission to drive it. Nice one don't you think, right back to the story.

Squid spent the rest of the day driving around his old hunting ground. He passed his old house nothing had changed there much. However Jenny's old house had been knocked down and a building plot had gone in of four new houses. Her father had obviously moved them away and sold the house and land. Disappointed he had been unable to find Jenny hung heavy on Squid's shoulders. He had this dream in his head that now he had enough money to look after Jenny properly and a new ID, that the two of them could just pick where they left off and live happily ever after. But, real life wasn't like that. A sad and once more angry Squid headed back to his home in Salisbury.

When Andrew walked in there was the smell of one of Auntie Brenda's roast dinners on the go that really did lift his spirits, the right food always seemed to have a way of doing that. With his spirits lifted he told Auntie Brenda and Uncle Bob all about his day out and his new car.

"Look Andrew, I hope you don't mind but we have been discussing all this money you have just come into, we think you should invest some of it. Both of us know you have been through such a hard time as a child, we want your future to be brighter.

I know a man at work and he can arrange for two hundred thousand pounds to be put into stocks and shares, an investment for your future." Auntie Brenda explained.

"Well funny you should say about that, but the man in the bank was saying the same thing so maybe he's right, I suppose it would make sense and the money would still be there should I need it." he replied.

"Andrew if you want to go ahead leave me the cheque tomorrow as I am seeing Mike at work, he will then set it all up this week for you, unlike a bank he's independent, so he's looking after you where the bank will only do a deal to suit themselves. It's seriously worth thinking about before you go spending too much." replied Uncle Bob.

"Okay, no problem I will leave the cheque on the kitchen table if I don't see you in the morning. I am not doing anything else with it anyway, so I think it's a good idea. Thank you. Auntie Brenda, Uncle Bob." said Squid as he gave them both a hug.

The following morning Auntie Brenda is washing up some cups in the kitchen when Squid comes to talk to her. He puts the cheque on the table as Auntie Brenda has wet hands, after a brief chat Squid then leaves in the Jag and goes for a drive. Then, like the old days, finds himself in town sat in a café thinking. Mobile phones had suddenly hit the market, so interested as to the prospects of an up and coming product like this he visits a couple of mobile phone shops and some property agents.

After returning home, Squid talks to his foster parents about his plans and ideas.

"I'm thinking about getting into either property or the mobile phone business, which do you two think I should do?" he asked valuing their opinion.

"Well my father always said bricks and mortar." replied Uncle Bob.

"I suggested you take a holiday love. You have just had your exam results through, taken your driving test and you've had all that nonsense over both your parents dying and now the disappointment of not finding this Jenny girl. Why don't you go over to the States like you've always dreamt of, spend a fortnight chilling out." Auntie Brenda replied.

"Hit the beaches chat up some of those American chicks, just chill out and decide what you want to do with your life." suggested Uncle Bob.

"Maybe you are right. I will go and book a flight tomorrow, I have always fancied learning to fly and it's much cheaper out in the USA. I really need to think about what I am going to do with my life. I really don't want to blow this opportunity. Thanks for the chat." replied Squid, whose head was now working overtime with ideas.

"Well I'm sure you'll do what's best. You're a smart kid Andrew; believe in yourself, the world is your oyster." said Uncle Bob as Squid headed for his bedroom.

After such reassuring words I remember jumping straight on a flight to the USA and returned six weeks later with my pilot's license. I was on top of the world; I didn't think anything could or would stop me making my fortune, but then I had let my guard down again, flooded with all this cash I had become distracted from reality and forgotten about the Brinks Mat curse.

Squid arrives home in the early hours of morning. Not wanting to wake Bob and Brenda he leaves his bags in front room, goes straight to bed. Waking around ten the following morning all was quiet which was a little unusual as Brenda would normally say hello before going to work. What with being away longer than expected Squid didn't let the absence of activity play on his mind. Getting up, Squid takes a shower and once dressed he goes downstairs for breakfast.

"Uncle Bob, Auntie Brenda anyone home. Hello anyone in?" he shouted.

The house remained silent Squid sees a note stuck on the fridge door, pulling it off he sits and reads it.

Dear Andrew. We have left for a new life abroad, Bob and I have decided to retire early thanks to your very generous gift and we wish you well in all you do. Love Bob and Brenda Ps: Sold the house so you have to be out by the end of the month.

We've left you some cash in the fridge to cover your costs in finding alternative accommodation, love you and thank you again, Uncle Bob and Auntie Brenda.

"What gift?" said Squid thinking out loud.

Opening the fridge door, inside on a plate was one thousand five hundred pounds in cash.

"What the fuck!" Squids screamed his head was thumping trying to take all this in. Squid picks up the cash and puts in his pocket. He then starts looking around the house, he opens cupboards and draws but they are all empty. Running upstairs to Bob and Brenda's bedroom, he soon discovers it was also empty. Every room except his own was empty.

"Gift . . . What gift? What the fuck's going on, what are they talking about? No-no-no not my money, please god, don't let it all start again." screamed Squid as his darkest fear became reality.

Grabbing his car keys, Squid runs to the Jag. He spins off up the road, screeching up outside the bank and runs in.

"Yes Sir how can I help today?" asked the cashier.

"Statement please, tell me, it says there's only sixty three thousand pounds left in this account there should be at least over two hundred thousand nearer three hundred. Is there a mistake?" asked Squid panicking.

"A cheque was banked five weeks ago for two hundred thousand pounds. It should be on your statement that went out of your account way over three weeks ago sir." the cashier explained.

"Damn it how could I've been such a twat! Bastards, I am going to kill the fucking bastards." Squid screamed.

"Sir is there a problem, if there is maybe I can help?" shouted the cashier as Squid left the bank.

As Squid gets out to the Jaguar in somewhat of a trance, he finds a traffic warden sticking ticket on the windscreen. The fact he had parked on the pavement outside the bank didn't even register with Squid.

"Wanker! Damn fucking wanker..." Squid screams at the warden. Taking off the man's cap, he sends it flying down the road like Frisbee, knees the warden in the balls then grabs the ticket from the windscreen and sticks it to the warden's forehead.

"Take that twat....and that and have this back." he screamed.

Squid gets in the Jag and spins off down the road heading back to the house. Once home he goes into the tool shed in the back garden, picks up an axe and walks into the kitchen. Confronting the fridge as if it's a person Squid has lost the plot.

"So think you can take the piss do you? Well meet my new friend Axa, Axa and I are going to teach you a little fucking lesson on how not to take the piss. There take that and that and this!" screamed Squid as he let the axe fly. Squid repeatedly takes swings at fridge with the axe which with every swing is moving from where it has sat for the last few years. By the sixth swing Squid hits the electrics, blowing himself across the room with an electric jolt knocking Squid out cold against the opposite wall of the kitchen. When he comes to minutes later the electric has tripped and the place is full of shadows from limited sunlight.

"Ok, so you think I am done do you?" moaned Squid as he pulled himself up from the kitchen floor.

Getting to his feet Squids fingers stretch and turn red as he takes a firm grip of the axe, running across the kitchen he swings the axe with all his might, the door of the fridge comes flying off, as it does so it covers Squid in sour milk which had sat in a carton since his foster parents had left a month earlier. This made Squid even madder and he proceeds to chop the fridge up into as many pieces as he can to let off all his anger.

It was at this define moment I changed, the boy in me was gone. Give me whatever name you want, but I am still Squid Ryan, I always will be and with that name comes the Brinks mat curse.

Julie Banks, the local estate agent, was having a very good morning. She had already done two viewings of houses close to Squid's and was now due to show a couple of newlyweds Uncle Bob and Auntie Brenda's house. Whilst Squid is now collapsed on the floor exhausted, Julie turns up with a viewing and enters the house with the keys left with them by Bob and Brenda. A recently married couple who are thinking of buying the house follow her in.

"And the owners have stated that any of the furniture left in here will be included which for a couple starting out like yourselves is a real bonus and that does mean things like the cooker, washing, fridge..."

Julie stammered on the word fridge as they all walk into kitchen, confronted by SQUID with an axe in hand, sitting on the kitchen floor gloating over the disembowelled dead fridge. The young wife's eyes met Squids and she let out a wailing scream that could be heard down the end of the street. Screaming she bolts towards the front door and runs from the house, followed closely by husband and estate agent Julie. The three run down the drive and are met by two police officers following up the assault on the traffic warden.

"Mad axe man . . . mad axe man, he's trying to kill us all, run for your life!" Julie screamed.

Unfortunately for Squid that wasn't actually the case but it was enough for the police to call for back up and a full on assault of the house ordered. Four hours later locked up in a prison cell, Squid has visitors from two familiar police officers, Morris and Maw!

"Andrew, my name's Sergeant Morris. You may remember me coming to see you at your foster parent's house. I organised the funds to be transferred into your account. I must say I am a little surprised to see you here. Do you mind explaining to me what the hell's been going on?" asked Morris

"The name's Squid-Squid Ryan and my so called law abiding foster parents have taken all my money and run off with it. This is the way my life is always going to be, cursed by this dammed Brinks Mat robbery. If they're not trying to kill me they're robbing me, bastards, they're all fucking bastards." Squid replied.

The officers sit and discuss what has happened and try to help Squid out. They've been dealing with him for a while and wanted to help the lad. They also hope it may lead to Squid divulging what he knows about the missing gold.

"You know it says in the note, you gave them the money as a gift. You also signed the cheque, it's going to take time this one. But you help us and we will help you." suggested Morris.

"I think I must have had some sort of a breakdown, due to the shock of it all, I am truly sorry. It's just so hard. I don't know who I can trust any more. What's going to happen to me now?" asked Squid feeling at an all-time low.

"Look, I will see what I can do to get you out of here and pull a few strings. But, you have to promise me nothing like this will ever happen again. Just because you are in a relocation program doesn't mean you can break the law whenever you feel the need. As for the money I am sure it's illegal for your foster parents to accept such a gift. As soon as I can I will inform their employers and I'm sure they will be as surprised as me when they find all this out. However it could take months or years to catch up with them and lord knows what money may be left or recoverable. All I can say is get on with your life. If anything good comes of it, count it as a bonus. I know you have had a shit deal so far in life. But don't let this ruin it for you, you have a nice sum of money still in the bank for someone of your age, so be sensible with it." replied Morris, giving Squid a little pet talk.

Two days later Squid leaves the police station. All his belongings are waiting for him in reception he loads them into the Jag. Sitting in the Jag Squid puts the key in the ignition, the V12 bursts into life. Squid smiles at least they hadn't sold his beloved Jag. In his heart he knew who he was now and what he had to do, putting the car in gear he heads to Croydon.

"You can't beat me you damned fucking curse, I won't let you, I am better than this." he said to himself as he headed out of town.

Before Squid reaches Croydon, he stops in at a garden centre, parks the Jag in the car park and pops in and buys a spade. He then drives to a secluded lane close to his old house in Croydon, reclines the red leather seat and goes to sleep. In the early hours of the morning, he wakes feeling cold, the windows on the car are frosted, turning the key he fires up the Jag and warms himself up.

After getting comfortable and warm, Squid turns off the engine and gets out. Walking to the rear of the car he opens the boot and grabs the spade. Sneaking into the back garden of his old house, Squid digs up the cash he buried there years earlier. Returning to the jag with the cash he once more leaves Croydon and heads for Brighton.

Chapter Five

Whilst Duke was trying his best to divert any enquires away from Squid's trail, every so often henchmen from one group or another insisted in thinking he knew where Squid was. This had led him to employ the services of an old military friend called Ox.

Ox was in his thirties, around 5'10" and built like a brick shit house, hence his nick name Ox as he was built like one. After a visit from a group of young men in a BMW, Duke had decided it was time to scare the hell out of them and let them know he was a force to be reckoned with. So, early one May morning, Duke found himself taking the BMW and its occupants to a dumping site he had often used in the past.

Duke and Ox drive down the isolated country lane in Wiltshire to a clearing, there the two get out and unload the BMW.

"Don't you think it is strange that every time we come back here the car we previously dumped has gone?" said Ox as he slides the ramps back under the rear of the truck.

"That will be the Pikeys, it's what they do." Duke replied.

Ox sits the two henchmen up in the car one in the back and one in the front he places a leaflet on their laps.

"Here's something for you to read. Now. We never want to see you ever again, do you understand? Now, tell your mates if anyone comes asking about Squid or Jenny next time we won't just leave you in the middle of no-where. The lord gives us all a path in life, it is never too late to seek forgiveness and embrace the lord." Ox preaches and smiles at them he pats one on the head as he shuts the car door. One of the thugs isn't very happy, he manages to free some of the gaffer tape around his mouth.

"Fuck you and fuck your god! I hope you all rot in hell!" he mumbles back at Ox"

"Blasphemer, I hate blasphemers." replies Ox as he punches the henchman twice knocking him out cold, he then smiles at the other one again. He then locks up the BMW with the remote and walks back to Duke and the two head off back down the track.

"Leave them something to read did you?" Duke asked.

"Yes, one of them was a blasphemer, but I think the lord has a plan for both of them." Ox replied.

"See how long it takes the Pikeys to find that one." Duke says laughing.

"Do you think they'll read the leaflet?" Ox asks.

"Who, the Pikeys? They can't bloody read, numbers, that's what the Pikeys know, numbers." Duke explains.

"No not the Pikeys, the blasphemer?" Ox replies.

"Like you say, the lord works in mysterious ways, so who knows." Duke says as the truck drives down the track. Ox winds down his window and throws out the key and fob. As the fob hits the ground there is a huge explosion and the BMW blows up. Duke slams on the brakes and both men look in the mirrors.

"What the fuck did you just do?" Duke shouted in a state of shock.

"Nothing mate, honest nothing, I just threw out the fob." Ox explained.

"Let's get the fuck out of here." Duke replied as he put his toe down. Changing gear, the truck bounced all over the track, it's springs creaking away. As they get a few metres on, a huge tank cuts across their path and loads of soldiers appear. Duke brakes heavily and the truck skids to a halt.

"I don't think it was Pikeys Duke, this is a bloody army assault course." Ox explains.

As the men move on unaware what they had done, Duke and Ox speed away.

Once again Squid finds himself sat in a café, this time in Brighton. He is totally unaware at what is going on with Duke and Jenny. He's confused on what to do and just wants to keep his head down for a while. He's lost, angry and has no idea what to do with himself. Seeing a copy of the Sun on the side he picks it up and starts to read, yet again there was an article about the Brinks Mat robbery, another victim of the curse had been killed.

"What can I get you?" asked a pretty young waitress.

Squid looks at the waitresses name badge.

"A Full English please Mandy." he said giving her a wink, the girl smiled back turned and went off to place his order. Five minutes later she returned with a mug of Coffee and ten minutes after that his breakfast was sat in front of him. The café was empty apart from an old man sat near the door looking out across the street.

"That was a great breakfast. You don't know how much I needed that. Haven't eaten in a day or two but there's nothing like a good old Full English is there to get you going again?" Squid stated to the waitress hoping to spark off a conversation.

"Well I thought you were hungry the way you polished that off. Right let's see that's toast, Full English, two coffees, one hot chocolate, two cakes, and a can of coke and a piece of bread and butter pudding to take away. I work that out to be £6.33."

Squid sits there looking at the till receipt for what seems like an eternity.

"It is correct." says Mandy looking concerned by Squids stalling.

"Six pounds and thirty three pence what are the odds on that?"

"Yes £6.33, that's a good price we're the cheapest in the area, it won't change no matter how long you look at it. Look, you are going to pay aren't you or do I have to call the manager? I mean it, if you're thinking of doing a runner we have cameras in here and the boss knows some pretty nasty people ... ... Please don't. He docks my wages. It will be me who pays." replied Mandy, putting her hand on Squids shoulder.

"What, sorry . . . yes,.. sorry . . . £6.33. Yes here it is, sorry."

Squid takes a wad of cash from his jacket and handing her a tenner tells her to keep the change.

"Bloody hell, had a bet on the Gee Gee's have we?" said Mandy seeing his wad of cash.

"More like life savings or what's left of it. It's not the bill. It's the numbers 633, they seems to haunt me for some reason. You wouldn't believe how often it crops up on a day to day, week to week basis.

"Maybe they're your lucky numbers." replied Mandy.

"More like my unlucky numbers to be honest!" Squid replied with a smile, she reminded him of Jenny.

"Well don't go flashing cash around here like that, we get some real arseholes in here, they will have the shirt off your back before you even know it's missing." Mandy explained.

"Tell me, I need to find somewhere cheap to live. Kind'a new to the area and would be grateful if you could point me in the direction of a cheap bed sit, flat or room." Squid asked.

"Well the governors got the house next door converted into flats, sixty three quid a week plus heating and electric. There is a meter in each room for both, it's a week in advance, plus a month up front and no dole wallers." Mandy stated pointing at her boss in the kitchen.

"As long as the door numbers are not six or three, I will take it." replied Squid.

"That's good then. Looks like it's your lucky day as it's flat nine." Mandy smiled.

"That figures, see what I mean six add three equals nine and it's sixty three pounds a week. Look I'll pay three months in advance but I want a receipt and a rent book. Like you, I don't trust anyone any more. I need somewhere to park the Jag where it won't get broken into or ticketed, any ideas?" Squid asked her.

"COSTAS" shouts Mandy.

The cafe owner comes into the seating area from the kitchen, he's been listening to Squid's conversation with Mandy, he's a large man who has a greasy look to him and is covered in tattoos.

"Twenty quid a week extra and you can park it round the back. My name's Costas, I own this joint, which makes me your landlord. Break anything in the flat and I break you, miss a week's rent and it doubles, do we understand one another?" Costas states as he points out the rear window towards the back of the building where his own car was parked.

"Totally understand. My name's Andrew, 'Squid' to my friends. Tell me is there a gym around here anywhere and is there a fridge in the room?" replied Squid as he shakes Costas's hand.

"There's a fan heater, shower and kitchen area plus one double bed, settee, a wardrobe and yes a fridge. The nearest gym is about a mile away anything else?" asked Costas.

"Yes would you mind removing the fridge, it's just I don't like fridges, had a bit of a bad experience with one once, so if you wouldn't mind removing it I would be grateful." Squid stated.

As he got up to leave Squid counted out three month's rent including parking and handed it to Costas.

"Like I said, a receipt would be nice please." said Squid.

"Mandy, go get my receipt book, I'll dig out the keys and leave them with Mandy for you to collect when you are ready." Costas replied.

Squid thanks them for their help, then leaves to go find a gym.

"One of those fucking yuppies everyone's talking about from the city I bet, wonder what the fuck he's doing here? That's the sort of kid you should be dropping your kack's to sweetie pie not the likes of those dip shits you normally go out with and what sort of fucking weirdo don't like fridges? When he said he had a bad experience with one do you think he was trying to fuck it or something? They do say those Yuppies are into some weird old shit." Costas says to Mandy as she clears the table.

"That's Cocaine Costas, not fridges. Mind you he is cute. Looks a little lost but I don't think he's the type to go around fucking electrical appliances." Mandy replies.

Squid finds the local gym and joins it, then takes the Jag around to rear of café and parks it up. Costas walks out as Squid is unloading some bags out of the boot. He notices the baseball bat clipped to the top of the inside of the Jaguars boot lid.

"Play or expecting trouble?" asks Costas

"What!" asked Squid, wondering what Costas was on about.

"The baseball bat, are you a sportsman?" says Costas

"Well I like to think so, I mean everyone deserves a sporting chance." Squid replied. He gives Costas a smile then taking the room key he carries his stuff up to bedsit.

Once his stuff was in his room Squid heads off to the shops to buy a duvet, towels and some toiletries. Squid gets back and tried to unpack and settle in. He takes a shower and after drying himself lays down on the bed where he swiftly falls asleep. It was around two hours later when he was awoken by a knock on the door. Squid gets up and answers the door he has a small towel wrapped around his waist.

"Hi-there . . . Squid wasn't it?" Mandy asked.

"Eerrrr yes, sorry just had a shower." Squid replied.

"There was some Shepherd's Pie left over and well I didn't know if you had been able to do any shopping so thought you might like some." says Mandy carrying a Pyrex dish.

"Wow, that's nice of you. I did go shopping bought every-thing, except food. Just forgot all about food, still not a huge problem when you live next door to a cafe and that has a beau-tiful waitress to bring you tea." Squid replied.

"You look hot. Looks like you work out too, how was the shower, if it plays up just thump it that normally sorts it out?" Mandy said as she eyed Squid up and down.

"Sorry, I um-should get some clothes on, Yes . . . it is a little warm, come in a sec. didn't mean to be rude leaving you stood in the door like that. After I had a shower, I fell asleep on the bed. I only just woke as you knocked on the door." replied Squid, trying hard to make conversation with the girl.

"I think the couple next door were having some sort of a tiff, they can be noisy at times, hope they don't keep you up too much." Mandy stated as she put the Shepherd's pie on the table.

"I didn't hear them to be honest. I'd better go put some clothes on." Squid replied.

Squid walks into the bedroom and is sorting out some clothes when Mandy enters the room with her dress totally unbuttoned.

"I thought it may help if I took something off sooner than you put something on." said Mandy letting the dress drop to the floor.

"I can go with that." Squid replied taking her in his arms and kissing her, she felt so good. He hadn't been with anyone since Jenny and now he was ready to move on . . . he needed this.

"I feel so fucking horny at the end of a day, what about you?" asked Mandy as she pushed Squid back onto the bed.

"Any time really, mornings more so, definitely after a workout in the gym but after works fine by me." Squid replies.

A squeaking in a repetitive rhythm is heard throughout the building, as Squid makes up for lost time. The squeaking was soon dampened out by the backing vocals of Mandy's pleasurable groans as the two make love for the next two hours. After a short break Squid runs a bath and Mandy joins him.

"So are you going to be around for a while or what?" Mandy asked.

"Yes, going to set up a mobile phone shop. They're all the rage you know, going to buy a dog and make loads of money." Squid announced to her.

The weeks went by and Squid is organising his life, slowly he is getting to know Brighton, but as much as Squid is trying to forget his past and move on, Brighton has someone who hasn't forgotten him. His face was recognised after the first week in Brighton and someone was waiting to make their move, then one evening Squid's past soon catches up with him.

Shutting the door to the flat, Squid walks out the back and down the alley alongside the café, it's late and the alley is dark. Squid didn't even know what hit him as he fell to the ground. Coming too he is in pain and bleeding, suddenly he is winded as another blow hits him in his stomach.

"Stop you are going to kill him!" screamed Mandy running down the alley and pulling at the man.

"Costas, quick it's Squid," She cried as the man turned and knocked her to the ground.

Costas in a string vest and black trousers with bracers hanging off the sides came running out with a bat in his hand, one swing later and the man was out cold on the ground.

The two helped Squid up.

"Who is he , do you recognise his face?" asked Costas turning the man over.

Squid looked out of his one good eye at the man as the other eye was too swollen to open due to the force of the beating he had taken, his eye widened in horror as he saw the man's face.

"He's my ex's old boss, runs a fruit and veg stall on the market, we had a grievance!" Squid mumbled as he tried to walk away.

The two carried Squid back to his room, leaving the man out cold in the alley way.

"You owe me boy for this don't forget it." Costas said as he left the room.

"Do you want me to stay with you, I don't mind?" Asked Mandy.

"No go, I'll be fine." Squid replied. As Squid lay on the bed in his room, the pain was one thing but what hurt more was thinking of Jenny. Sleeping with Mandy didn't help the guilt he was feeling, maybe it was karma catching up with him for not being stronger and staying with Jenny. That night his sleep was restless as he tried to figure out everything in his head, once again the curse had stricken.

After six months Squid tires of living next door to the café and decides it is time to find a new place to live. It wasn't long before the perfect property became available. He had been looking at some empty commercial properties in the town centre which might be good for opening up a mobile phone shop but the location had to be right. Within a couple of months a unit presented itself to him, with a heavy electric roller shutter at the front to protect the contents of the store. This shop was perfect and it had a three bed roomed flat above which went with it and was on a two year lease. It was roomy, in a prime location, so Squid signed the contract and within six weeks the shop was ready to open. He decides he wants a companion, so Squid buys himself a Staff and calls it Vinnie. He employs two very pretty girls to work in the shop, Pippa and Cindy, knowing all too well first impressions are important and he knew he needed good eye candy to entice the customers in. Pippa and Cindy were just that, slim well dressed, perfect hair and nails. Cindy always wore bright red lipstick it was her trade mark which wore well with her long blonde hair. Pippa however was always a little more modest, whereas Cindy would love a short skirt, Pippa would wear trousers, but most importantly both girls knew how to make a sale.

"Right Cindy, Pippa, today's the first day. Do well and you will both have a job tomorrow. Keep doing well and you will have full time employment. Reach the targets I have set and you both get bonuses. Now come on snap, snap lets open up and make some money. Whoever makes the most sales will get a twenty quid bonus at the end of the day." Squid announced.

The first day was a huge success, as were the days that followed, people wanted phones and within a month Squid had two guys out fitting phones in vans, business was booming.

After twelve months Squid was offered a buyout deal by a large national phone company. Taking advantage of the booming mobile phone business, he soon hammered out a deal that was very profitable to himself and sold his complete business, the shop lease, lock, stock and barrel. Squid found himself with no ties and a lot of money in his bank account. After tax he had made a two hundred thousand pound profit and was on an extremely good salary working as area manager for the company that bought him out.

"All locked up Squid." said Pippa as she walked into the back office where Squid was adding up the days takings.

"Pippa, get Cindy and come back in my office a minute please." Squid replied very formal.

"Here boss, what's wrong, is everything ok?" asked Cindy.

Squid puts three glasses on his desk and opens bottle of champagne, as the cork pops out Vinnie barks and chases it around the floor.

"Girls it's been just over a year now, business has been very good. A month ago I sold the shop and made a huge profit. The names going to be changing soon and there will be a lot more stock coming in, the very latest smaller units. They are keeping me on running this store as area manager. There will be new higher targets to meet but I have every faith in you meeting them. I am proud of you both, so here, I wanted to give you a bonus. Some of that's from my buy out deal, if it wasn't for you two, it wouldn't have happened." Squid announced as he handed them each a cheque for ten thousand pounds.

Girls came and went over the years, none of them came close to Jenny, it was just good sex. I stopped counting past twenty, all I wanted was a normal life, settled without police or gangsters on my back.

The girls are over whelmed and the three soon find themselves having a party up in Squids flat, a party that ended with both girls in bed with Squid. Waking up the next morning with these two beautiful girls either side of him Squid was once again on top of the world, he felt amazing, his working out at the gym had paid dividends and he was now a huge muscular frame of a man. Over the next six months Squid and his team blasted their way through all the targets set, all three were getting huge and regular bonuses. Squid's bonuses were now happening daily where the two girls were concerned, they seemed to enjoy sharing him and Squid wasn't going to argue with that.

It was now late 1986 and Squid had once again forgotten all about his past, it was like a distant memory. But the Brinks Mat bullion robbery had changed the face of how the criminal underworld did their business, they now realised that there were huge amounts of money to be made in other things apart from cash. It was 9.33 on a Monday morning in September, Pippa was under the desk giving Squid a blow job, when Cindy bursts into office, followed by man with sawn off shotgun. The man's face is covered by a balaclava. He has two accomplices with him.

"What the Fuck!" shouted Squid, unable to move.

"This is a hold up. Now do as you are told and no-one will get hurt. You, Mr Manager stay right there at your desk and don't fucking move." Well "Thank fuck for that!" Squid thought unable too if he wanted too. Every so often Squid let out a little murmur. Pippa's under the desk giving him head with her head phones on listening to music and is oblivious to what is going on the other side of the desk. The thug gives him a strange look, whilst the gunman's two sidekicks take the phones from the shop and load them into the van.

"Now don't you go getting all nervous on me sunshine, I would hate to have to put a few pellets into that handsome looking face of yours. Just let my pals here load up the stock in the van and no-one will get hurt. It's all insured so don't be a hero." the thug explained.

The thug then makes Cindy stand over at the desk behind Squid, Cindy notices Pippa under the desk working Squid's tool with perfection. Pippa sees Cindy and winks at her. In the heat of the moment, Squid lets out a cry as he releases himself deep down Pippa's throat. Cindy looks at Thug, who suddenly looks worried.

"I am sorry I think he's having an asthma attack. He needs his inhaler." She splutters out not thinking of anything else to say.

"Well find out where it is, don't want him choking on anything, I don't want to hurt anyone, my boss just wants the stock that's all." replied the thug looking a little nervous.

Unbeknown to the thug, the only person with a chance of choking on anything is Pippa and he doesn't even know she's there.

"Squid sweetie, I just need to search you to find your inhaler. Can you tell me where it is please, point if you can't speak

Hun?" Cindy asks trying to stall things till the guys have loaded up their van.

"Oh fuck!" Cries Squid as Cindy puts her hand down Squids pants taking a grip of his tool and slapping Pippa's mouth with it.

"Right, we have all the mobile phones. We're out of here. You best sort him out I don't want him dying, I am not a murderer you know. Don't call the police for at least twenty minutes and you won't hear from us again. Ok?" said the thug as he got ready to leave.

"Yes . . . yes ok, just go, I will sort him out now." Cindy replied as she squeezed at Squids tool.

All three thugs leave the shop and head off in the van which is loaded with all the stock from the shop.

"Now don't move Squid. Don't think you are going anywhere until I've had my turn." announced Cindy as she moved the desk and pulled Pippa to one side.

Getting up from under the desk topless Pippa is well pleased with herself, and singing away walks back into the front of the shop whilst re-arranging her clothes. As she walks through the short corridor between the office and shop front, she notices the open and closed sign on the door reads open her side, which meant to the public the shop was closed, then as she walked towards the door to change it, she sees all the shelves are empty and the stock gone, she runs back into Squids office confused. Cindy is now bent over the desk being banged from behind by Squid.

"Squid I think we've been done over, all the stocks gone!" Pippa says looking very confused as to when this might of happened.

"I guess you missed that bit." replied Cindy as she gripped the desk.

"Like the man says, it is all insured." Squid replied.

"He did?" asked Pippa.

"Yes, now come and bend over the fucking desk here next to Cindy, you two girls are just so damned naughty." Squid replied as he continued to make love to the pair.

The three thugs roar away out of Brighton in their van towards London. The thug who has been holding the shot gun over Squid turns to his accomplices as his brain works over time.

"That girl back there called her boss Squid. Wasn't that the name of that kid the boss was looking for, the one whose father hid some of the Brinks Mat gold?" he asked the other two.

"Dunno, before my time mate." one replied whilst the other shrugged his shoulders.

After their little session in the office, Squid realised he should act on the robbery, before any more time is wasted.

"Better call the pigs, damn it! They are going to want to see the CCTV footage and all they're going to see is us three screwing." Squid announced.

"Just say you were just loading it when that thug barged in. In the mean time I will put the blank one in its place." Cindy replied.

"I will take this one home and run us all off a copy no-one will ever believe this is for real." said Pippa, as she took the video from Cindy.

"Good thinking. We better check our stories all match up before they get here though and Cindy go and put that tape in your car so no-one will find it. In future I will make sure I bring Vinnie to work with me all the time. That was just too close. The stock is covered by insurance and I am sure the new owners will have us up and running within a few days, girls, are you both ok?" said Squid.

"Yes were fine, I didn't even know they were there Squid, sorry." Pippa replied.

"I think I cum in my pants, it was a real adrenaline rush, that's not to say you shouldn't keep comforting us Squid." replied Cindy giving him a kiss.

"Yeah if only every morning started with a shag like this." Pippa replied giving Squid a wink.

"You know they didn't make me open the safe, and this is all covered on insurance so I say we open the safe and we split what is in it three ways" Squid said as he looked at the safe on the wall.

"Good thinking Batman!" Replied Pippa,

"Cindy go check the shop. See if there is any other stock left there that they missed, if so, go put it in your car and take it home, we'll split that three ways as well." Squid replied knowing that his father had taught him how to take advantage of a gift horse.

But little known to me, a seed had been set that day and my bubble was about to be popped big time. Once again the Brinks Mat curse was about to rage its fury.

It only took about two weeks for the shit to hit the fan. Until that Monday morning a fortnight later, a well-dressed man entered the phone shop.

"Hello Squid, well I must say when I got a call last week telling me that you were in Brighton running a mobile phone shop, imagine my surprise. Shall we go into your office for a little chat? We can catch up on old times." announced the smart dressed man who was in his late fifties.

"Do we know one another?" Squid asked knowing straight away trouble was about to brew.

"In a way, you know a friend of a friend. The name's Charlie, Charlie Adams." Charlie replied.

"Doesn't ring any bells, were you wanting some phones?" Squid replied.

"The big boss really wants you to come with me he needs to have a little chat with you regarding some missing gold. But, then you know all this, don't you Squid my boy, so let's not waste one another's time having silly chats about phones." Charlie explains as he plays with the gold Rolex on his left wrist.

Charlie puts his phone on Squids desk next to Squids phone.

"Amazing how the tables can soon turn, all because of technology." Charlie replied looking at the phones.

"What makes you think the tables turned?" Squid replied.

"When my phone rings in five minutes time, either you tell the boss what he needs to know, which will save a lot of unpleasantness, or in ten minutes the boys, who are sat in a car around the corner come in and we'll break up this place and the people in it." Charlie replied very calmly.

"Like I have always told you lot and the pigs, I really don't know a thing." Squid replied.

"Pretty girls you have out there, it would be horrible if something happened to them just because of you, then of course, even after I have hurt them, I will still have to hurt you. The choice is yours, the easy way or the hard way." Charlie replied as he clearly started to get agitated.

"That's all very well but I really can't help you. Do you seriously think that if I knew where there was millions of pounds worth of Brinks Mat gold I would be working for a living?" replied Squid.

"I do hope you are pulling my pisser son. I ain't pissing about you know. If I don't have an answer for the boss, things will turn ugly around here do you understand me? Am I highlighting how serious this situation is for you? We're not just talking about concrete boots here it's the full multi-story car park job. You seem very calm for a dead man walking." Charlie said as his whole attitude turned more aggressive.

Squid realised at any moment things were going to kick off and he had to protect Pippa and Cindy. They were innocent to all this and he couldn't bare anything happening to them. Suddenly Squid saw his opportunity as Charlie's phone rang, it's ring tone was that of a cat meowing.

"Meow-meow . . . meow-meow . . . meow." rang the phone.

"You know that really is not a good ring tone to have in here today." Squid replied, ready to make his move.

"Why do you think that is?" replied Charlie punching the table so that the phone falls on the floor. But before Squid could utter a word, Vinnie bolted out from under table and eats the phone whole. Vinnie then stands looking at Charlie growling. Charlie immediately pulls a knife from his jacket pocket.

"Call the fucking mutt back to you and hold him down, I need that phone back this is definitely going to get messy." Charlie screamed.

"Kill Vinnie kill!" shouted Squid.

Vinnie dives at Charlie's crotch, takes mouthful of trousers with it Charlie's left testicle. Charlie lets out huge scream which causes the girls to run to the office door. Squid punches Charlie in the face, knocking him out cold.

"I seriously need to answer that call Vinnie." Squid says grabbing Vinnie.

The phone rings once more inside dog. Squid puts the dog down and Vinnie tried chasing himself to get to the noise. Putting his arms around both girls, Squid hurries them through to the front of the shop.

"What the bloody hell's going on Squid?" asked Pippa.

"Call the police now, then get the hell out of here. In about five minutes all hell's going to let loose." Squid replied.

"Right, can everyone please leave the shop, we have an emergency situation and for your own safety you need to leave now!" shouted Squid to all the customers who were looking at phones.

"What is it Squid, what's happening?" asked Cindy.

Squid gave both girls a huge kiss.

"I'm not who you think I am, I'm on a relocation program, these men are very, very, nasty people. I have to go and I can't return. When the police arrive tell them it's all to do with the Brinks Mat heist. My real name is Squid Ryan. Tell the police The Brinks Mat gang are on to me again and that I will be in touch." Squid explained.

"Will we ever see you again?" asked Pippa.

"No, I doubt it, sorry girls, I love you both but, you are safer not knowing me anymore, now go, run before you get hurt." shouted Squid at the pair.

"Squid Ryan, Brinks Mat, gold." mumbled Cindy.

"Yes that's it, have you got all that? Now run." Squid said ushering them out of the door.

"Yes, Squid Ryan, yes-no problem, take care Hun." said Pippa as she kissed him then ran from the shop her eyes moist with tears.

"I know the way these guys work, this place will be full of bullet holes in a couple of minutes, now run and don't come back." said Squid as he shut the door behind the girls.

Squid grabs his car keys and runs out back to the Jag.

"Come on Vinnie, in the car quick." shouts Squid to the dog. Moments later he spins off down the back road from the shop, he's well aware they probably know his car so he hides it in a car park whilst he gets himself back close to the shop. Before the police can arrive at the shop two series five BMW's screech up with the hit men inside.

"Go find Charlie then shoot the place up lads, shoot the fucking lot of them." screamed this six foot five thug.

Five armed men from the car run inside the shop, they carry out Charlie who is covered in blood. But just as they get him in the car the Police arrive.

"Let's get the fuck out of here." screams one of the thugs to the others.

The men turned their fire power from the shop to the police cars disabling them both and getting into the BMW they flee.

The girls walk out of a café where they had been hiding looking at the destroyed shop they hug one another sobbing. The two police cars are reduced to smouldering wrecks.

"Holy crap, I didn't know Squid was into shit like this." sobbed Cindy.

"Me neither, I hope he's ok." Pippa said as she continued to hug Cindy.

Both girls look around for Squid. Whilst they wait the police to take control, looking towards the bottom of road, Cindy sees Squid's Jag. He looks up the road content that both girls are ok, putting up his hand he waves to them both. Climbing back into the Jag Squid heads off to a nearby car sales garage and ditches the Jag. With Vinnie on a lead he then walks to Brighton Police station.

Squid explains what has happened and how the criminal underworld now know who he is. They go to Squid's flat where they recover all his documents, ID, and cash.

"We've changed your identity again Squid your name's now Steve Carr and we have booked you a flight to the USA leaving tonight. We suggest you stay away for a while and keep your head down." explained the police officer who was dealing with his case.

A week went by, Pippa and Cindy are on leave whilst they wait for the insurance company to repair the shop and a new manager is brought in.

Pippa is still in bed when there is a knock on her door, as she opens it she is nearly knocked to her feet by an excited Vinnie, she thinks Squid has returned to see her but instead looks up to see a police officer stood in the doorway.

"Excuse me Miss, I have been asked to give you Vinnie and in the bag is some money for you." said the policeman handing her a package.

"You best come in. What am I supposed to do with Vinnie?" she asked.

"I think that's up to you Miss. He asked me to give you this as well it is a letter from your ex-boss." explained the man.

Pippa takes the note and reads it:

Dearest Pippa, You once said you always wanted a dog, well now you have one. I've had to go away and will not be returning. In the bag is ten grand in cash. It should help out with food and vets bills. Please give Vinnie the same affection you showed me. If you can't, then please find him a nice home for him. Wish I could explain but it's all too complicated. Stay well and thanks for some great times Love Squid.

A tear runs down Pippa's cheek as she shows the policeman out then she climbs back into bed sobbing her eyes out. They had all got closer than any of them had realised and now it was over they were all left feeling empty. Vinnie sat by the bed wining so pulling back the covers Pippa beckoned the dog into bed where the two cuddled up together. Squid knew Vinnie would protect Pippa should she ever need it.

Chapter Six

Christmas of 1987 came and went, I found myself on a flight to the USA where I stayed for eight months. I kept myself busy upgrading my pilots licence and working out in the gym. But I knew I had to return to the UK and I had to make yet another new start.

Squid landed at Gatwick then he caught a train to Somerset. It was out of the way from Croydon and a good place to start a new low profile life. This time there would be no business, he had money in the bank, he would simply keep his head down and get a job.

Being able to look after himself, Squid found himself working as a doorman at the night clubs in Taunton and Tiverton. At first he rented a small bedsit in Taunton, he then moved to a flat in Wellington, as it was an ideal town to live in being half way between the two work places. One of the club owners in Taunton had overheard talk of Squid having a pilot's licence. Having his own plane he decided he would ask Squid to be his personal pilot.

"You know I could use a big strong lad like you Steve, what with you having a pilot's license and all. You are wasted as a doorman fancy moving up the ladder a bit?" asked Rob Curtis, who owned the club.

"Sure, always looking to better myself. But, I won't fly drugs, not for anyone, as long as we're clear on that and understand one another, then yes." Squid replied eager to be doing more.

Over the next few months Squid started to do more and more flying for Rob, discovering the man had his finger in several pies. Christmas was soon upon them and Squid was able to spend it in the warm on the Costa del Sol on Rob's boat that was moored in Torremolinos . As a new year approached and a new decade, Squid was on the move again this time down to Exeter so he was closer to the airport for Rob, who was now using his plane most days. Squid was determined to tread very carefully in what he was doing this time not wanting to get recognised again.

Instead of the Jag, Squid drove a Ford Escort, he didn't want to attract any attention to himself. It was in April of 1990 Squid was reminded of how the Brinks Mat curse was very much alive. He picked up a copy of the Sun newspaper to read the headline *"Great Train Robber Murdered."*

Charles Frederick 'Charlie' Wilson had been killed, shot dead in Marbella Spain by a hit man. The article went on to say that the shooting was related to the laundering of gold from the Brinks Mat bullion robbery. Squid recalled Charlie visiting his house when Squid was a child. He knew the two had been friends so he really wasn't surprised Charlie had become yet another victim of the curse.

One morning in May, Squid is sat in Morgan's transport café on the A38 outside Wellington. Supping on a hot chocolate he looks through the property section of the Wellington weekly.

"Nice hot chocolate." Squid announced to the waitress as she walked passed him.

"Glad you like it, not from around here are you, not seen you here before." she replied.

"No, been down in Exeter for a while, looking to buy a house around here so having a flick through the papers. Was thinking of Wellington again, used to rent a flat there for a while and liked the place." he explained.

"I have a mate Dominic. Give me your number and I'll get him to call you. He's a financial adviser, knows loads of properties going at sensible prices." the waitress explained.

"Lovely job, here's my number. Tell him to call me. My name's Steve Carr." Squid replied

"Mine's Louise, maybe see you around then." she replied walking off with a smile.

With money sat in the bank Squid really didn't need to work like he did, he also didn't need to get a mortgage in order to buy a house, but he realised it was in his interest to do so. It made him look like every other hard working male of his age. A week or so after chatting with Louise, Squid arranges to meet up with Dominic who was short around 5'3 but weighed around 16 stone. His hair was curly and grey was starting to come through, the guy was a sales man and this showed the moment the man opened his mouth. Together they go looking at houses on the outskirts of Wellington. By the afternoon Squid had seen the perfect house that he wanted to buy. "The Swallows" a four bed roomed detached house with drive and garage. It wasn't too big it was just a normal sized house, one which wouldn't attract any attention to himself.

Squid had soon built up a reputation as a man not to be messed with. Under this new name of Steve Carr, he had now become the local businessmen's debt collector. His muscular build was now very intimidating. After a year and a half in Somerset Squid was established there with a new but small group of friends he felt he could trust. It was August of the following year when Squid bumped into Dominic again at a pub in Wellington.

"How's life then Steve, still knocking off Louise from the cafe? I picked up this lovely bit the other night in Taunton, Dawn, I tell you, nothing like getting up the crack of Dawn." Dominic joked with him.

"No, Louise and I fizzled out months ago, there's been about ten others since, can't even remember their names, just can't find that special one." Squid replied.

"Well, enjoy it whilst it's there. Anyway look, I've got word of another nice little earner it'll suit someone like yourself with a bit of spare cash to invest. Fit in with the others you have with me a treat." Dominic replied.

"Go on then, not even going to ask what it is, but the others have been doing ok, you seem to know what you are doing, so as long as you've invested in it as well, count me in." Squid replied.

"Look without sitting here turning the night into a business meeting, just want to suggest to you of amalgamating the three other ones into this one deal. It's what I've done and so have a lot of my other customers. We're already reaping in the rewards, it's a bloody good opportunity Steve." Dominic explained briefly.

"Go on then, drop the paper work in next week and I will sign it." Squid replied.

It was a time when things were going a little crazy. In 1991 Squid had his busiest year ever. He was flying nearly every day, earning a damned good wage again and was enjoying his bachelor life style. Then driving back from Dunkeswell aerodrome in the May of 1992 Squid passes through the village of Hemyock where he sees a stunning metallic blue MK2 Jaguar. Pulling up outside the garage in his escort, Squid wanders over to look at it. The car was like new.

"Beautiful isn't she?" stated the salesman.

Squid peered in through the window looking at the stunning light blue leather seat with a dark blue bead around the edge of them.

"Yes, this can't be original, can it?" Squid asked.

"No, they never made them this good, it's one of those revamped ones from those yuppies in London. He was down here on business and bought a BMW off me. Apparently these Jags are all the rage in the city, spent a bloody fortune on them they have. This particular one has had all upgraded brakes and suspension, discs all around, new engine and box, new interior, paint job, the list goes on." the salesman explained to Squid.

"Can I have a test drive?" asked Squid.

The salesman looked over at Squids Escort then back at the Jag.

"I don't want to be rude sir, but I should mention, the car might be beyond your price range. I can see what the finance company can do, but like I said these yuppies were spending over a hundred thousand having these cars modified and rebuilt. Even resold by someone like myself they are still a very expensive car." the salesman explained.

"It's ok, I understand, I won't want finance, but I will expect a good price for cash. What are you asking for her?" asked Squid.

"Let me go get the keys, the trade plates and if you like her we can discuss price whilst you enjoy the drive." the salesman cunningly suggested.

Ten minutes later Squid was powering this stunning car up Hemyock hill, the car performed like a new one.

"Ok come on hit me with it, what do you want for her?" Squid asked.

"Well as I said sir, this car has had a very expensive rebuild, the paintwork is of the highest quality, the re-spray alone was well over ten thousand pounds. I have all the receipts from the re-build and this interior was over twenty thousand pound. I don't want to put you off, but I did allow the man far more for it than I would have liked." the salesman explained.

"Look, you can cut all the crap with me, just give me a ball park figure." replied Squid, who had already decided he wanted this car.

"Well the asking price is sixty five thousand pounds sir." the salesman replied sheepishly.

"Look you know as well as I do, you are not going to get that sort of cash for this car here in the West Country. Tell you what I will do I'll give you forty five thousand cash" Squid announced as he pulled up back at the garage.

"I couldn't let it go for that sir, fifty thousand and we have a deal and with that I will put twelve months mot on her as well as twelve months road tax and a full service." the salesman offered, holding out his hand to seal the deal.

"Tell you what, you do all that, take my old Escort as part exchange and I will give you forty nine thousand in cash on Friday. That gives you three days to get it all done and I have the car for the weekend." Squid replied.

The salesman smiled at him then nodded his head and shook Squids hand.

"You drive a hard bargain Sir, but yes I can do that. But I will need a deposit today before I can start to get the car ready for you." replied the salesman.

Squid walked to his car, opened his briefcase and took out five thousand pounds in cash.

"Here I want a receipt." Squid replied handing the salesman the money.

"Not a problem Sir and I will have the car all ready for collection on Friday afternoon." he announced.

Squid knew this was one of those reckless moments he might live to regret but he wanted this car, he had fallen in love with it. What with buying the car and Dominic's investments, Squid's bank account was now greatly reduced but money seemed plentiful. He was having no problems earning it and people were constantly chasing him for work. Money really wasn't a worry.

But, it wasn't until Squid came to insure the car he had a huge shock, one that bought the past right back to the present.

"Yes sir that's all in order, all I need now is the estimated value of the car and the registration number?" asked the insurance woman.

"No problem, the value is sixty five thousand pounds and the registration number is . . . oh hang on, I haven't even looked, let me just go to the window and see." replied Squid as he walked to the window. Looking out at the stunning Jaguar sat on his drive Squids heart sank as he read back the registration to the insurance woman.

"It's 633BMR!" he replied almost choking on his words.

September of 1992 Squid was as busy as ever, his car had become his pride and joy. When Squid's not working he would be polishing and detailing it. Once again his old life seemed to be a distant memory. He was doing a lot of work for a businessman called Reginald Greenslade at this time, whom he had met through his other boss Rob down at Exeter. Squid had also decided to take in a couple of local lads as lodgers, this helped cover his mortgage payments so he was sitting pretty comfortable again. Reginald had a King Air which Squid was flying for him regularly. Then one morning a flight for Reginald meant going down to Squid's old hunting ground West Sussex.

"Squid I need you to fly me down to Shoreham today for a business meeting with some chap from Spain. He's talking about building an air-park over there." Reginald explained to Squid.

"No problem boss let me know if it's any good, may invest in it myself." Steve replied.

The King Air didn't take long to reach Shoreham. Squid taxis it to the parking area close to the terminal building and shuts off the engines.

"Keep your phone on Steve, just in case I need your services in Brighton, but I think it's pretty straight forward. The taxi should be waiting for me now and I should be back in three or four hours depending how the meeting goes." Reginald explained as he disembarked the aircraft.

"Sure thing, boss I am going to hit the cafe, get myself a Full English." Squid replied.

After eating his breakfast Squid goes to the toilets to freshen up, as he heads back towards the reception area a huge dog pounds towards him, flat on his back with face being licked Squid was left wondering what had hit him.

"I am so sorry, that's just so unlike him, bad dog Vinnie, bad dog." shouted the owner as she ran towards Squid.

"Vinnie . . . Pippa?" Squid squealed with joy.

"Squid!" she cried looking so surprised.

"How are you sweetheart? It's Steve Carr by the way not Squid, if you don't mind. Squid died a long time ago now." he said in almost a whisper.

Getting to his feet Squid gives Vinnie a huge cuddle, Vinnie immediately rolls on his back enjoying the rub. Squid looks at Pippa stood in front of him and pulls her in for a hug.

"Wow look at you, you're huge. You must have been into some real heavy shit to get a new identity and judging by the uniform you're a pilot now as well. That body, where did you get that body you look great." Pippa replied trying to get her arms around him.

"Look at you two as well and Vinnie he's so big, obviously you feed him well. I'm so glad you kept him, I have never stopped thinking about you both, I'm so glad you are both well." Squid said.

"Have you got time for a coffee or are you about to do another disappearing act? I mean an explanation would be nice, what happened to you? ¬Where you been?" she asked.

"I suppose now this has happened, the least I can do is answer some of your questions. How do you fancy going for a flight? We can talk better with no-one else around. I still have to be careful." Squid explained.

"That would be nice, but let me put Vinnie in my office first, he doesn't like flying my husband and I tried a couple of times with him but it makes him sick." she explained.

"Husband, so you're married then?" Squid asked.

"Two years, you?" asked Pippa

"No, my life style wouldn't allow for a wife at the moment, but I would like to one day." Squid replied.

Squid takes off in the King Air with Pippa, he flies her to Alderney where they land and have coffee. He keeps an eye on his phone in case Reginald texts or calls him.

"You supposed to be somewhere? You keep looking at that phone of yours." asked Pippa.

"Only Shoreham, but ok for a few hours. Sorry, I am supposed to be working that's all, not got my own business anymore and thought it was safer to keep my head down." Squid replied.

Over the next forty five minutes and two mugs of coffee, Squid explains his life story to Pippa.

"I guess we should head back then before this boss of yours calls, I was kinder hoping we could have a bit more time, for old time's sake?" Pippa replied giving Squid a wink.

Squid leans forward and kisses her.

"In which case, we should head back to the plane." he replies.

Squid shuts the door of the aircraft behind them as the plane sits out on the apron at Alderney. He turns to walk towards the cockpit. Pippa unzips her little black dress and lets it fall to the cabin floor. Squid didn't need any more encouragement than that and for the next fifty minutes the two made love. Once again Squid had just gone with the flow, it seemed a natural outcome to him, after all the two had been very close.

Back at Shoreham Squid lands and parks the aircraft in the same spot. He still hadn't heard from Reginald so he and Pippa had a drink together just to settle the lunch they had eaten, whilst he waited.

"I must tell you, a week after you left, this blue Rolls Royce pulls up next to me the driver is huge built like a bloody ox, anyway the back window goes down and this smartly dressed middle aged man starts asking me questions about you. I told him I didn't know where you had gone, he gave me a £50 note and said if I ever hear from you to give him a ring and that there would be a lot more cash where that came from if I did. He had some blonde bimbo in the back, I heard her call him Yoda, just thought I should mention it as it might be important." she explained.

"Did you keep the number?" asked Squid

"I did for a while but then it just got lost like things do and to be honest I forgot all about it until just now." Pippa explained.

After lunch Reginald returns eager to depart. Squid says goodbye, as he walks with Pippa back to her office.

"No Vinnie you can't come with me, your job is to look after and protect Pippa and you Pippa look after Vinnie for me, I will really miss you guys. Say hi to Cindy when you see her." Squid said as he hugged Pippa.

As Pippa let go of him her face expression had change to one of sadness,

"Of course you wouldn't know, Squid. Cindy's dead, a car crash whilst on holiday in Spain, it was awful she was left in a coma and died three weeks later, I am so sorry." Pippa explained.

Squid's heart sank, leaving him with a troubled mind.

It had been nice seeing Pippa and Vinnie again but there was never any shortage of woman, after hearing about Cindy maybe it was good not to get too attached.

"I thought it was just sailors who had a woman in every port." joked Reginald as Squid flicked the 'gear up' switch as the King Air climbed away over the West Sussex country side.

"Just an old flame, can't believe we bumped into one another down here." Squid replied making it sound like he had never been to Shoreham before.

A few days later Squid climbs out of bed, takes a shower and relaxes back into the sofa with mug of coffee, turns on the TV and starts to read paper. The headline isn't good: 16 September 1992 — Black Wednesday is written across the front page. He looks at the date on the top of the paper thinking he had got his days muddled up but he hadn't. It was Thursday the 17th of September, the day after. Squid turns on the news and listens to what is being said and his heart sinks. It is very bad news for anyone with investments, worse for those who hadn't been keeping an eye on them like Squid. Grabbing his phone Squid calls Dominic to get some advice on what he needs to do.

"Come on Dominic answer your bloody phone." Squid moans as Dominic's cell phone just rings and rings.

By late afternoon the situation was grim all the news is talking about is how the financial market has collapsed. Squid picks up the keys to the car and drives to Dominic's house, by the time he arrives, there are three other people already there banging on the doors and windows.

"Dominic are you in there? Answer the fucking door, you arsehole." shouted Squid much like the others.

"I think he's done a bunk mate with all our money. Bastard needs shooting he's done loads' of us apparently." said the first man, who was now sitting on Dominic's step, rubbing his hands through his hair.

"I've lost everything. The bastards conned me out of my life's savings, it's gone everything, just gone." he cried.

Squid returns straight home, he needed to check his investments. It didn't take him long to discover they all turn out to be bogus, the two men were right Dominic was a conman.

"Damn man, this shit isn't worth the paper it's printed on. Back to square fucking one, all my money lost!" Squid screamed as he kicked over his coffee table in anger. Within days Squid finds himself with no work, his bosses fall like flies, their businesses failing or they're leaving the country to escape other more serious problems. Squid searches for Dominic to no avail. Then he gets a call from Reginald.

"Steve that short fat little bastard . . . Dominic Nash, I have this contact out in Spain apparently this chaps got a place out there." Reginald explains.

"Brilliant! Ok thanks Reginald, I wondered why I couldn't find the wanker so that's where the little shit is hiding out. I will get my arse down to Spain. See if I can't put him under some pressure to release some funds my way." Squid replied.

"Steve look, whilst I am on the phone, it looks like we are all going to have to squeeze in our belts a bit so, going to have to let you go mate, I've lost the King Air. If I hear of any work going I will get in touch and pass it your way. Take care of yourself Steve, I am sure we'll speak again soon." Reginald replied as Squid sits down on his sofa realising he is now totally unemployed.

A week soon passes and Squid finds himself once more in Torremolinos. Dominic enjoying the weather climbs out of his pool only to see Squid standing there looking at him with his arms folded.

"Look man I can explain, I'm sorry, it was an accident, a bad investment. I got hit too. It's not just you." Dominic spluttered as he tried desperately to dig his way out of what he knew was a very serious situation.

"Yes loads of others got caught, but your investments were not real were they? So, I never really had any investment. So my way of thinking is I haven't lost anything." Squid replied.

Squid walks towards the man, but panicking Dominic jumps back in the pool, he stands in the middle of pool refusing to move. His method of thinking being whatever end or side Squid may jump in to get him he could reach a closer side and escape the man.

"Dominic we can do this all day and night if you want, but at some point you will either have to get out or drown. Of course I can't promise you won't end up drowning anyway, but that depends on how our little chat goes. I know about the made up investments. I know how you befriended us all and conned us. At the moment it's just me, but I know some others who are also doing their best to find you. So, please no more crap, get out." Squid replied.

"But, you're going to hit me, I know you are. Promise me you won't hit me and I will get out. I was just trying to make a bit of money, you know the score . . . you know how it is." the man replied looking terrified at Squid's presence.

"I had a girlfriend once who said the very same words to me. She was getting into a car and running off with all my cash at the time. Now, I promise you I won't hit you and yes, I know how it is, you're a chancer. Did you know two of your investors committed suicide? One left a young wife and two kids behind. So that makes you, my friend, the lowest form of scum in my books. Now get out of the pool." Squid replied.

"I've got all your money Squid-all of it. It's just invested, please don't hurt me?" said Dominic as he slowly walked towards the edge of the pool.

As Dominic climbs out, Squid grabs him by the nuts, squeezes them tight and frog marches him into his house. Seeing the fat little man in trunks walking like this and squealing like a pig put a smile on Squids face.

"You promised you wouldn't hit me, please!-please! I beg you I have a weak heart." he squealed and then cried as Squid released his grip.

"I haven't, I'm just trying to take control of my assets by putting the squeeze on yours. Now, tell me about these assets, now what do I own?" Squid asked sitting down next to Dominic.

"I own...I mean you own a canal boat with mooring at Newbury. Then there's the motor yacht in the local marina, a Sunseeker Renegade 60, the rest is tied up in a few clubs and stuff. I have some bonds here if you don't want the boat, here take them." Dominic replied as he walked to his safe and opened it.

"Right, you get the documents out and you sign it all over to me and I just might let you live. By the way, make sure it includes the deeds to your house. There's a fatherless family that's going to need a home." Squid replied.

"You can't take it all, you only invested two hundred thousand with me, the boat alone worth far more than that." Dominic announced.

"I'm not here just for me you selfish bastard, I'm making sure I take enough back to give that poor young wife who won't even be getting the life insurance money because her old man committed suicide. Hopefully I can get back before that guy Harry does the same before he loses his home." Squid explained.

"You can't do this to me, you will leave me with nothing." Dominic replied spreading out the contents of his safe on the front room table.

Squid slapped him hard, and Dominic fell back against the wall.

"Just be grateful I'm leaving you with this house and whatever you have in the bank, now sign it all over to me now." Squid demanded feeling extremely pissed off with the guy.

Shaking like a leaf on a tree in autumn, Dominic does as Squid tells him. Sliding all the documents into a briefcase, Squid pushes Dominic back into the sofa. Unfortunately for Squid it was one shove to many. Dominic had been telling the truth and he did have a bad heart and the stress of Squid turning up gave him a fatal heart attack.

"Bugger, this is awkward." Squid said as he tried in vain to revive the man. Squid realised there was only one thing to do so carrying Dominic to the pool he threw his body into the water. As far as anyone would know, the man died whilst having a swim. Squid went back inside and removed all his finger prints from the house before making a move to the Marina.

"Nice doing business with you Dominic." said Squid as he walked away leaving the guy floating in the pool.

This was a very borderline moment for me, I had never wanted any of this, being the wrong side of the law I hated it, and killing someone was something I didn't want haunting me for the rest of my life. But, this had been close, all I had wanted to do was to give Dominic a bit of a slapping, scare him and make him see sense. But, suddenly fate was reminding me how this wasn't my game I was just a player.

Two weeks later Squid arrives with the Sunseeker at Bournemouth. With cash in the bank again, a nice home, car, house boat and now a stunning yacht. Squid is feeling very secure. His first move was to sort out the wife of the poor man who killed himself. Driving to her house, Squid posts the bonds and deeds through the letter box, there was little else he could do but he hoped it would make a difference, as for Harry hopefully he would be ok.

Squid heads back to his house, but as he turns up the road to his house he glances at the clock in the car, 6.33pm it reads. His heart sinks and suddenly a feeling of nausea hits him like a train. On the right where his beautiful house once sat, is a smouldering pile of rubble.

"No . . . What the fuck, no, no, no, not my fucking house!" Squid cries as he sees what remains.

Then he notices the Police tape around house, parked on the drive a fire engine still douses the remains. Two SD1 Rover police cars are parked close by. His first thought is that he's been found again and the gang behind all the Brinks Mat murders have burnt down his house.

"Hi I own this house, what the fucks happened?" asked Squid.

"Did you know a Mr Cross, Martin Cross?" asked the officer.

"Yes he is one of my lodgers." Squid explained looking distraught.

"From what we can gather, one of your lodgers had set a pan on fire, tried to throw water over it, thus destroying the house and himself in the process." explained the policeman.

"Oh my god, you mean someone's died?" replied Squid.

"Sorry yes, a Mr Cross, Martin Cross, his family have been informed." the policeman replied.

"Look I have a canal boat in Newbury I will be staying up there till the insurance company can get this mess sorted. Is there anything salvageable I need to go through? What do I need to do, where do I go from here? This is awful, and Martin's family do they know? Sorry I just wondered what the procedure is in a case like this." replied Squid.

"Well we're going to be busy here for a week or so, leave us your number so we can get in touch with you. There is little else you can do for now Sir." the policeman explained.

Squid climbed back into his car and headed off towards the motorway. He had no idea of the condition of the house boat or where it was exactly but it was pointless him hanging around Wellington. The drive to Newbury took around two and a half hours and Squid couldn't find the boat when he got there, so he decided to spend the night in the travel lodge.

The next day Squid managed to locate where the boat was moored. It was clean, tidy and up together which allowed Squid to move straight in. The first thing he had to do was to go shopping, not only did he need food but he also needed clothes. So it was two days before he was in a position to find out the details of his insurance company and give them a call. He was unable to speak to anyone as the lines were busy so he left a message with all his details for them to get back to him. The following day Squid receives a devastating call.

"Hello, Mr Carr, I am from the Co-op, it's about your claim and insurance policy. I am sorry to have to tell you this and be the bearer of bad news but the policy lapsed 3 months ago. I am afraid you are uninsured." the man explained.

Squid soon realises that not only is he uninsured but he is going to be responsible for the clean-up operation. On top of that he receives a call with regards the mooring of the Sunseeker, suddenly he realises he's haemorrhaging money. Dominic's victims had received most of Squid's spare cash, as he thought it better to keep the assets in the Sunseeker and his house. Well the house was gone now, he wasn't in work and the Jag was worth about five grand now as the market had fallen away on the MK2's. He could sell the canal boat and live on the Sunseeker but that wasn't a practical move as the mooring on the Sunseeker was more expensive than renting a house. The Sunseeker had to go.

This was about the lowest time in my life. I started drinking heavy and feeling sorry for myself. It seemed pointless fighting anymore. I lost track of what day, week or month it was. All I could think is "Why me?" What the fuck have I ever done so damned bad I deserve all this shit. Thanks old man, thanks for the damned curse. Brinks Mat gold, wouldn't have it if it was given to me.

Squid gets up morning after morning hung over. All his mail box delivered was bills, one from Somerset County Council for the clean up on the burnt out house. Then there was electric, gas, rates, car insurance, road tax and mooring of the yacht. It turned out Dominic was even behind with the canal boat mooring fees. Everything was coming at once.

It took nine months to sell the Sunseeker and due to the recession, it was for a pittance of what it was worth just a year earlier. With a now full length beard and long hair Squid is looking ruff. He watches the yacht sail away with its new owner then heads to the bank in Newbury with a suitcase full of cash.

"Good morning Mr Carr, how can I help you today?" asked the cashier.

"I want to pay off my mortgage." Squid replied as he starts pushing the piles of cash through the cashier's window. It took an hour to sort out but walking out of the bank Squid lent against the wall and breathed a sigh of relieve now he owed nothing and his mortgage was paid off. He slid down the wall and sat on his heels, taking in the midday sun. As he sat there in a moment of thought, an old lady walked out of the bank and put fifty pence in his hand.

"There you are love, get yourself some chips." she said smiling.

Squid looked across the road at his reflection in a shop window, it was at that moment he realised how low he had fallen. His thoughts were broken by his mobile phone ringing. A woman walked past with her daughter.

"Look mummy, that tramp's got a mobile phone."

Shaking his head but smiling to himself Squid answered the phone as he walked back to the Jaguar.

"Steve Carr . . . Hello?" answered Squid.

"Steve, it's Reginald, I have a job for you . . . look I know this guy needs a pilot, no questions asked . . . " Reginald explained down the phone.

"Hi Mate, long time no speak....yes...you know me if its cash I will do it . . . Ok call me later or fax me the details." Squid said.

Finally he had a job come in, what with that and the old lady giving him fifty pence, his spirits have been lifted. As he drove through the town he spotted a hairdressers. Parking the Jag out the front of the shop, Squid went in and had a haircut and shave. He felt like a new man by the time he returned to the car. Getting himself organised again, Squid retrieved the fax from the business centre he had been using. All the details he needed were there. Piper Seneca G-BSPG at Compton Abbas, the owners name was blanked out it simply said "Mr H", and that the aircraft was grey in colour with a Blue, Yellow, and Orange stripe. The Key will be left under the nose wheel, and the aircraft will be fully fuelled and read to go, read the fax.

The thing with a recession is, people who thought they were something often end up becoming nothing, suddenly they are vulnerable and that's where my services come in useful.

It was a cold fresh moon lit morning in May, the year was now 1993. Squid looks at his watch, as he warms up engines on a Piper Seneca aircraft.

"Come on-come on, you are late, I don't fucking believe it, six minutes and thirty three seconds late, don't turn up yet for fucks sake, that's not a good omen." Squid said talking to himself.

Minutes later a Rolls Royce arrives at Compton Abbas Airfield. A short well-dressed man appears from the back of the car and heads towards the plane. He's carrying two brief cases and he's followed by a man who was also carrying four more bags. They head towards Squid who throttles back the engines to idle, climbing out onto the wing Squid jumped down onto the grass to greet his passenger.

"Come on, come on, I was told no baggage." shouted Squid.

"Mr Carr, you have done everything I asked?" said the man that Squid recognised to be Asil Nadir.

"Yes, it's all in place, whose this with you?" Squid demanded to know.

"This is Peter Dimond, he's coming with us." Asil Nadir explained.

"I was told Mr Dimond would be waiting in France, and that he would be continuing the journey with you to Cyprus and I will return in your private jet to Biggin Hill later this morning and I said no baggage. The deal was one man and one bag only." Squid explained.

"There is a slight change of plan. I am afraid the baggage is necessary, it cannot be left behind." the man announced.

"I am sorry. A deal is a deal. I don't haul drugs for anyone. The bags stay." Squid replied.

"My dear man, who in their right mind would be taking drugs out of the UK. No, no, this is business papers, very important business papers and they must come with me. Shall we say an extra five thousand pounds cash?" Asil Nadir replied.

"Hurry then, we are running late and I want to see the cash first." replied Squid.

"One more thing, Mr H would like his aircraft returned straight away, so the Jet has been cancelled. Mr Dimond has arranged another plane that is waiting in France." Nadir replied.

"Too many changes, I don't like this, but I am here now, so shall we say another 5k for the return trip to Compton Abbas, and like I said I want to see the cash up front." Squid demanded.

"Of course you do Mr Carr, of course you do." replied Mr Nadir.

The short balding man sits the briefcase on the end of wing and flips it open. Inside is thousands in cash. Opening the other case the man counts out an extra ten thousand pounds. He hands it to Squid with the other fifteen thousand which has been agreed for Squid doing the job.

"Here twenty five thousand in cash, not bad for an hour and a half flying. Now can we please get a move on, I really need to leave this dreadful country now. Despite what you may read in the papers over the next few weeks, I am an honest man, a man of my word and remember that should we ever need to do business again." Mr Nadir replied.

Squid laughed.

"I know a lot of honest men Mr Nadir, I still wouldn't turn my back on them, neither would their mothers." Squid replied.

"Now we have determined we are both men of our word, can we get the hell out of here?" replied Nadir.

"As the man from Del Monte says, YES!" Squid replied chuckling to himself.

Asil Nadir climbed in the back of the plane, Peter Dimond sat next to Squid in the co-pilots seat, within minutes the three were taxiing towards the runway.

"I know all about newspapers and what gets written, so you will understand I was never here, I know who you are Mr Nadir." Squid said making conversation.

"I have my reasons for fleeing the UK like this, there are certain government members who have got it in for me, you can't fight governments, they just steal and lie." Nadir replied.

"I am not interested in your reasons for leaving, I don't want to know what any of this is about, none of this is my business, but if the shit hits the fan, just remember Peter here is your scapegoat. Do we understand one another?" Squid said determined to make his point.

"My friend you worry too much. Do not be troubled we understand one another." Nadir replied patting Squid on the back.

No sooner are the wheels off the turf at Compton Abbas, Squid puts the gear up and points the plane south east. Dawn was breaking and visibility is perfect for Squids skilled flying, staying low the Seneca headed towards France.

"There's plenty of sick bags should you need them." Squid said as he banked the aircraft hard around to the left. Forty five minutes later, Squid touches down at a private air strip in France. There is a stench of vomit in the used sick bags from Nadir and Squid sees another plane waiting for his passengers. As the three disembark Squid grabs hold of Peter by the shoulder.

"As I have said to Nadir, I was never here. If anything goes wrong and my name should be mentioned then I will track you down and cut you up into a thousand pieces and feed you to the birds. Do we understand one another?" Squid said to Dimond as he handed over the remaining couple of bags.

"Really!" mocked Peter Dimond in a sarcastic tone.

Grabbing the man by the throat Squid pushes him against the side of the fuselage, Peter drops the bags he is holding.

"Yes REALLY!" he replied as the man choked.

"Yes-yes, I understand, I'm no grass." Dimond replied.

"Don't concern yourself with the aftermath Mr Ryan, Mr Dimond is being paid extremely well for his part in this, you are and will remain the invisible man." said Asil Nadir.

"Mr Ryan . . . How do you know my real name?" asked Squid.

"Did I say Ryan, sorry just a slip of the tongue I meant Carr." Nadir replied.

Squid climbs back into the Piper Seneca and within minutes is heading back towards Compton Abbas. By 11:00 am he is driving through the gates of the airfield after enjoying a hearty breakfast in Compton Abbas's restaurant. However, his mind was troubled, that slip of the tongue by Nadir made him question who was behind all this. It made him feel like a puppet and that some where someone was pulling his strings.

Squid banks some of the money then heads home to the Narrow boat. The following morning he's up early and back in the gym for a workout. He can't help but see the papers headline, Nadir is all over the front pages. It also seemed that his flight from Compton Abbas was also in the headlines, some saying Nadir left in an executive jet, others in a small Cessna. Squid tries to focus on his workout. After two hard hours pumping iron, Squid decided to treat himself to some time in the steam room, followed by a massage. He then headed back to the boat and cleaned all the empty bottles out. There had been too much drinking, too much feeling sorry for himself.

Chapter Seven

Squid's afternoon was then spent cleaning the boat and getting his washing up to date. Whilst he cleaned he listened to the news on the radio, it seemed a certain little airfield on the Dorset and Wiltshire border was now receiving a lot of attention. Then by early afternoon he heard something that put his mind at rest, reports were coming over the radio that Asil Nadir had fled the UK from Compton Abbas airfield in a Piper Seneca flown by a pilot named as Peter Dimond. Nadir had kept his word, Dimond his, there was no mention of who the real pilot had been that day.

By early evening Squid decided to do some shopping and stock up his cupboards. As he left the store Squid found himself singing along to the music coming from his cars stereo system.

"Finished with my woman 'cause she couldn't help me with my . . . " sang Squid.

Glancing down at the clock on the dash the time was 6.33pm Squid is not impressed.

"Why is it not 6.32 or 6.34 why 6.33? What is all this shit with the numbers about?" he said talking over the music. As he drove out of the store the song changed to D Ream (Things can only get better) which makes Squid smile as he remembered when he and Jenny were fleeing the bedsit. He stops at Junction and a car behind him touches the back bumper nudging his car slightly.

"Things will only get better my arse! They didn't last time and they are not going too this time." Squid mutters under his breath as he gets out of the car.

"Damn it!" he shouts walking to the back.

"Sorry mate I wasn't concentrating." explains the other driver who is a man in his late sixties. He is obviously intimidated by Squid's build. Squid inspects the car for damage. Slight graze on bumper is all he can see and that will polish off. He takes a deep breath and sighs.

"Here this is my phone number, if there's any damage call me. I will settle it with you, I'm so sorry." said the old man.

"It's OK chap, accidents happen. Have a nice evening, it will polish out I am sure." Squid replied.

Squid takes the piece of paper and glances at man's number, he gets irritated when he sees it ends in 633. Squid puts the piece of paper in his pocket and watches the man climb back in car. He drives away looking very apologetic for what had happened. Squid leans against side of Jaguar and smiles. However his attention is suddenly moved to a child's cry, this wasn't a sobbing but a cry of panic.

"Help, my mummy please someone help!" cried the girl.

Squid looks round to see where the cries are coming from, as he moves to the front of the car a little girl runs straight out of a Passageway and heads straight into path of oncoming car. The car's tyres screech, Squid moves and manages to catch the girl with one arm and the other arm thumps against the bonnet of the oncoming car. The driver blows his horn as the car stops.

"Woo, sweetheart you nearly got run over then." Squid says to the distraught child.

With the Child tucked under his arm he gestured to the driver to move on. Squid then stands the girl on pavement by the Jaguar.

"Have your parents never taught you the Green Cross Code? You nearly got mowed down by that car sweetheart, you could have been killed!" Squid lectures the girl.

The child stands there in shock, sobbing and breathing heavily then Squid hears a woman's cry coming from the same passage way.

"My mummy-some muggers, they are robbing her, my mummy, please help her please." sobbed the girl who looked so small with a fragile frame.

Squid opens the back door of Jag and sits the young girl in the seat. The Animals 'The House of the Rising Sun' can be heard coming from the car stereo.

"Stay here and no matter what happens don't move. Do you hear me don't move." Squid said.

Squid walks to the back of the car and opens the boot and removes a cricket bat. The name 'Mary' was carved in the wood. It was a personal joke of Squid's since it had a little blood on it, the bat became 'Bloody Mary.' With the bat slung over his shoulder, he turns and heads up passageway. As he walks his foot hits a bag of sugar bursting it open then he feels the crunching of broken eggs, there is a smell of old urine where people have been using this short cut to relieve themselves. Squid then comes across other shopping bags which are split open. He sees a silhouette of three people, one is on the ground and two others are stood over the one on the ground.

"Step away from the woman." Squid ordered in his deep masculine voice.

Two youths look up to see Squid's huge frame in front of them blocking out the light from the end of the street. Pulling out a knife, the first youth lunged forward focusing on trying to attack Squid.

"Mind your own business fuck-head and piss off before I knife yah." Screams the youth who is in tracky bottoms and hoody.

His accomplice dressed much the same, struggles with the girl's Mother. The bat swings and a youth goes flying through the air, he lands on his back at the feet of his friend and with a last moan the lad is knocked out cold. Dribbles of blood and saliva dripping from his mouth, blooded snot from the nose. His accomplice charges at Squid who swings the bat once more as the song still echoes down passageway.

"I am not going to ask twice. Some criminals have no morals." Squid replies as he helps up the woman.

"Mummy!" screamed the girl.

"I'll fucking teach you to rob an innocent young mother and daughter." Squid says as he walks past the lad and kicks him in the nuts.

The youth falls to the floor in agony, gasping for breath and turning a shade of red as the pain from his groin shoots up like an Apollo rocket to his diaphragm winding him and he too was drooling saliva, but mixed with vomit which seeped down his blooded top. His eyes rolled back in his head as he lost control of his bodily functions and a stronger smell of urine wafted down the alley.

"You're ok luv, your girl's in my car and she's fine. Are you OK? It's all over." Squid tried to reassure her.

Both attackers were out cold and the little girl stands at end of passageway waiting to see what was happening. She could see a huge shadow carrying something coming towards her. Then she sees her mother cradled in one of Squid's arms as the other hangs a swinging blood covered bat.

"Mummy!" she cried, worried for her mother's health.

"Mummy is fine sweetheart." Squid replied as he put the woman down in front of her daughter.

"I thought they were going to kill me." she sobbed reaching for the girl.

"Hey you're ok, try not to think about it." Squid replies comforting them both.

They head back to the car passers-by avoid them giving Squid a dirty look. Not one of them had listened to the woman's cries for help.

Squid sits the woman in the Jag, Mother and child hug one another both are sobbing their eyes out. Squid walks to the rear of the car, wipes the bat down and then clips it back in position. As he walks around the front a traffic warden approaches the driver's door.

"You do realise you shouldn't be parked here?" States the warden as he points to the yellow lines on the road.

"Seriously, where were you five minutes ago when this poor woman was screaming for help and being attacked by a couple of druggies?" Squid replied.

Squid gives the warden a disgusting look, gets in his Jag.

'Wet, Wet, Wet, plays 'Love is all around' out of the cars stereo. Squid starts up and heads toward A&E.

"I am taking you to the hospital to be checked over." Squid announced.

"Thank you!-Thank you! I really mean it you are my guardian angel that's for sure." she replied.

"It was nothing I am just pleased I was there, just in the right place at the right time. If it wasn't for that old man hitting my car I would have just driven past unaware." he explained.

"He's a giant mummy. He saved me from being run over by a car, he held out his arm and stopped it dead. He's a hero twice over mummy you have to buy him a drink or something. That's what Daddy would do, oh yes and your car smells funny." announced the girl.

"The car was braking nipper, it was nearly stopped. I simply lifted you out of the way, as for the smell that's leather." Squid explained trying to brush off what he did.

"If only Daddy were here, he would buy you a drink for saving us. I know he would, he's like that." said the girl.

"Well I am not a huge drinker, so don't worry." He replied smiling in his mirror at her.

"My shopping, that was my week's shopping! I need to go back and pick up my shopping." panicked the woman.

"Don't worry about your shopping we can sort that out later. Here I have a mobile phone, call your husband let him know where you are." Squid replied.

"I don't have a husband. I am a single mother." she replied.

"Oh sorry, it's just I heard your daughter say she wished her Dad was here." Squid said.

"She was just wishing. He doesn't even know she exists. I never had the opportunity to tell him, but she knows who he is. May be one day she'll have better luck than me at trying to find him. In the mean time she's dreamt up this image of this guy in her head, haven't you sweetie?" the woman explained.

"Daddies a pilot as well, mummy said he loved aeroplanes." replied the girl.

"See what I mean. I do love the smell of these old cars takes me back, Jags bit of a badboys car back in the day." the woman said as she gave her daughter a big hug.

"I see, life goes like that sometimes. We lose track of the ones we love, fate seems to have its own idea on what it wants to happen." Squid stated.

"You sound like you are talking from experience." she replied.

"Let's just say I know how you feel. I had a very special girl-friend once and we were separated. I tried to stay in touch, but I couldn't find her and one day she was just gone." Squids tone was sad as he explain to her.

"Mmmmm, it's similar for me, even though I didn't treat him very well he was there for me. But it was complicated." she explained

"Life often is." said Squid.

"Oh! Squid Ryan Where the hell are you?" she sobbed out loud very distraught. Squid slams on the brakes and the Jag screeches to a halt.

"Now what, it's not a cat is it?" she sobbed

"What did you just say?" asked Squid wondering if he had heard her right.

"I said now what? I figured something must have happened for you to brake like that." she replied.

"No before that." he asked.

"I said where are you, Squid Ryan, that's the name of my daughter's father. I just haven't been able to find him and he needs to know he has a daughter. God everything's such a damned mess." she cried.

"It's ok mummy, we will find him one day and he will be big and strong like this man." she replied hugging her mum.

"Jenny, Jenny Davison?" he asked.

"Yes-how do you know my name?" she asked.

"My name was once Squid Ryan." Squid announces.

Turning to the rear of the car, the two come face to face for first time in ten years.

"Squid?" she murmurs in a state of shock.

"Pulling on the hand brake, Squid jumps out of the car, runs to back and flings open the door. He pulls Jenny into his arms hugging her real tight.

"I tried to find you sweetheart, I tried many times honest I did. Is it true I have a daughter, she's mine-she's really my little girl?" he asked tears run freely down his face.

"Yes, she's yours Squid. Look at her. Can't you see it? She's the spitting image of you. Her name's Sophie. It was my Gran's name, I hope you like it. She must have been conceived that night before you dropped me off. She'll be eleven next birthday." Jenny explained sobbing her eyes out.

"Oh Sophie, my Sophie, come here and have a hug sweet-heart." cried Squid as he cradled them both in his arms.

Sophie pushes back and looks at Squid then at Jenny, she is shaking and the tears are running down her face.

"Is he really my Daddy mummy, for real, to keep for ever?" Sophie cried almost hysterical.

"Yes sweetheart, to keep. Sophie, meet your father Squid Ryan,........... I don't need to go to hospital Squid, please can we just go home?"

"You sure?" he whispered almost choking to find his voice.

"Please take us home, its 63 Goldman's close I'll show you the way." Jenny begged.

Squid gets back into the car and follows Jenny's directions to her house. He pulls up at the house, and walks up the path with an arm around both Sophie and Jenny. Suddenly he stops and looks at the car parked on the driveway.

"Is that my Dad's Jag?" he asked looking a little shocked.

"It is, I was visiting Duke Smith a few years ago and he had it sat in his yard, he explained someone had brought it in and that he had kept it in the hope of meeting up with you again.

"Duke Smith, how is the old bugger?" asked Squid

"He's good, he's Sophie's godfather so we talk every so often, he told me to keep the Jag in the hope you might see it and recognise it. It was our only hope and connection to you we just hoped you might turn up one day asking about it. But, then it just sat here, the MOT ran out and I just can't afford to get it up together. So, she's a little worse for wear at the moment." Jenny explained.

Squid ran his fingers through his hair this was too much. Jenny opened the door to the house and walked in. Squid looked at her gesturing him in and he smiled at her. It was a struggle taking all this in, there had been so much crap in his life and yet here was another side of his life which he had known nothing about. Squid stood there a few seconds in a bit of a daze.

Out of all the crap, I had produced this beautiful child, conceived in chaos she was the only thing that was perfect in my life.

"Welcome home Daddy." Sophie smiled.

"Home, you know nowhere has felt like home for a long, long, time for me." Squid said as he still hugged the two girls too scared to let got in fear they might vanish.

"I think we could all do with a cup of tea and a big cuddle on the sofa." announced Jenny.

"Can I make it mummy?" asked Sophie.

"Be careful with the kettle. Do it how I have showed you." Jenny explained.

"OK.....Mum we've got no tea. Shall I do coffee?" she asked.

"Oh no, that was one of the things on the shopping list." said Jenny

"Don't worry...Coffee is fine darling. I have so many questions and I don't know where to start." Squid replied, his mind racing.

"Me too, are you married, have you got kids, where are you living these days and what were you doing in Newbury?" asked Jenny.

"No, not married. No kids, not even anyone special. My house burnt down in Somerset, so I moved here, I have a Canal boat moored about eight miles away. I have been living in the area for a while now. What about you, does my daughter have a step dad or is there anyone special in your life?" asked Squid nervous at what the answer might be.

"No, only you. You have always been that special person in my life. I can't believe you have been so close all this time." Jenny replied

"Here Daddy I have a coffee for you, white with two sugars, Mummy has always said that's how you like it, is that right?" asked Sophie wanting to please him by showing him how grown up she was.

"It's perfect. Now come here both of you I want a really big hug." replied Squid taking the two in his arms.

"Daddy, are you going to stay? Are you going to be a proper dad and come and live with us? You can share my room if you want there's loads of space." Sophie announces keen to keep her father close by.

"I would love too sweetheart, but that's up to Mummy. Mummy and I need to have a long chat and catch up a bit first." Squid explained.

"Do you mean it, that you would love to move in?" Jenny ask, her heart pounding with excitement.

"Of course, I mean it babes. You two are my family, you're everything to me and if you want me I am here for good. Here for you both, I've wanted this for so long." he explained.

"Oh please yes, stay with us." they begged, wanting nothing more than to be a proper family.

"Ok I would love too, give me an hour and I will drive back over to the house boat and get all my stuff." Squid explained.

"Can I come? I have never been on a boat." asked Sophie

"Yes-If it is ok with Mummy that is?" asked Squid.

"Yes take her, she is yours after all. I'll try to make some space whilst you two get to know one another." Jenny replied giving Squid a big kiss.

As Sophie pulls away from Squid she lets out a scream there is blood on her dress from where she had been cuddling her father.

"Daddy you are hurt. You're bleeding." the young girl sobbed.

Squid looks at his arm, blood is dripping down and the arm of his shirt is soaked in blood. Pulling off his shirt it drops to the floor and they are able to see the wound.

"Guess one of the little shit's caught me. It must have been all right whilst I was driving and the excitement and adrenaline must have numbed it all." he replied as he picked up his shirt and wiped it down.

"Quick let me put something around it then we can get you to the hospital." Jenny announces, taking control of the situation like a mother hen.

"No, no, no! I don't do hospitals, let's just clean it up and stick a plaster on it." suggested Squid.

"You will do as you are told Squid Ryan, that wound needs stitches, tell him Sophie." Jenny replied as she wrapped a bandage around the gash.

"Go get me a needle and cotton, I'll soon have it done." Squid announced to the shock of the two girls.

"I'll do nothing of the sorts, hospital NOW!" Jenny demanded.

"It's pointless arguing, we know what's best and how to look after you, if Mummy says hospital then so be it." Sophie announced trying to be very grown up.

Squid really didn't see what the fuss was all about. He had hurt himself before, this was just a graze compared to some he had received as a doorman. As Jenny rolled the bandage around his arm she couldn't help but look at his body there were a few other scars, one on his chest another on his side, she ran her fingers over them. His body was so different to the last time she had seen it. Sophie giggled.

"I think Mummy likes all your bumps." she said laughing, Jenny blushed.

"Right, get your jacket on let's get you to the hospital." said Jenny pulling his jacket over his arm for him.

"Keys." she announced holding out her hand.

"Eeerrr NO, I remember you're driving!" said Squid, looking rather worried.

"Best give them to her daddy or we will be here all night." Sophie says placing her hand on her hip looking the proper little madam.

Squid hands her the keys and gets in the passenger seat.

The hospital wasn't too far away and after a short wait Squid was taken to a cubical to have a few stitches put in the wound.

Sophie holds Squids hand as the nurse injects the area and numbs it. Squid screw's up his face as the needle enters his arm. Jenny laughs and points it out to Sophie.

"Look at you, Mr Hunk, terrified of a little prick!" Jenny said finding it most amusing.

"It's OK Daddy. Hold my hand I am here." Sophie said holding his other hand. The nurse smiled and let out a giggle.

"It's not funny, I don't like hospitals and that needle hurts more than the cut." Squid announced wincing as the nurse put the needle in again.

Squid looks at the clock hung on the wall in the hospital it was now another day, his first with his family. He smiled to him-self as he indulged in the thought.

"What's with the smile?" she asked.

"My first new day as a family," he replied pointing at the clock.

"Oh yes it's got late hasn't it." she replied.

"Or really early, why don't we all go back to mine? I have to bring some stuff back anyway so how do you fancy spending a night on a Canal boat Sophie?" asked Squid.

"Oh yes please, can we Mummy, can we please?" begged Sophie.

"I suppose, but I need to go home. I need to get Sophie and my night clothes and a change of clothes for tomorrow. Look at us we're a mess the pair of us." she replied.

"You look good to me. Don't think you will need any night clothes." Squid replied winking at her. Jenny blushed.

"Seriously, do I look that easy, you have 10 years of making up to do Mr. Maybe I won't need mine but Sophie does." she whispered.

All three leave the hospital and walk back to Squid's Jaguar hand in hand. It doesn't take them long to pull up outside Jenny's house. She runs in doors leaving Squid and Sophie sat in the car waiting. Running up to her bedroom she catches a glimpse of herself in the mirror.

"Bugger, I need to look sexy . . . how do I do sexy, it's been so long." Jenny said out loud.

She lets out a little screech in frustration as she panics to find something nice for Squid, searching her draws in a hurry she tries to find some sexy knickers and a nice dress to wear. Throwing off her clothes she runs from draw to draw naked, catching sight of herself once more in the mirror she lets out another scream of frustration.

"Fuck...pubes! Where's that damned trimmer? Shit I can't let him see me like this." she mutters to herself.

Squid and Sophie talk in the Jag, getting to know one another.

"Aren't you tired young lady, it must be way past your bed time . . . Mums taking her time, maybe I should go check on her." Squid said feeling a little awkward around Sophie, part of him just wanted to cuddle her whilst the other half felt cautious but he didn't know why he felt that way about his own flesh and blood.

"No... It's not every day you get to meet your dad for the first time. Mums ok, she will be out soon, its woman's stuff. She's making herself nice for you." Sophie explained.

"Really for me, oh I see and you know this how?" he asked.

"I am a woman too, I know these things." she replied.

"A woman, more like a proper little madam." said Squid as he started to tickle her.

Five minutes later Jenny comes running out to screams and giggles blasting from the car, she's clutching an overnight bag, and looks stunning.

"I see, can't leave you two alone for two minutes can I without you terrorising one another. As they drive to the boat, Sophie falls asleep in the back of the car. Once at the boat Squid makes Sophie a bed up in the spare room whilst Jenny sits with her in the car till Squid is ready. Then picking her up in his arms Squid carries his daughter to the small cabin and lays her on the bunk leaving Jenny to tuck her in.

"You have done an amazing job bringing her up. She's a great kid, I feel so guilty I have missed so much, I am sorry it didn't occur to me this might have happened." Squid explained.

"How could you? I didn't even know, it wasn't until three months after you dropped me off that day that I found out. As soon as my dad knew he insisted on moving. Then one day we just went. I had no notice, I couldn't warn you. I tried and tried to find you but Squid Ryan seemed to have just vanished." Jenny replied.

"Your Dad was just protecting you. I was the enemy remember. The Police changed my name and everything changed. The mob kept trying to finding me and it's because there is still such a lot of gold missing and of course the value of it keeps going up, that they had to make me invisible." explained Squid.

"I was worried they might, luckily your plan worked and they left us alone. Mum and dad decided to emigrate to the USA, I went with them for a while, but returned in the hope of finding you. They weren't very happy with me taking their Granddaughter away from them." Jenny replied.

"Anyway, I worked at changing things my way and for the last few years the Brinks Mat gold thing has all gone quiet. Most of the people involved are either dead or locked up. Its old news now and the missing millions, gold and diamonds are lost forever." Squid stated.

"Good, it can stay lost, from the day your father took it. It was never your problem in the first place, our biggest worry now should be the curse." Jenny stated.

"There both dead now you know mum and dad that is." Squid replied.

"No, I didn't, I am sorry Squid so you really have been all on your own." Jenny said hugging him.

Opening a bottle of wine, Squid poured them both a drink and the two sat for almost two hours talking.

"You can't imagine how lonely and empty my life has been. No matter how hard I tried, I never felt complete. Not like I do at this moment." Squid replied.

"We want you too Squid, this time it will be different. I promise you I'll be loyal to you. I've grown up a lot and I'm not that silly little kid anymore." Jenny explained.

"You were never a silly kid. We were both just too young sweetheart. God I can't believe we made such a beautiful child together she is so amazing, can't wait to see some pictures of her when she was little. I will do my best to be the greatest dad ever, I promise, no more struggling I want to know everything I have missed." Squid stated.

Jenny puts her finger to his lips to stop anymore guilt, they both had too much of that. Getting up Jenny slips out of her dress and stands in front of Squid in panties, stockings and bra.

"Where's the bathroom, I just need to sort myself out. I haven't done this in a while you know." Jenny announced.

"Look before we get all carried away here, I need to ask something. You said you found out you were having Sophie three months after we last saw one another, I am sorry but what about Barry . . . you know Barry the bakers boy?" asked Squid.

"Wow, you know how to kill a moment don't you!" Jenny replied grabbing her dress to put it back on.

"Please don't get funny. I had to ask. I know how close you both were." replied Squid.

"Look if it makes you feel better, Barry could only fire blanks. I knew this back then that's why he was a safe fuck and he's now called Shirley and lives with a transvestite called Thomas." Jenny answered.

"Thomas eh, bet there's some shunting going on in Shirley's tunnels." Squid replied laughing, he grabs Jenny's dress from her hand and he sees a smile come back over her face.

"Guess you're glad you picked a real man." Squid said.

Squid starts flexing his muscles and prancing around the room showing off, Jenny giggles and suddenly Squid winces as he flexes where his stitches are.

"Oh yes a real man." Jenny replies.

"I'll go make the bed, the bathrooms through there to the right, it's a bit small, but you should be able to manage." replies Squid, pointing the way and trying to recover from looking a fool.

Squid makes the bed then comes back in and sits down. He polishes off the last of the red wine the two had been drinking while he waits. He smiles to himself as he hears a small electric motor buzzing away convincing himself she was trimming off her bush. His eyes wince as he hears the motor change tone as if it was working hard.

"Christ I know she said she hadn't done this for a while but how hairy can she be?" Squid thought to himself then he almost choked on his last mouthful of wine as the motor nearly stalled and then buzzed away at full speed again.

"You OK in there sweetheart? What's up the old bush turned into a forest has it?" he said teasing her.

"What was that, sorry I didn't hear?" mumbled Jenny, as she stuck her head round the door with an electric tooth brush in her mouth. Squid chuckled to himself realising it was the tooth brush buzzing he could hear must be a man thing he thought.

"Was just asking if you were OK in there?" he replied.

"Yes, just cleaning my teeth." she replied, stating the obvious . . . well what was obvious to her, not Squid that it. He headed to the bedroom and undressed then waited for Jenny on the bed in just a pair of briefs.

Moments later Jenny walked in looking stunning. A little shy and embarrassed she slid under the covers.

"Look this body isn't like it used to be, I've got stretch marks, saggy tits and wrinkles. You're sure this is what you want? I mean I bet you have the ladies dropping at your feet looking like that." Jenny said feeling very insecure. Squid pulled back the covers and ran his hand over her tummy.

"So where are these stretch marks then? I can't see them, you look stunning to me." he replied running his hands over her.

"They are there believe me." she replies.

"And the wrinkles?" he asked kissing her on the neck.

"You are just flattering me because you want to get in my pants." Jenny replied.

"You are stunning babes, stop putting yourself down sweetheart. We're both older and yes I seriously want to get in your pants." Squid said as he slid his hand down her tummy and his fingers slid straight down under the elastic waist of her panties and down to her sex. Jenny took a deep breath and Squid felt a shudder run through her body. He took her in his arms immediately unable to resist her another moment. Re-mapping her body with his lips and tongue he pleasured her, she smelt just heavenly. For the next hour the two made love, until worn out with the day's events they collapsed against one another, falling asleep.

The next morning at nine, Sophie goes into her Mother and Father's room and slides in bed between the two of them. They wrap their arms around her and all three falling back to sleep together. Squid wakes first hours later, looks at the clock by his side which tells him it is midday. Slowly getting up they sit together at the table eating toast and drinking coffee.

"You are coming home to stay aren't you, with mummy and me forever?" Sophie asked.

"Forever sweetheart and today you me and mummy are going shopping. Then tomorrow you can pick out whatever you want to do for the day and we will have a family day out." Squid announced.

The family leave the house boat by one and head over to Jenny's house in the Jag. Walking up the path, the door to Jenny's house is a-jar. Squid can hear things being broken. Jenny looks at Squid panic stricken and he orders Jenny and Sophie back to car. Entering the house Squid is confronted by two raiders armed with baseball bats.

"Morning chaps. I think you must be lost, wrong house maybe?" Squid asked.

"Who the fuck, are you?" asked the first thug.

"Probably the bitch's latest fella." the other replied.

"Now I know I don't know you, but I seem to be feeling some sort of hostilities here. Now I think this may be due to your interior designing skills on my part. But, come on chaps is this really necessary? So before you demolish one more thing why don't you explain what it is you want or do I just have to relieve some of my hostility on the pair of you?" Squid replied.

"What!" the pair answered in unison.

Whilst the two are looking confused for a moment, Squid grabs one of the baseball bats from them and then proceeds to beat the crap out of them both.

"See all you had to do was just tell me what this is all about and then maybe I could stop with all this negative energy" said Squid.

"Ask that bitch, she knows and whilst you're at it tell her Jimmy says the debts doubled." the larger one of the two replied trying to get to his feet. At that moment the thug's mobile phone rings and Squid pushes him against the wall. With the bat across the man's throat Squid put's his hand in the man's pocket pulls out the phone, 'JIMMY' is lit up on front of the screen.

"Hello." said Squid

"Who's this? Where's Joey and Matt?" asked Jimmy.

"Well! Which ones which? I mean Joey could be on the Matt, and Matt, well if it is Matt, he's on the floor where a Matt belongs.

"What who is this?" Jimmy replied.

"Hang on a sec . . . Oi mate which one are you, Joey or Matt?" asked Squid.

"Joey" the thug replied.

"It's Joey who's against the wall and Matt who's out cold on the floor." Squid explained.

"You are messing with the wrong person sunshine. If you know what's good for you, you will get that bitch to pay up today and tell her the debts are now tripled for my inconvenience." Jimmy shouted down the phone.

"No, you listen. The debts cancelled and it's you who has no idea who you are messing with. Now, I suggest you reel in Stan and Ollie here before I lose my temper. If this doesn't stop then I will find you and you and I will have a game of tennis with me using your head as the ball. Do we understand one another?" Squid replies, he then throws the phone on floor and stamps on it.

"Now take your mate and fuck off" Demanded Squid.

"Do we have to stay in the back of the car? Daddy may need our help." asked Sophie as she eagerly watched the door of the house. Suddenly two men appeared one helping the other to walk.

"Look mummy, do you think Daddy did that, he's so brave?" Sophie states as she points at the two Hench men limping arm in arm down the road past the car.

"Come quick mummy, let's check on Daddy." she said jumping from the car.

Sophie starts to runs to the house then stopping she turns and runs towards the men and starts kicking them in the legs.

"That's for scaring mummy and that's for being horrible." she shouted as she kicked each one.

"Ou . . . Ow . . . Ou . . . ow . . . leave it out kid!" the two men moaned as each kick is felt.

Squid looked out the door and whistled at Sophie, "Come here sweetheart stop playing with the bad men." he shouted.

Sophie runs up the path and catch's her mother up but as they walk in the front door, they see the front room is wrecked.

"I think we need to talk." said Squid, swinging the two baseball bats over his shoulder with one hand and hugging Sophie with the other.

"I took out a loan two years ago for Christmas . . . It's been hard Squid, I only borrowed £300 and I paid it back by the following May but then they tripled the debt, saying I owed £900 with interest. Now they say it is £3,000. I have been going out of my mind with worry. I am sorry I didn't mean to involve you in all this." she replied getting upset.

"Involving me is not the problem, this is what I do remember. Idiots like this is how we came together. It's been my life, but I don't want Sophie growing up in an atmosphere like this, it's not good." he replied.

"I know, you can leave if you want, I'll understand?" Jenny started to sob last night had been so perfect.

"What I want is you both to move to Somerset with me. I know it means Sophie changing schools, but we need to get you away from these thugs. I will rent a house for us until we can afford to buy a place. Get everything you want together and I'll take you back to the houseboat. Do you know who this moron is?" Squid asked.

"All I know is he's called Jimmy and the two blokes you just beat up are his rent collectors. I have no idea where they come from. They're just hired thugs. Do you mean what you just said? You really want us to come with you?" Jenny asked.

"Yes. No daughter of mine is growing up in an atmosphere like this if I can help it. I don't care how I have to struggle, we are starting a new life together ok?" Squid said in a commanding tone.

"Yes Squid, yes, we will do anything you want us to do. Isn't that right Sophie?" she replied with excitement.

"Yes Daddy and I will try to be a good girl for you. Please don't leave us, not ever." Sophie starts to cry thinking her fathers about to leave.

"I know you will sweetheart, it's not about being a good girl for me it's about doing the right thing, and right now we need to be a family. Right, let's start sorting things out." he replied as he hugged the two of them.

The three spend most of the day packing up the house, important bits they load onto the back seat of the car the rest is put in boxes and bin bags.

"You can drive the Jag Jenny, I'll hire a van then I'll find a recovery company and get Dads Jag moved today. There is a garage I use in Somerset they can fix her up for me. Make some calls, only tell who you need to we don't want this following us." Squid explains

"Ok, get me on your insurance, I'll phone up the gas and electric and speak to the council about the rent I owe," she replied.

Squid hands Jenny a credit card.

"Pay everything off, I don't want to give any forwarding addresses and we're going to make it look like you just disappeared. It's the only way who knows what connections this guy has." Squid replies.

"Are you sure, Squid I am not going to lie to you there is about three grand's worth of debt you sure this card can cope with that." Jenny replied.

"It is fine, I have the money we'll be ok for a while." Squid reassures her with a hug,

"I'll nip down and get some boxes from the supermarket whilst you make the calls." Squid replies.

"Can I come?" asks Sophie.

"For sure then I will give you a hand to pack up your room, it will be an adventure." Squid says smiling at her and ruffling up her hair.

As he walks to the car with Sophie, Squid pulls out his phone and calls his insurance company and insures Jenny to drive the Jag. As they drive to the supermarket they pass a van hire company so Squid calls in and books a van for later that day. Four hours later they're loading up all Jenny's things into a Transit Luton. Sophie was fully enjoying the experience, it was fun, an adventure like he had said. Squid constantly messed about making the two laugh, Jenny realised she hadn't laughed so much in years, she watched him with Sophie, it made her feel complete. Every time Squid walked past her she felt goose pimples flow over her skin like a morning tide ripples up a shore.

As evening fell, Squid settled Jenny and Sophie into bed together whilst he kept an eye out. Making a coffee he walked outside to his father's Jag. Opening the door he sat inside relaxing and sipping his coffee, straight away the aromas of the car sent memories shooting back. He could smell his father's cigarettes and his mother's perfume or maybe it was just his mind playing games with his heart. As he sat there he looked around the car it had weathered well considering. He could see a few jobs that needed doing, stitching on one of the seat was letting go and for some reason the clock was hanging out of its housing. Squid picked it up and pushed it back into the hole, it sat there a few minutes before dropping down again, Squid moved about searching for things of sentimental value. He felt a connection with the car it was the only thing linking him to his parents. He smiled to himself as he remembered trips out with his Dad in it then trips with his mother visiting his father. Squid's eyes became wet he had never cried for them. They had never deserved it as far as he was concerned, but now years later seeing life for what it is, he felt he understood them both a little more. They both just wanted things and that wanting sent them off in the wrong direction to which they both paid a very high price.

That night Squid slept lightly just in case another visit came but it didn't, for now it looks like Squid had scared them off.

The following morning he saw the Jag off on the back of a recovery truck, moments later they then head off together Jenny following Squid in the Jaguar. Squid headed to the houseboat first to collect some belongings. But as they pull up in the car park, all that is sticking out of the water is the Chimney stack. The boat has been sunk, that's why it had been such a quiet evening.

A small gathering of people are stood by the mooring looking into the canal.

"Oh your lovely boat Squid. I am so sorry." Jenny gasped as they walked towards the other people.

"Did those bad men do it, have they sunk Daddy's boat Mummy, are they going to kill us?" Sophie asked worried.

"No one's going to hurt you sweets, it's just a little set back. Let me salvage what I can a minute." Squid replied.

"Anyone know what happened?" Squid asked as he reaches the sunken boat.

"Bert in the next boat down heard some commotion in the early hours, apparently there was a load of hammering then he saw two men running up the track. He then noticed the boat starting to lean to one side but by the time he reached it there was nothing he could do. They must have holed her." the man explained.

"I'm guessing the police have been informed?" Squid asked.

"Yes, you missed them they left about an hour ago." the man replied.

To everyone's amazement Squid starts to undress.

"What are you doing sweetheart?" Jenny asks.

"There is some stuff, personal bits I need to get before we can leave, here hold these a minute." he replied, as he continued undressing and handing his clothes to Jenny until he was down to his boxers. Then jumping in the canal he dives down into the cabin and retrieves what he needs. Squid surfaces a couple of times passing Sophie all the important bits, cash, cards, jewellery etc, all were hidden in a secret compartment Squid had put in just in case of a situation like this. A couple of the men grab his hands and help him back onto the tow path. Squid proceeds to dry himself down with his t shirt, he then pulls on his clothes.

"I am so sorry Squid, it must be me. I must be cursed every time we get together all we get is shit from people. I must be fucking jinxed!" she said looking absolutely distraught.

"It's not you sweetheart it's me and this damned Brinks Mat curse that's been with me all these years. I am used to it now nothing surprises or shocks me anymore. But, they're messing with the wrong person this time. My first priority is to protect the two of you." Squid replies looking as if he's planning something. Jenny then spots Sophie holding the necklace she bought Squid when she was 14 years old.

"You're shivering! I don't want you getting a cold. Sophie run and get dads jacket from the van please?" asked Jenny, taking the belongings of Squid's the child was holding.

"Thanks babes. That water's colder than it looks, but I had to get certain things I don't have much of sentimental value, but what I do have is important to me. Can't do anything without cash and cards if we want a fresh start." he replied checking through a tin he had recovered.

"Squid you still have the necklace." she said smiling as she held it up.

"Of course!" he replied.

"Oh Squid, you sentimental old fool, look please don't do anything? Let's just leave here like you said and have a fresh start somewhere. I don't want to risk losing you and Sophie needs her Dad right now." Jenny begs as she clings to the chain and kisses Squid.

"Do you still have your bracelet or did you have to sell it?" Squid asks.

"I still have it sweetheart, I wouldn't sell it for the world, no matter how bad things got." she replied.

"Now whose been sentimental, come here babes." he replies giving her a big hug.

"Surprisingly enough these idiots may have done us a favour, the police have no idea what this is about at the moment, but if we get to Somerset and go to the police saying we've had to flee here because of this, they will presume it's related to the Brinks Mat robbery." Squid explained smiling.

"And that's a good thing why?" asked Jenny.

"Time to turn a page babes, I am on a relocation program, they will have to sort us out. Let's go to Somerset shall we? Leave these horrid men and start a new life together." Squid announces.

"Don't worry Daddy it will be okay, you have Mummy and me to look after you now." Sophie replied.

The new family head to Somerset. Three hours later they arrived in Taunton with the van and car. Squid books them into a guest house for a few nights until he can sort something out.

"Jenny I have two aliases, Andrew Mathews and Steve Carr. If I go into Taunton police station and they can track down a chap called Morris, he's the guy who sorted things out for me years ago. I can probably swing it so I get you both new identities as well. You will both have to call me Steve, not Squid. I know that's not a problem for Sophie, as I will be Dad but you will have to be careful not to slip up." Squid explained.

"Squid, or should I say Steve, do what you must. What's in a name as long as I have you and Sophie has her Daddy, nothing else matters. Andrew . . . can't imagine you as an Andrew." She said screwing up her nose.

"Right then tomorrow we will all go to the police station and see what we can sort out." Squid replied.

That evening they sat together discussing what they wanted for the future and making plans. Despite the chaos Squid was happier than he had ever been.

Chapter Eight

Squid, Jenny and Sophie head to the police station the following morning. They get interviewed over the Newbury incidents and the changes and paperwork are put in motion. They are soon married as Mr & Mrs Carr, sadly Sophie could not enjoy being a bridesmaid as there wasn't even a ceremony as such just a meeting in a room with some coppers and signing papers. Within a week they are able to find a property to rent, a terraced house with large rear garden and parking for three cars at Springfield Road in Wellington. They sign the contract and move in a week later.

Things just seemed to fall into place, either fate was on my side or someone was pulling some strings and mapping my life out for me again. I tried not to think about it, but I still remained very cautious of the new people coming into our lives and new job offers.

Squid decides it is best to hide the Jaguar away for a few years and decides on getting a car for Jenny and a van for himself. After putting the car up on blocks and taking the battery off Squid heads indoors for some lunch.

"Sophie I have moth balled the Jag. Please try not to scratch it with your bike. By the way Mummy and I were talking last night and we've decided to try for a little brother or sister for you. Are you going to be ok with that?" he asked not wanting Sophie to feel left out of the decision.

"Ok I will be careful. Really Dad that's brill, can I name it?" she asked excitedly.

"Well let's see what mum says, it may take a while yet, it's not like when I went out and bought that bike you know so don't get too excited." Squid explained.

As the days and weeks went by Squid got everything organised to give his family the best protection he could. He knew at some point the curse would wriggle its ugly head again, but until it did, he would simply take all the steps he could to ensure safety for them all. Squid's old house was still fenced off and boarded up from the fire years ago. Arriving in his transit which was now his main means of transport, he makes up a brick letter box and then sticks a plaque on it with the house name on so that mail can be sent to that address. Things were coming together, life was suddenly very different. Squid's sex life was amazing. He and Jenny had been at it like rabbits, the two seriously couldn't keep their hands off each other. He had new meaning to his life being a father to Sophie was an amazing thing for him and they had become so close.

"I have set up a PO box number at my old house so all mail can go there to keep us safe. I have bought you a Land Rover Discovery sweetheart, it is strong enough to get you out of trouble should any come your way and I am not with you. I will be driving the Transit. Dads Jags will be done soon but best keep that one out of the way for a while too I think." he explained.

"Ok Squid, I feel like I have just come back into your life and burdened you with problems and talking of problems we have a bigger one to deal with right now." she replied looking a little nervous.

"Really, what is wrong, babes?" he asks.

"I am pregnant! I know the timings crap, but what do we do about it?" she replied.

"Shit, so quick. What do you mean do? Anyway I know a certain little girl who's going to be over the moon." he smiled.

"What about you Squid? How do you feel? You do want this baby don't you? I think being apart all these years have got to us a bit. We have been at it none stop, it doesn't surprise me I am up the duff!" she replied

"I want this more than you know. I have dreamt for so long of being settled and having my own family. I love you and Sophie to bits sweetheart, this is what we wanted so yes, it's good news, I for one can't wait. If either of our pasts catches up with us then we deal with it as it happens. My family's safety has priority over everything." he explained as he hugged her.

"We have each other. We'll work out whatever comes our way as a family. Now while Sophie is at school, fuck my brains out before I become fat and ugly." Jenny said.

"You will never become fat and ugly my dear and your wish is my command." Squid replied picking her up in his arms and heading up the stairs.

"God you always say the sweetest things" Jenny replied.

The following day Jenny is busy decorating the house preparing a nursery room. With Squid at her side she is happier than she has ever been. But there was another surprise heading Squids way which Jenny had organised, but she was a little nervous as to how it might go.

It was 11.00am Squid had just sat down with a cup of coffee when Jenny came in to the front room talking on her mobile. She hangs up and then looks at Squid she smiles and then grabs his hand.

"Come with me I have a surprise for you." said Jenny as she pulled Squid to his feet.

"A surprise, now I am worried. Not sure I can handle another surprise so quickly, what is it?" Squid asks.

"Come with me?" she replied as she led Squid out of the rear of the house and up the garden path to the garage. The two of them walk hand in hand.

"You have that smile on you, that Jenny smile when you are up to no good. I remember that smile, that Jenny," Squid said as they walked.

"Good that Jenny's still here, now get in the garage and say hello to an old friend." She said pushing him through the door.

"Look at you, after all these years, you're still bloody pussy pissed!" a voice said as they entered.

"Oh my God! Duke, Duke Smith!" Squid moved forward and hugged the man. The embrace was that of a long lost father and son.

"I can't believe you are here! Come into the house the kettle has just boiled." said Squid his eyes full of water once again.

"So Bonnie and Clyde ride again." Come on stand back let me see what that scrawny young lad has turned into." said Duke taking a seat at the table. Squid steps back and holds out his arms.

"Not so scrawny these days, and getting a little fat now what with Jenny's cooking." Squid replies patting his tummy.

"I'll say, looks like someone's been spending time in the gym. I have a guy who works for me doing odd jobs, OX he's called, he's like you all beefed up. He's just gone to get himself some lunch. I let him drive me about these days, can't be doing with all the hustle and bustle of today's traffic." Duke explained.

"Well you haven't changed a bit, you are just how I remember you. Even down to those fingerless mittens you still wear, thought you'd be retired by now." replied Squid.

The two talked for hours, reminiscing of years gone by both men looking at one another remember the people they used to be.

"I'll never forget the first time I taught him to use the cutting torch Jenny, the silly prat stood there cutting away, he hadn't seen a red hot lump of metal land on his jeans and burn a hole. Then as if that wasn't enough they burst into flames where he's spilt some petrol on them earlier in the day. Never seen anyone get their trousers and pants off so bloody fast in my life and there you were streaking around the yard looking for some water." Duke explains chuckling away to himself as he tells the story.

"I was 12, and had a burn mark on my arse for a week after that" Squid replied.

"That explains how he learnt to get his pants off so fast." replied Jenny laughing at the story.

"So, lad what's the story with the Brinks Mat thing, ever worked it all out?" asked Duke.

"No and not interested as far as I am concerned the hidden gold is gone lost for ever, I told you last time we saw one another.

I am not my old man, all I want is a normal life with Jenny and the kids." explained Squid.

"Kid's . . . yes Jenny told me the good news, well it's nice to know you are safe and that the buggers never got to you because it's still going on you know. Even the other day I had some copper in the yard asking me questions about your old man, I just told him, the bugger died owing me £30!" Duke replied laughing it off.

"I do miss him, but as for my old dear, well never given her a second thought." explained Squid, Jenny put her hand on Squids shoulder and squeezed it reassuringly.

"Well I for one think some bits of the past are better off not thinking about. It's our future now and stuff that lot." said Jenny smiling.

A couple of hours later there was a knock on the door, it was Ox ready to drive Duke home.

"Well boy it's been nice seeing you, don't be a stranger, stick your head in when you are down south next." Duke said as he stood up to leave.

"I will and Duke thank you, for what you did back then. You are the closest thing to a decent father I have ever had and for putting your neck on the line for me back then. What you have done for Jenny means a lot to me and if ever I can return the favour let me know, I owe you." Squid replied squeezing Dukes hand as they said goodbye.

"By the way this is OX, you two haven't met. He's my right hand man these days, you two will get on for sure." Duke explained.

Ox and Squid shook hands both were equal in size.

"Now there's a team not to be messed with." said Jenny seeing Squid, Ox and Duke all stood together.

They all said their goodbyes and then Duke and Ox headed back east.

Later that evening once Sophie was in bed Jenny and Squid were cuddled up on the sofa, Squid was very quiet. Jenny could sense something is troubling Squid.

"Sweetheart what is it, what's wrong? Was it seeing Duke again after all these years or is it the thought of another child?" she asks.

"What, what . . . no sweetheart neither and please don't doubt the pregnancy, I so want this." replied Squid.

"What's bothering you and don't say nothing because I know something is wrong. I can see it in your eyes. Is it work then sweetheart? I know things are quiet, but you have the part time work up at the farm." she replies.

"It's just a number of things, that Ox guy, I feel sure I have seen him before somewhere, by the way I sold the canal boat. We didn't make much I am afraid, after the cost of getting her floated as well as patched up and liveable again, we came out of it with eight thousand pounds profit." Squid explained.

"Eight thousand, why that's fantastic, why so gloomy?" she asked.

"Because that's it sweetheart, we have no other money. All my accounts are down to their last five hundred pounds. The only assets I have are the land where the house is which I can't touch because we need it for the PO Box number. The two Jags, and I don't want to sell either of the Jags. This leaves eighteen grand in total with what I put in your account and I don't have a job, the baby will be here in a few weeks. There is the rent and bills to pay I am just so scared of failing you and letting you down. This is the best either of us has known I want to keep it like this." he explained.

"Well look at it this way, everything we have is either new or as new. We need nothing, we don't owe anyone and if the worse comes to the worse, once the money has gone, you can sign on the dole. The rent will be paid so enjoy being a dad and stop your worrying." she replied relieved it wasn't her he had, had enough of."

"Never the dole sweetheart, I am not having our kids start out in life like I did. I want more for Sophie and Harry than this." Squid said.

"Harry! Where did Harry come from? I am not having Harry. What about Barry, it's like Harry with a B instead of a H." she explained giggling.

"You said Sophie could help choose a name remember? Definitely not Barry, all I will see is that bloody Mark Three Cortina of Barry the Bakers every time you call his name." Squid laughed.

"Anyway might be another girl yet. Guess this means we need to discuss names and just forget about everything else for now." she suggested.

Over the next few months Squid is kept busy, he becomes a flight instructor at Dunkeswell on a part time basis and on other days his time is spent working on a friend's farm. Two evenings a week he works as a doorman at a night club in Taunton so his worrying had been for nothing and he is able to provide well for his family.

"See, didn't I say not to worry and that things would work themselves out?" Jenny states as she cuddles the little one in hospital.

"Yes you did my sweets, that's because you are the smart one, I just have the brawn remember." he mocked.

The weeks soon flew by, having a baby had brought the whole family closer together.

Pulling Jenny onto his lap he gave her a cuddle and a kiss. " Little ones asleep Sophie's playing big sister and watching over the baby, god this all feels so right. I do love you so much." he whispered to her.

"I got a call from Mum and Dad the other day they've decided to retire in Taunton. They want to be closer to us all, I am thinking it is time you met them again." Jenny explained.

"That should be interesting, bet your dad loves the fact you are back with me, but on a plus, we're going to need baby sitters." Squid replied.

"Squid, that isn't what I was thinking. It's going to be awkward for you isn't it?" Jenny said running her fingers through his hair.

"As long as they can see we are together for good then I don't have a problem, but I don't want reminding of the past every five bloody minutes. I am not that little kid he told to stay away from you, your Dad has to realise were married now and that's that." Squid explained.

"He understands, still you can catch up tomorrow, they are coming around for tea." Jenny replied.

"Shit Jenny! Tomorrow! Thanks for the warning!" Squid replied slapping her arse.

"You'll be ok, you are a man remember . . . go on flex those muscles for me." Jenny mocked.

Squid picked up Jenny and carried her upstairs.

"I'll flex something for you alright." he replied as he rolled her onto the bed.

By some miracle the curse left us alone for a number of years. Sophie blossomed into a beautiful teenager. We had another three children in all, another beautiful daughter Penny, and two sons Bradley and Lewis. Jenny opened up a lingerie shop in the town and we were able to buy the house we had been renting. I would never have believed I could be this happy. Duke was a regular visitor and was like an uncle to the kids, but I was happy, very happy. Once again I had become comfortable in my life-style, even forgetting all about the Brinks Mat missing millions. It was Christmas of 2001 everything changed.

There was a knock on the door. Squid looks at the digital clock on cooker it reads 6.33pm his body tingles then he feels as if a ghost had just walked straight through him. As he walked to the door he felt cold, he sighs and his heart sinks as he feels its trouble. Squid walks to the front door and answers it.

"Hello Squid how are you? Do you remember me? I was one of the original coppers who had changed your identity back in the early days. I arranged for the funds to be put in your new bank account when your Mother had died. Merry Christmas!" said DCI Morris.

"Sergeant Morris, Yes I remember you well, Merry Christmas! to you too. Is something wrong, I haven't heard from you in years? Is there a reason for this visit or is it just a social call to see how we're doing?" Squid asked.

"Well DCI Morris (Retired) it's just a social call, I've just called it a day with the force and thought I'd look up my old friend Squid and see how things are with you. I also wanted to give you this, it's your mother's urn, you never picked her ashes up from the station." Morris explained.

Squid looked at the man, he was now fat and balding with a small tash, his teeth looked rotten and yellow from too much smoking.

"So, that's what happened to the old grass? Thought you guys had disposed of her?" Squid replied.

"No, kept her just for you, anyway all that aside, I see you have a nice home. Fancy you and Jenny getting together again like that. Strange how things happen don't you think?" Morris replied.

"It's been you driving the blue BMW which has been fol-lowing us around the last few days. I was getting a little worried our pasts had caught up with us again. Come on into the kitchen I'll put the kettle on." Squid gestured, beckoning the man in from the porch.

"Yes, I see you are as vigilant as ever. The families grown to four now hasn't it? said Morris, making conversation.

"Yes" replied Squid.

"Jenny's shop seems to be doing well." Morris said.

"You're well informed for someone who's retired." replied Squid.

"You have a lot to lose now, if that old Brinks Mat curse does catch up with you" Morris said as he leaned back against the work surface.

"That seems a strange thing to say! Milk, sugar in your coffee?" Squid asked.

"Please." replied Morris.

"So you're retired. Who will be dealing with my case now, should I need them?" asked Squid.

"Your case is long forgotten now, most of the people involved are either banged up or dead, you know that." replied Morris.

"Really, because I see it still pop up in the papers every so often and now what with the internet and that TV program about it, I would have said it's all very fresh again. said Squid.

"I even heard a rumour Asil Nadir is having problems." stated Morris.

"Nadir, why mention Nadir?" asked Squid.

"Come, come Squid, this is me you are talking to, there's always someone who would be interested in getting hold of all the information, information like I have saved on this CD. Names, addresses, bank details, car registration numbers, case file info . . . it's all here Compton Abbas flight as well." Morris replied holding up a disc.

"I see!" replied Squid.

"So I will have to be very careful to make sure it doesn't fall into the wrong hands, if you know what I mean?" Morris said.

As the two are talking an eighteen year old Sophie runs into kitchen, chasing Bradley who's now five, and Penny who's seven, the three run around playing chase.

"Sophie, take the kids upstairs and play with them. Watch one of the DVD's or something, I need to talk to the nice man a minute." Squid replied in sarcasm.

"OK Dad, but Bradley's being a real sod today, he keeps winding up Penny." replied Sophie.

"What lovely girls you have there, it would be such a shame if certain people found out she was your daughter. It must be such a worry for you, an attractive innocent young girl like that. In the blink of an eyelid they can just disappear." Morris said, as he played with the CD in his hand.

"Before this conversation goes any further, I suggest you remember who you are dealing with." Squid replied looking Morris straight in the eyes.

"Of course Squid, I remember your back ground well. One can't forget it's all on here, even the Asil Nadir flight, do you really believe that we would take Peter Dimond's story for real?

But, you need to remember who I know. I've dealt with some pretty disgusting low life scum in my day. Just imagine what would happen to your girl? A pretty girl like Sophie or Penny, how old is Penny now? Seven years old, they would keep her alive for months, probably taking her around all their friends making videos." said Morris.

"You sick bastard. Enough of your riddles, what the fuck do you want Morris? You're starting to fuck me off!" shouted Squid.

"Good old Squid straight down to business. Did you ever work out the old riddle your father left? What was it now: Mark, 633 squadron, a 303." Morris said.

"Something like that." Squid replied.

"I mean what was all that about? We never did find the 303 bullet or the aviation video, I guess someone has them just innocently sat in their house, not knowing inside are the directions to a hidden treasure. That is unless, of course you found them? Well did you Squid? Ever find that lost cash, gold, and diamonds did you?" quizzed Morris.

"Do you think I would be living like this if I had? I am not my father." Squid said through gritted teeth.

"I thought maybe you were holding out on your friends." Morris replied.

"I think it is time you left, whilst you can still walk." Squid replied.

"I have to think about what I am going to do for the next twenty or thirty years. I want a little bit of paradise, find somewhere nice and warm to go. I think I am entitled to that after all the scum I have put away, don't you Squid? Morris said.

"Like I said, I know nothing." repeated Squid.

"Let's say one hundred and fifty thousand, then you and I can smash up this disc." Morris suggested.

Squid had heard enough. Walking over to Morris he grabs the disc and smashes it up with his hands.

"I have copies you don't think I would be that stupid do you?" Morris replied.

"Are you an idiot man? I don't have that sort of cash. I would need to re-mortgage the house. It would take time." replied Squid as he stalled, whilst trying to think of a way of dealing with the situation.

"I give you a week? If you don't come up with the cash by then, well let's just say, keep a close eye on that little girl of yours." Morris threatened.

"No one threatens my family. I will kill you before I would let anything happen to them, you should think about that before you utter another word." Squid expressed.

"Suit yourself. Just think of what someone would pay to break in that daughter of yours." Morris replied ignoring Squids threat.

Jenny had just finished her last day at the shop before the Christmas holiday, tired after a busy day she walks through the front door. She lets out a scream, as she finds Squid holding a man by the throat up against wall of kitchen.

"Squid NO!" she screams.

Morris is blue in face and gasping for last breath. Sophie runs down the stairs to see what all the fuss is about. She is confronted with her father trying to strangle Morris up against the wall. The man's legs are dangling and kicking in mid-air as Squid's mighty frame pins him against the plaster. She joins her in trying to coax Squid to release the man before it's too late.

Squid can't even hear them. The mist had come across his eyes, he was turning into a killer. It was the touch of Sophie's hand on his face that brought him back to reality, he could see their lips moving but still could hear no words.

"Squid-no sweetheart no, you are killing him. Squid please hunny, please stop! Squid look at me sweetheart, look at me. Put the man down before it is too late. You are no good to us in jail, who would protect us then? Please! Baby, please let him go." Jenny begged.

"Dad listen to mum, please dad, please let him go." Sophie cried.

Like a clap of thunder he suddenly heard them and he drops Morris to the ground and not a moment too soon. The man falls to the floor panting and gasping for breath.

Jenny and Sophie look at Squids face, this isn't the person they know and loved, the look in his eyes was one neither wanted to see again.

"Get the fuck out of my house and don't ever come back. If I see you around any of my family then believe me next time they won't be around to stop me." Squid replied.

"You're a foolish man Squid Ryan. You should have taken my offer whilst you had the chance. I hope you can live with the consequences." Morris replies as he staggers down the hallway to the front door.

Squid yells and punches a whole straight through the wall.

Morris holds himself up against the wall as he wobbles out onto the path and staggers down to the gate. Squid walks back into the kitchen, looks out of window in a daze, his fore arm is bleeding.

"Sorry sweetheart." Squid replied, his head sinking into his hands.

"What's going on Daddy, who is that man?" asked Sophie.

Jenny pours Squid a large malt and puts the glass in his shaking hand.

"Come sweetheart, sit down and tell us what's going on?" Jenny said as she led Squid to the kitchen table.

"Sophie that man who was in the kitchen, can you remember what he looks like?" Squid asked.

"Yes Daddy." Sophie replied.

"If you ever see him around or near Penny, Bradley or Lewis, call me and run like hell with them. Then find me or your Mother do you hear me, you run." Squid replied in a harsh tone.

"What is it Squid? You are scaring us." asked Jenny.

"Sophie, go check on the little ones upstairs awhile. I need to discuss matters with your Mother." Squid replied

"Well don't go leaving me out of this, I want to know what's going on OK?" Sophie demanded as she headed upstairs to check on the others.

"That man was Sergeant Morris, or DCI Morris "Retired" as he now wants to be known. He was the man who dealt with my case back when we were teenagers. He's retired now, like all the other scum bags seems to think I have the hidden Brinks Mat gold somewhere. He wants one hundred and fifty thousand pounds to keep his mouth shut or things will start happening. He threatened to have Penny kidnapped by paedophiles and abused on film. That's when I lost it and you came in." Squid explained.

"I should have let you kill the bastard. We have to go to the police babes." suggested Jenny.

"It will do no good. He's wiped the files and my ID everything, it's all on this disc he had with him." replied Squid showing Jenny the broken disc.

"I am scared, what are you going to do Squid? I mean why, why now?" she asked.

"Retirement I suppose. Once the kids are in bed we need to sit Sophie down and tell her everything. At least that way we have another pair of ears and eyes out there. She's old enough and sensible enough now to understand it all and help." Squid replied.

Squid pours himself a scotch then goes and sits on the sofa with Jenny.

"Dad, Paul's coming round in a minute to take me into Taunton for a while. We were going to watch a movie. Is it still ok to go out or shall I cancel him?" asked Sophie, shouting down the stairs.

"Not tonight sweetheart, call him and put it off, please." Squid replied.

Sophie comes down the stairs and sits with her parents.

"Is everything OK?" she asks.

"We need to have a chat, it's important, but after the kids are in bed." Jenny explained.

"Look if this is about sex and boys we have done all that before. Didn't we have this chat when I was twelve?" Sophie replied trying to make her father smile and lighten the situation. Squid looked at her and smiled.

"I remember those chats. You were so innocent back then, to think it won't be long before I will be doing it all again with Penny." Squid smiled.

"Well, I still am Dad. Just because I am at college doesn't mean I am sleeping around. I'm still a virgin you know. I am not the sort of girl to sleep with any Tom, Dick, or Harry and Paul knows it." Sophie replied.

"Sweetheart, I am not worried about Tom or Harry or Paul." Squid replied.

Jenny frowns at his mocking of the situation.

"Squid, this is all very amusing, but a little beside the point." Jenny replied.

"Sorry seriously, I am glad you are still a virgin, but this is way beyond all that. I am proud of you and I love you to bits. You're a smart girl which is why your mother and I need to tell you a story, a true story. Some of it you will remember and some of it goes way back to when you were conceived." Squid started to explain to Sophie.

Sophie sits with her parents listening as they explain to her what went on before they met up again. She listen's as the pair tell her about the Brinks Mat bullion heist carried out by Squids father. Together they explained how they have been chased and pursued over the years. But, Sophie was more interested in the romance behind the robbery.

"So you and mum were childhood sweethearts, wow, you are like soul mates." Sophie replied.

"So, you see Sophie this is the reason that I made you go to all those Martial Arts classes, I needed to know that if anything happened, you could get yourself out of trouble. I thought it was all over then that idiot turned up tonight and well he started making threats." Squid explained.

"Sophie the thing is, it's not a story and the threat is now serious. This man and the people he knows are dangerous, he threatened to harm you and Penny. That's what made your father flip just now. So you have to be on your guard all the time from now on. Be sure to look out for your sister and brothers." Jenny explained.

Squid gets up and walks to a cupboard drawer, takes out a stun gun and pepper spray and hands it to Sophie, to keep in her bag.

"Keep this on you at all times and I mean all times. Even if you are in the bath have it close by. If anyone gives you shit use it on them. Either one will put them out of action long enough for you to make an escape. Always make sure your phone is on you and that it's charged. I don't want to scare you sweetheart but you have to remain vigilant all the time." Squid replied.

Christmas passed and the New Year was seen in. It was still a good Christmas although all the elder members of the family were a little on edge. Sophie started practising her Martial Arts again, often sparing with her father in the garage. Squid decides on other ways of protecting his family and gets both vehicles up the farm and reinforces them. The transit has an RSJ running from end to end with RSJ bumpers, something he remembered from his days with Duke at the scrap yard, when he was a teen-ager. He then did a similar job on the Discovery, if anyone tried messing with his family they were going to suffer.

Squid keeps looking out of the window, checking to see who's around. Sophie calls Squid over as she watch's TV with the other kids.

"Daddy, chill out, I am looking out too, this isn't all down to you anymore. I'm not that little 11 year old kid any more, I've grown up. I can help this time, now come here and give me a hug." She demanded.

"What's all this, family cuddle time?" asked Jenny as she walked into the front room.

"Come here mum you can have a hug too." Sophie replied.

"We are going to be safe, aren't we? Or are things getting worse, do I need to be worried for the kids?" Jenny asked. But, before Squid could answer the phone rang.

"Hello, yes that's me... On fire! Oh my god, I will be straight round." said Jenny.

Putting the phone down Jenny turns to Squid.

"What's up sweetheart?" he asks.

"It's the Lingerie shop, it's on fire." Jenny replied.

"That damn Morris is behind this, I just know it." Squid mumbled in anger.

The family watch as the fire service put out the blaze, but whilst they watch the fire, Squid looks for something more sinister and when he sees Morris's BMW slowly drive past, his suspicions are confirmed. Now he knew it was time to act. That evening Squid, Jenny and Sophie talk about recent events. Squid explains he has a plan.

"If anything goes wrong and I get caught just remember stay safe. And look after yourselves" he expresses hugging them.

"Now you are scaring me, we don't want to lose you Squid." Jenny replied.

"If I go down, sell the house and land along with the Jag and move out to Florida. The exchange rate is very good at the moment. You will probably double your money. It would be enough to live comfortably for quite some time." Squid explained.

"Daddy no, we won't leave you, never!" sobbed Sophie.

"Listen, under the back seat of the Jag is seven thousand pounds I have managed to put aside in case anything should happen to me. It's not much I know, but with the exchange rate like it is, it will give you about fourteen thousand dollars. It will be enough to get you going." Squid replied.

"Squid no please, let's just go to the police." Jenny begged.

"I want you two to promise me you will leave and forget about me and all this shit, and damned curse. Give the boys and Penny a new life and a chance to be something." Squid asked.

"No mum you can't, it's not fair!" Sophie sobbed as glances anxiously at her mother.

"You start a new life out there. Don't write or get in touch with me in any way. Do you understand? You must promise me you'll do this?" Squid begged wanting to free his family from the curse started by his father.

No, no, I don't want to lose you, No!" she said hugging her father.

"Sweetheart, I have some people who owe me a few favours, now let's stick to this plan for now, if shit happens then you know what to do end of story. That's the way it has to be." Squid replied as he ran his fingers through Sophie's lovely dark hair.

"Come here Jenny, give me another hug, you know the score Sweetheart, we have been here before." Squid said as he hugged them both.

"I know what has to be done. Like you say, we've been there before remember. Same sort of shit just a different day." Jenny replied.

"Mum no, you can't agree to this, no." Sophie argued.

"Whatever we need to do we'll do it, just never ever forget how much we love you Squid." Jenny said getting tearful herself.

"No mum no, don't agree, please! I don't want to lose either of you." replied Sophie.

"It will be fine honest sweetheart, I don't want to lose you either but mum knows what these people are like. They won't go away." Squid replied.

"Then count me in, I am helping" Sophie stated.

Squid and Jenny's eyes meet across the sofa and they nod and smile at one another. OK, we do this as a family then. Squid runs by the two what he has planned for Morris. Emotions ran high that night and when they went to bed Jenny made love to Squid like she did the first night after they had met up again. If it was to be their last night together she was damned sure he was going to remember it.

At 7:00am the door to the front of the house opens. In a screaming rage Jenny throws four large bin bags of clothes out of the door into the street. A huge row erupts between her and Squid, Sophie then gets involved and pushes her father from the house, she hands him his mother's ashes telling him to leave.

"Now get out Squid I can't take any more of this!" Jenny screamed.

Grabbing the bags Squid throws them in the back of his Transit and then wheel spins off up the road. This wasn't what he wanted his family's life to be like.

Squid drives to the farm and moves into an old caravan. With Dave his mate who owned the farm being away for a month, Squid had realised this was the perfect time to deal with Morris. A week goes by and he works the farm returning to the caravan every night. Then early one evening Squid gets a call on his mobile he's been waiting for.

"I have someone here who would like to say hello." screamed Morris's voice down the phone.

"Squid, Morris has got Penny, Bradley and Lewis. I don't know where Sophie is, she's not here. Help us, please help us." screamed Jenny.

"It seems you thought I was joking, that little incident with the shop didn't seem to get the message through to you so, maybe now you will take me seriously." shouted Morris.

"OK, OK, please just don't hurt them. I have managed to get a one hundred thousand together. It's all I have it's everything. Bring them up to the farm I will meet you here. Just don't hurt my family please I beg you leave them out of this." Squid replied.

"OK, now that's more like it. See I can be a reasonable man. I'll be there in half an hour and no funny stuff. Otherwise I won't stop until I have Sophie as well." Morris replied.

"Sweetheart I need you here at the farm in ten minutes." Squid said as he spoke to Sophie on the phone. She had deliberately been making herself scarce most days allowing Morris to come after either her or her mother.

"OK Dad, I am on my way, I should be there in five." she replied.

Squid carried on working around the farm whilst he waited for Sophie. He parked the tractor in the yard lowering the loader, he removed two bales of hay and put them into one of the feeding troughs. Once Sophie arrives Squid hides her car out of the way and then explains to her what he wants her to do. Morris isn't long behind her and enters the farmyard in his BMW only five minutes later. As Squid looks towards the approaching car Morris puts his lights on full beam blinding Squid for a few seconds. Squid holds up his hand to his eyes and tries to see what he can, which isn't much. He had to hope Sophie would act at the right moment.

"Where's the money?" shouted Morris out of his car window.

"It's in the cab of the tractor in a holdall." Squid replies.

"Get it and no funny stuff with the tractor or your family gets it, do we understand one another?" replied Morris.

"Yes." Squid replied, getting the bag from the cab and walking back towards the headlights of Morris's car.

"Throw it in the back window of the car. Any funny business and you'll never see any of your family again." Morris threatened.

"Where's Jenny and the kids?" asked Squid.

"They're at your home safe with a friend of mine. You don't think I would attempt this alone do you? Unlike your father, James Ryan, I have thought this through." Morris replied in sarcasm.

"Enjoy it whilst you can arsehole." Squid replied as he throws the bag in the back window of the car.

"Now stay back whilst I check the cash." Morris demanded.

Morris waves a pistol at Squid, undoing his seat belt Morris twists around, fumbles trying to reach and inspect the contents of the bag.

Sophie has been watching, waiting for the perfect opportunity.

"Let's see how you like a bit of body piercing...Wanker!" Sophie announced

The transit had been sat behind Morris's car silently ticking over in the barn with Sophie at the wheel. Slipping it into gear she flicks the lights on full beam and the spotlights light up the yard dazzling Morris momentarily. She shoots out of barn and the Transit rams the rear of Morris's car. Keeping her toe to the floor Sophie push's Morris's car into the front loader of the tractor. Morris lets out a horrifying scream as the prongs pierce through the windscreen and into Morris's neck and chest pinning him to the seat.

"Good girl! Now go and sit in the caravan whilst I deal with this problem. I don't want you to witness what I am going to do next sweetheart." Squid shouted to Sophie.

"Ok Daddy, be careful he still has his gun." Sophie replied as she turned off the Transit and headed to the caravan where Squid had been staying. Walking around to the driver's door of Morris's car, Squid opens it, to see Morris is still alive gasping for breath, blood is everywhere.

"See! This is what happens to people when they mess with me and my family. Looks like you have made yourself another victim of the Brinks Mat curse. Dear oh dear, I thought I could trust you especially with you being a copper and all." gloated Squid.

"Help me-please-just help me." he spluttered.

Squid walks back to the tractor, reverses it back pulling the spike from the neck and chest of Morris who then starts to bleeds out fast.

"I wish you could see what I have planned for you but unfortunately it's a bit shit. Bet that pension seems quite rosy right about now." Squid replied making sure Morris was well aware of how grim his situation was. Squid opens up the passenger car door he picks up Morris's gun from floor. Squid then tips out the content of the bag in front of Morris.

"It's paper, all paper." stated Squid waving it under the dyeing man's nose. Squid gets in the Transit and reverses it out of the way. Climbing back into the cab of the tractor Squid pushes Morris's car around with the forks and lines it up with the slurry pit. Climbing back out of the cab Squid walks to Morris's car and winds down all the electric windows. He goes to the boot of the car checking none of his family were in there. Then walking by the side of the driver's door he grabs Morris's hair and pulls his head up from the steering wheel. Morris tries to speak but is too weak.

"Well you wanted to retire somewhere warm, well sorry, all I can offer you is a slurry pit for now full of nice cold shit." Squid replies holding up the man's head and pointing out the dark cold slurry pit in front of him. Squid attaches a piece of rope to the towing eye of the rear of the BMW then once more he gets in the tractor and pushes Morris's car into slurry pit. Slowly the shit rolls over the open windows of the doors and fills the car with slurry. Morris panics with his last breath his eyes filled with fear. Squid keeps pushing the car until it is completely submerged in the pit out of sight.

"Are you Ok Sweetheart? Sorry I had to get you to do that but it had to be done." Squid said to Sophie hugging her.

"It's OK Dad, it was him or us." she replied.

Squid strips off his clothes and changes into some fresh ones in case he had any DNA from Morris on them.

"Let's go get your Mother, brothers and sister. Morris isn't going anywhere for now." Squid said.

"He asked for it and I am not going to live without my father again. I'll do anything for you Daddy, anything." Sophie said hugging her father.

"Same here sweetheart same here." Squid replied.

Squid walked over to the Transit and pulling out his pocket knife he cut off the tyres that were hung over the RSJ and throws them back onto the silage clamp. He and Sophie headed back to the house. Sophie clung onto her father's arm as the headed home in the transit.

"Sweetheart whatever happens and whatever is said by the police you deny knowing anything OK? As far as they're concerned you were off riding one of the horses and simply rode back down here with me in the van, you didn't see or hear anything, remember that." Squid ordered.

"Yes Dad, what are you going to do about Morris's girlfriend, she still has mum and the kids?" Sophie asked.

"Well that's an unknown, will have to just play it by ear as we go. My plan is to let her think Morris has double crossed her, I will say I gave him the money and he drove off hopefully she will just go." Squid replied as he pulls up outside house.

Squid walks straight into the house as if nothing has happened. Sophie follows close behind. As the two enter, Morris's Girl friend is there holding a gun over Jenny and kids. She was a thin woman a lot younger than Morris, she had tattoos on both arms covering over scars. At some point in her life she had been self harming. She points the gun at Squid.

"Where's Morris?" she asks looking very unstable.

"What are you doing still here? Morris has the money. He said he was calling you to let them go. He's got the money, he's gone." Squid replied.

Squid takes Morris's gun from the pocket of his jacket.

"Now we are equal, you have a gun pointed at me and I have one pointed at you. But, look all I want is my family back safe, Morris has his money, whatever you two had going on was between the two of you. This is nothing to do with us so just go, please walk away I promise I won't even call the police." Squid explains.

The woman grabs Jenny then holding the gun out towards Squid she starts to panic.

"He wouldn't do that to me, he loves me, he said to stay here till he called me, he wouldn't leave me, he wouldn't." shrieked the woman who clearly had mental issues, no doubt brought on by years of drug abuse and Morris taking advantage of her.

"Look all I know is I gave him the cash, he left, now keep calm. I'll put my gun down . . . see as a good gesture, I want no trouble just my family back safe." Squid replied, as he placed his gun on the floor

"Just walk away." Squid repeated.

But, the woman was obviously on something. Jenny could see her finger starting to squeeze on the trigger and her hand was shaking in desperation. Not knowing what to-do and worried for Squids life, Jenny swiftly turned punching the woman on the face with the back of her elbow. As she fell away the woman squeezed the trigger and the gun went off. The bullet ricocheted off the log burner shooting Squid in the arse. He fell to the floor, screaming with pain. Jenny thinking the worst beat the hell out of the woman knocking her out cold. Running to Squid she feared the worse.

"Squid sorry sweetheart are you ok?" Jenny cried.

"She shot me in the fucking arse, how, how the fuck did she do that?" Squid cried.

"I thought she was going to pull the trigger, I am so sorry Squid please don't die!" Jenny sobbed.

"I am ok sweetheart, I just got a bullet in my bum that's all. I'll live. Quick, call the police, but wipe Morris's gun and stick it in her pocket. Sophie in the cupboard draw are some tie wraps. Put her hands behind her back and tie them up, then do her feet. She can stay there till the police arrive." Squid explained.

Jenny wiped the gun and did as Squid said putting it in the woman's jacket pocket. Then she ran to Squid and hugged him.

"Get me something to stem the blood flow sweetheart, before I do bleed to death." Squid asked.

"Don't you dare go dying on me Squid Ryan." Jenny replied.

"Then get me something to stick in this hole in my arse." Squid replied.

"Roll over babes let me take a look." Jenny said.

Squid loosened off his trousers whilst Jenny pulled them down a bit.

"Shit babes, you got a hole in your arse. It's bleeding badly. What shall I do?" she asked.

"Stick your finger in it!" Squid replied.

Jenny quickly puts her finger in the hole, stemming the bleeding. Squid let out a groan of pain just as Sophie walked back in.

"Oh my god you two what are you doing, that's disgusting?" Sophie said screwing up her nose."

"I am just sticking my finger in your father's hole" Jenny replied just as a police woman walked in.

"Really, at a time like this." The police woman replied.

"No, no it's not what it looks, my husband's been shot in the bottom. I am trying to stem the blood I need something to shove in here till the ambulance arrives." Jenny explained.

"Here mum use this." replied Sophie handing her mother a small tampon. Jenny pulls out her finger and pushes in the tampon which immediately stems the flow. A policeman walks in and looks at Squid.

"Well that's something you don't see every day a guy with a tampon up his arse!" stated the policeman.

"It's not up his arse it's in a bullet hole by his arse." explained the police woman as she escorted the Morris's girlfriend from the house.

"Oh, well looks like a guy with a tampon up his arse." the copper replied.

Minutes later the ambulance turned up. Feeling dizzy with the loss of blood Squid passes out and is rushed off to hospital. Outside the neighbours had gathered round being nosey.

"What's happen?" asked one.

"Apparently, they were having some weird sex game, her husband came out with a tampon up his arse. He'd been bleeding terribly, god knows what they were inserting up one another, its weird shit and even the daughter was involved." replied Mrs Jones from two houses down.

"I overheard a policewoman say when she arrived the wife had her finger inserted right up his Jacksy!" said another.

"Always thought they were a bit of a weird family." replied Sandra Brown who lived opposite Squid and Jenny.

Chapter Nine

Squid wakes in hospital. He has tubes and drips coming from his body. Jenny is by his side. A Police Officer is outside the room guarding the door.

"Oh Squid you're awake. They had to operate to remove the bullet from your bum." Jenny said.

"That explains why I have a sore-very sore arse! Is everything OK?" Squid replied.

"Well you only have one hole in your bum now and the doctors think you won't have any problems going for a poo." Jenny explained.

"Not my arse silly, is everything ok with regards Morris's girlfriend?" Squid replied.

"Yes, they have found other discrepancies in Morris's files. It turns out he is under investigation. They are searching for him at the moment." Jenny replied.

"Guess he's defiantly in the shit then. Hopefully they won't find him before I have a chance to deal with the situation. How is Sophie, Penny and the boys?" asked Squid.

"They're fine. The little ones found it all very exciting and Sophie...Well she's just relieved she still has her dad." Jenny replied.

"And I am not handcuffed to the bed, so I guess things are OK for now." Squid stated.

"Do you think it is over now Squid or do you think there're still others out there?" asked Jenny

"That depends on how I get on when I get out of here, but I don't know. I never for a moment suspected Morris. Most of the others are all dead. Hopefully, we have heard the last of it." said Squid.

Sophie comes running into the room and hugs her father. She was followed by a police officer.

"Daddy you're awake." She screamed.

"That was a close shave you had there, how are you feeling today Sir?" asked the officer.

"Too close. Another couple of inches and she would of blown me nuts off." Squid replied.

"We do need to take a statement from you Mr Carr, as soon as you feel up to it, just to get your side of the events." the officer replied.

"Ok, but can it wait till tomorrow? I still feel like shit to tell the truth." Squid replied.

"No problem. I will let the station know and they will send someone down from CID tomorrow." the officer explained.

A Doctor soon arrives in the room, checks Squid over and then he gets the nurse to change his dressing.

"How long before I can get out of here doc?" asked Squid.

"You seem a very fit young man and the wound is healing well. I should say 48 hours and we'll be happy for you to go home." the doctor replied.

"We'll look after you Dad." said Sophie.

"But you must take it steady. Once home you rest up and take things easy. You will have to have daily jabs for the next week just to prevent any blood clotting but this can be administrated at home." the doctor explained.

"Cool, can I do it Mum?" asked Sophie

"I worry about you sometimes girl, first you shove a tampon in my arse and now you want go sticking needles in me. I am going to be watching you young lady. I think I'll let your mother do it." Squid replied.

"We're staying in Taunton at a secret location. They're talking about changing our identities again, just in case." Jenny explained.

"I could really do without another name change. I am sure everything will be just fine." Squid tried to re-assure her.

The doctor, nurse and police woman leave the room. Squid whispers to Jenny once they are gone.

"Sweetheart, can you get me a protein drink and something to eat please? I need to get my energy up to get out of here." Squid whispered.

"I'll pop down the corridor and get something." Sophie replied.

"Pop home and get me some clothes babes too." Squid asked Jenny.

Sophie returned moment later with an energy drink and a beef sandwich.

"At around mid-day tomorrow Sophie, I want you to distract that copper I need to get out of here and back up to the farm pronto." Squid explained.

"Ok Dad, but please just rest up for today." she asked.

"Yes, sweetheart I will." Squid replied.

"Squid you've just been shot. Let Sophie and me do as much as we can, we are all in this together." Jenny replied.

"I know sweetheart I know." Squid replied

"I will tell the Police I need a sitter to watch Penny and the boys whilst I sort stuff out. We will go up the farm together OK?" Jenny explained.

"Sure thing Babes sure thing, now I really need to sleep. Squid said as his eyes start to close.

The medication and trauma had taken its toll, Squid was drained and needed to rest.

The following day as planned, Sophie distracted the policeman and Squid was able to get away.

An hour later he was at the farm pulling Morris's car from the slurry pit. Getting out the other tractor they had at the farm, Squid attached it to the forage harvester and connected up the

PTO (power take off) drive. Putting some bales in front of the pickup feed the machine was ready to chop up Morris's corpse.

Squid lined up the chute so that it sprayed the remains onto the covered yard, where the cows are held ready for milking. Sophie and Jenny blocked off the lane to the farm to prevent anyone driving down to where they were disposing of Morris's body. Squid handed Sophie his mother's ashes.

"Right first things first take this urn down to the twelve acre field and spread the ashes on the grass. The pigs will soon tread her remains into the soil." Squid replied.

"OK Dad, you going to be OK here or shall I come back and help?" Sophie asked.

"No you stay with the car till I arrive with the shit spreader and make sure no one comes past. If you get a problem call me." he replied.

"Jenny, whilst I am getting rid of Morris, can you crush his car up with the loader on the tractor, then when you have finished smashing it up, load it all up in the trailer ready for me to take to the breakers yard?" Squid asked.

"Too true, sounds fun." Jenny replied.

Opening the car door Squid was faced with a grim scene, blood curdled with slurry, and the stench of death. He took in a deep breath as the severity of his actions, seeing Jenny smile through the tractor windscreen he remembered why he had done it. Squid dragged Morris's body from the car, laying it out on the bales in front of the forage harvester. Walking to the tractor he starts up the engine and engages the PTO then opening the throttle wide he walks back round to where the drum blade is spinning with rage. Slowly Squid fed the body into the machine, the tractor puffing out black smoke as the engine worked under load.

So my friends this was the moment I totally crossed the line. I tried being good, been the bad boy, now I had just got downright ugly. I had now become everything I was trying not to be. Who was I, or am I even? Because still even today I question as to whether I am the good guy or the bad guy. I convince myself I had to do it for love, for my family, but then doubt runs through my mind and I start to wonder whether I am just evil and it's in the blood, and Jenny and Sophie have been dragged into the lie. How this would affect Sophie long term worried me and still does to this day.

In the meantime Jenny wanted to do her bit, there was still a side to her he didn't know about, she still had her own connections so picking up the phone she made a call.

"I need a favour, Squids taking a crushed car down the breakers yard we need it to disappear completely, no trace what so ever can be left, is that understood!" Jenny emphasizes to the man on the other end of the phone.

The call was brief but what she asked for was put into action.

Squid, who was constantly looking around in case anyone turned up. He noticed two ramblers walking towards him he had to stop them before they came too close. Leaving half the corpse on the bale, Squid hurried over to them.

"I am sorry you can't come any closer Health and Safety, I am afraid. I must ask you to go back to the public foot path." Squid explained.

"But, we always take this short cut that way we don't have so far to walk." the man replied who was dressed in tweed from head to toe. As he stood talking to Squid, he tried looking past him at the machine which was still whistling away.

"But, isn't that the point of being a rambler . . . you walk?" Squid asked as he looked at the man's wife who seemed to be wearing matching tweed, hats, coats, her skirt even his trousers all seemed to be tweed, must be a ramblers thing thought Squid.

"Burt can't keep going for as long as he used too so, if he can sneak in the rear, he finds it's quicker for him." the woman explained leaning on her stick which had once been the part of someone's hedge row many years ago. Her fingers rubbed the Y at the top of the stick impatiently as she talked as if she were in a hurry to get walking again.

"Well I am sorry. There can be no nipping in the rear today, too much shit, don't want you getting stuck." Squid replied.

"I get a little stiff you see, don't I Shirley?" Burt explained as he lent on his stick which matched Shirley's except his had the addition of little badges running all the way down.

"You do Burt, you do. Once my Burt's stiff, I find the best thing is to get him home and lay him down. He likes a nice massage, don't you Burt?" the woman replied in a very domineering manor.

"I do Shirley, I do." he said re arranging his small round glasses that sat on the edge of his nose.

"Well I am sorry, stiff or not, there's no nipping through the rear today. If you slip, health and safety will be on me like a tonne of bricks so, please if you can turn around and follow the path on round behind the hedge." Squid explained as he went to turn and walk back to the tractor.

"Nice tractor you have there, Massey Ferguson isn't it? Burt loves his tractors, don't you Burt." explained Shirley.

"I do Shirley, I do." replied Burt taking off his glasses and wiping the lens with his white cotton hanky.

"Then Burt will know that's a New Holland, its blue not red, Massey's are red. Now please, I really do have to get back to work so please stick to the footpaths." Squid asked, as he turned to walk away again.

"Nice forage harvester? Isn't it the wrong time of year to have that going, what make is it?" asked Burt.

"Burt likes his forage harvesters don't you Burt." Shirley explained standing up right and moving her walking stick to her left.

"I do Shirley I do." Burt replied trying to look past Squid who was clearly doing his best to block their view.

"Well I would like to show it to you but, I still have the last rambler who trespassed through my yard to put through it. So if you don't mind, I would like to get on with my work, some of us do have to work you know." replied Squid, getting angry with the couple.

"Well I say, how rude, I have never been spoken to like that before, tell him Burt tell him." the woman replied feeling quite offended.

The woman puts her scrawny husband in front of her and then pushes Burt towards Squid, whose huge frame looked very intimidating. The man stood there took off his glasses once more and gave them a wipe before putting them back on. Looking at Squid, he stepped forward another step.

"Look here, I am a reasonable man . . . and I am sure you are a reasonable man too so as a pair of reasonable and civilised men, I think on this occasion Shirley and I will go back around the footpath but. we do so in protest. I really don't think it could have hurt us to have gone through your yard." said Burt.

Squid smiled at the man as he reminded him of Stringer Davis the actor, he then let out a slight giggle as he realised the woman reminded him of Stringers wife and famous actress Margaret Taylor Rutherford.

"Oh it could, believe me it, could hurt very much." Squid replied.

The couple turned and walked off back to the foot path, Squid watched them disappear behind the hedge before going back to his machine and pushing the rest of Morris's body through the rotating blades.

The machine made easy work of the task and within a few more minutes the job was done. Now in order to complete the task, Squid had to scrape up the remains into the shit spreader and then spread them on the twelve acre field where Sophie was waiting. Squid ran a couple of bales through the forage harvester to clean it through then loaded them into the shit spreader as well. Once finished he let the cows back in the yard.

Sophie waited for her father to return whilst keeping a firm eye open for anyone approaching, she breathed a sigh of relief as she saw Squid driving towards her with the tractor and shit spreader. Squid pulled up by Sophie.

"Sorry I have been so long, had a couple of ramblers I had to deal with." Squid explained.

"Oh no, are they in there too." cried Sophie as she put her hand to her mouth.

"No, no sweetheart, deal with . . . not DEAL with." Squid explained.

"Oh thank Christ for that! We don't want the police looking for any more missing people, ones enough. I spread your mum's ashes over there." Sophie explained pointing to a green patch of grass.

"Ok, time to spread some shit on the GRASS and put at least one part of my past to rest. You go up to the farm sweetheart and give your mum a hand. She's squashing up Morris's car, we need to get the power washer going and wash down the machines." Squid explained as he engaged the PTO drive on the tractor.

"OK Dad." Sophie replied giving Squid a kiss on the cheek.

Squid spread the load over the field and it wasn't long before the pigs trotted over and nibbled at any of the larger remains. Squid then headed back to the farm. Morris's car was already loaded in the trailer ready for Squid to dispose of and the two girls sat waiting.

Squid gave Jenny a big hug.

"Thanks for helping you two I'd be lost without you both. Now whilst I'm gone, if you can steam off the forage harvester as well and put it back out in the paddock for me. That would be great and then feed the animals so everything looks as it should." Squid asked.

Squid drives the tractor and trailer to his friend's breakers yard, he hands over five hundred pounds in cash, then he watches as they grab the BMW's remains out of the trailer and put it straight in the crusher. It then gets loaded on an artic lorry with a whole bunch of other scrap cars and is taken away. Squid leaves the yard reminiscing about working with Duke Smith as a kid, it was the first time in years he had thought about his childhood working for Duke. He had been a good friend and Squid missed those innocent days. As Squid arrived back at the farm the police were there waiting for him.

"We wondered where you were. You had us worried for a while. You shouldn't be working and we still need a statement." Glen Maw announced.

"I still don't know who I can trust, figured I was safer looking after myself and my family. After all Morris is a copper." Squid replied.

"I understand that, but the quicker we get your statement the sooner we can catch him." Glen Maw explained.

"I feel better on my own turf with my family close by. I'm not one for just lying in hospital. Had to get back to work, despite what everyone thinks I don't have the Brinks Mat gold. I need to work for a living." Squid replied.

"Can you come to the station now?" asked Glen Maw.

"Have you sorted everything out, are we safe?" asked Jenny.

"Don't tar us all with the same brush Squid. I worked with Morris remember in the early days? We've met before and Morris was an arse then." replied Glen Maw

"I remember, but that's what is worrying me." said Squid.

"Look for now, you are all safe but you know this will never ever go away. Well not until you hand over the missing gold." Glen Maw explained.

"See, you're all so convinced I know where it is." Squid replied.

I have to make sure. To be honest I have never thought for one minute you knew where it was. However, I do believe if we can solve this damned six, three, three, Squadron and a 303 riddle we could find it." Glen Maw explained.

"If I did, don't you think I would have tried to do a deal by now? I would have given up the cursed haul a long time ago. I wish I did know, but I don't. I just want to enjoy my family. I can't help what my father was and what he did. You've seen the statements and notes you must believe me when I say I have no idea where it is." Squid explained.

"The trouble is Squid, it's not going to go away. Not until we have something to put the case to rest with." replied Glen Maw

"Then tell me, who's the man at the top? Where's the man I need to talk to, the one who thinks I have the gold? Take me to him, I will explain to his face, get him to understand I have no idea where the Brinks Mat gold is and never have." said Squid

"Well you see that's the problem, there is no top man. It's just a story that is passed down through the force. Every new copper that joins at some point hears the story about this gangster dying and leaving his son a clue as to where he hid the gold bullion. Then at some point in their career they look up the notes and walk away thinking maybe now he will give it up, maybe now he's had enough of being hounded and threatened." replied Glen Maw.

"I had, had enough years ago! Do you think anyone with kids enjoys living like this?" asked Squid.

"We need to work out this riddle. Just imagine finding all that gold and remember once the gold is found the case is closed. So let's work together and let's make this problem disappear. Work with us." replied Glen Maw.

"You were starting to sound a little like Morris there for a moment. There is only one problem, I have no idea where my father stashed the haul." Squid explained.

"This is pointless Squid, come on lets go." Jenny replied tiring of the conversation.

"How many more times, he doesn't know where it is so what's the point in talking?" shouted Sophie.

Walking across to Maw, Sophie pushes him away from her father.

"I don't have to tell you, you've read the case notes after all that's happened to me in my life I can tell you, it's not worth the hassle. Read all the material you have on the Brinks Mat robbery maybe then you will see it's cursed. Everyone ever involved with it is either dead, banged up or vanished. Or like me hounded by everyone. Believe me if you did have just a single bar, you wouldn't want it." Squid explained.

"You see, I hear what you are saying except for one thing. You are the only connection to this robbery not dead, not banged up and still here. That's why it keeps coming back to haunt you." Glen Maw replied.

Sophie gets in Glen's face she's heard enough and is very protective of her father.

"Stop hounding my dad, leave now! We can look after ourselves it's worked for us up 'til now." Sophie said, as she tries to get Glen Maw to leave.

Jenny gets between Sophie and Glen. Squid also moves in as the conversation gets heated, but as he moves he twists too quickly and holding his arse cheek realises he's ripped his stitches.

"See now look he's hurt himself again." Jenny says.

"Dad, come and sit down." Sophie said.

"I don't think sittings the answer sweetheart." says Squid.

"I am simply trying to offer you a way out, whilst I am still in a position to do so. Once I've left the force there will be a whole new generation of dreamers wanting to be the ones to get their hands on it. You will never ever be left alone. I had to ask, couldn't have lived with myself if I didn't. I believe you." Glen Maw announces.

Squid sits on a concrete milk churn stand and gets comfortable.

"Do you mean that, that you believe me?" asked Squid.

"Yes I do. I have dealt with enough scum in my life to know when I am being lied to. Also you don't follow the pattern. You strike me as quite a sensible man, a family man, but I feel for you as I know this case will never go away Squid." Glen Maw replied.

"How sure can you be that we can stop these idiots coming after us and bring closure to this whole Brinks Mat bullion thing?" asked Squid.

"Are you telling me you do know something?" asked Glen Maw.

No, but I knew my father. If you're being honest with me and you think we can do this, then you know far more about the case than I do. You have access to the case files bring them around, let's go through them together. Maybe then we can work out what my father did with his share of the gold, but I want to know what your plans are. Let's say we do find whatever's left from this Brinks Mat heist, how will you ever make it all go away?" Squid asked as Jenny and Sophie sat either side of him with their arms around him.

"That bits simple, there's a reward for the missing gold so we go public with the find. By going public with the story we drag any of the worms associated with the Brinks Mat robbery out of the wood work. Then you'll have the reward and give me a drink for my troubles. Then the gold is given back and everyone will know the lost Brinks Mat gold is found. Case closed." Glen Maw explained as if it were simple.

"You realise trying to do this could take months, even years?" Jenny replied.

"If you're being straight with me then yes, go for it, I can put up with the media interest in me once again, but I want my family taken away and put in a safe house until it's all over." Squid explained.

"Dad No, you can't do that, it's not fair." Sophie replied.

"I can't risk you, mum and the kids being hurt anymore. If we go public who knows what shit might turn up on our door step and we might not be able to come out of it safe next time." Squid replied.

"Leave this with me for a few days to get this all in motion and then I will call you to let you know when everything is in place. Since the files are boxed and there are lots of boxes, it will be best for you to come to the police station to go through them." Glen Maw explained.

"Ok, you move my family to a safe house. I will stay at our family home in Wellington and it's a deal." said Squid, holding his hand out for Maw to shake.

I'd had a close shave with Morris, too close, but what do you do when your back is against the wall and your family threatened? I had to try to break the curse and if that meant working with the old bill then so be it. People say you chose your own path in life, well that's bollocks. You have a plan on the path you want in life, but then every fucker else changes it. So you fight, you fight or you'll end up one of those idiots we see sat in shop doorways with their dog begging, that or pushing up daisies.

The weeks and months rolled by Squid had adapted to living on his own again and his family without him. None of them were happy at the situation, but knew they had to try. Glen Maw spoke to Squid regularly to discuss the case and when he could he popped over with papers and documents related to the case and the two would sit and discuss them over a beer. Jenny and Squid were reduced to secret meetings in hotels or days out with the kids far away from home.

"How's your arse, what's it been three months? Family all ok are they?" asked Glen joking with Squid.

"Yes fine thank you, they've settled in well and my arse is as good as new, except I have a new dimple on the right cheek I never had before. Would you like to see it?" asked Squid, jesting with him.

"No, too much information thank you, I will take your word for it you keep your arse to yourself." Glen replied.

"Have there been any sightings or news of Morris, what's the story with his girlfriend?" Squid asked.

"Nothing I am afraid. I expect he is half way around the world by now. He must have realised we were on to him. As for the girlfriend she has mental health issues and has been sectioned, she can't even remember that day." Glen explained.

"I see, so hopefully things have died down for a while. When's the publicity starting?" asked Squid.

"We've already put out a press release, just a case of seeing which papers pick up on it. The Sun will for sure. I see you're back in the gym, don't know how you do all that gym stuff it would bore me crazy." Glen replied.

"That's why you have a bit of a belly and I don't." Squid jested as he looked at Glens beer belly, the man was always so skinny in the past but now with his middle age spread and receding hair line Glen was starting to look older than he was. Squid put it down to the man's job.

"You're right there, too many burgers and beer. You know one has to give your old man's gang a bit of respect, they changed the face of organised crime overnight. The day your father went on that job, it was just supposed to have been cash only which got me thinking he wouldn't have had time to hide the gold properly. Between them they removed 6,800 ingots of gold. Can you imagine that? I mean hats off to these guys and that's without taking into consideration the cash and diamonds." Glen explained as if his father was some sort of genius.

"Wow, the Ryan's are famous for something then." Squid replied sarcastically.

"The underworld had been a strictly cash business until then. Your Father changed how things were done. Before that the talk of the town was the Great Train robbery, anyway, we've your old man's cut of around one thousand seven hundred bars, but there are two people per van so that means the missing van should have around three thousand four hundred bars in it. You'd have to plan ahead to hide that much gold." Glen replied.

"Give or take a few we know, each of them took gold away with them. I never thought about that before I guess you are right. So what you are saying is, where ever the van is hidden it's a fluke just pure luck no one has found it" Squid replied.

"Your old man only went on the job in a getaway car, that Jag of his. You know when they found all that gold they had to improvise so they steal the Brinks Mat vans to load and move it all. We know he had to hide it but he had to hide it fast, but only temporary as they intended to come back to it." Glen explained

"He was bloody lucky then to escape like he did. Are you saying you think that the van has just sat in a barn or something all this time and no one's discovered it?" asked Squid as he gets up and pours Glen and himself a drink.

"Well, yes sort of. As for your old man being lucky that'll depend on how you look at it. If he hadn't done that job and stuck to being a small time crook, he'd probably be still alive and out by now." Glen replied.

"True, can you imagine their faces when they discovered what they had stumbled on?" Squid replied.

"Not many people know it, but they didn't get it all. There was just too much there, then, there were the Diamonds and the cash. We know they had around £600,000 between them in cash, but we know they took some of that cash with them till things cooled down. The truth is we think there was more, much more. How crazy's that?" Glen explained.

"You think that's crazy imagine at sixteen years old going down to breakfast and tipping the cereal into your bowl and having wads of cash fall out into it. I thought it was my birthday and Christmas joined into one, I should've known. I did nick some of it, it wasn't much just a few grand." Squid replied.

"I can imagine you did, I think I would of at that age." Glen replied whilst they both flicked through the notes.

"I can't believe this, just looking at all these names: Brain Pringle, Holly Northam, John Fordson, Mickey, Kenneth and John. Then you have my old man and my old dear. All are either dead or doing time. There are even coppers here and security guards not to mention my old man's team." Squid said looking a little shocked at the list of victims.

"I know, who would have thought it would claim so many victims over the years." replied Glen as he dumps a load of newspaper clipping on the table. Whilst they looked through them they continued to talk.

"What about Auntie Sandra, did she ever know anything? What happened to her?" Squid asked.

"Unfortunately she died two months after your father. She committed suicide I am sorry to say." replied Glen

"So many gone, I realise now how lucky I've been. I never realised it was all so complicated." said Squid.

"Maybe now you can see why everyone keeps coming after you. You are literally the only person connected to the case who has come away unscathed." replied Glen.

"You think!" replied Squid.

"By unscathed I mean not dead or imprisoned. I checked this morning and the reward for the gold is up to three million pounds. To be honest, if we can find this I don't need to skim anything off the top. I'd be well happy with one million if you would be happy with two." replied Glen.

"I tell you this Glen, if we find it leave the gold alone, how many times do I have to remind you it's cursed." Squid replied.

The two read through Glen's paper work together and looked at pictures and maps. Squid has a large board on his wall which has pins marking things on a map of the south of England. Several routes are highlighted in marker pen as to which route they may have taken, but it's not easy and still the months roll on. Then it turns to years and it is Christmas 2003 when they are reminded the curse is still there. Squid visits the police station to give Glen a bottle of scotch and a Christmas card.

"Hi Squid, this is nice my favourite tipple, thank you. By the way they got George West yesterday. That's another lead gone. Goes to show they're still looking for it." Glen explained.

"I could have done with some better news things are hard at the moment, Jenny wants to come home. All this sneaking around visiting each other as and when we can is taking its strain on us, the kids are growing up, they think there fathers some sort of spy." Squid replied laughing to himself.

"Well may be I can make a difference, I have a nice present for you too, I didn't want to say anything until I knew for sure, but here........... You and your family have a really nice 2004." Glen Maw replies handing Squid an envelope.

"What's this?" asked Squid.

"Open it and see." Glen replied.

"It's a cheque for £120,000. I don't understand, what is this?" asked Squid.

"After getting involved with you on this case and reading what a raw deal you've had over the years, I started to understand a little of what you've been going through. I didn't say anything at the time, but I did notice that Morris was also chasing your old foster parents in Spain." Glen explained.

"Really!" Squid replied.

"Morris had an address I am guessing he was going to move onto them once he had dealt with you." Glen replied.

"Greedy bastard." said Squid.

"Yes a very greedy man and he obviously wasn't going to stop until he had got as much as possible out of this case as he could. Anyway to cut a long story short, remember six months ago I had to go away for three weeks on another case, well I was in Spain tracking them down." Glen replied.

"Really!" Squid muttered, still shocked at the cheque.

"Yes really, I had them both arrested and due to their age when I threatened to bring them back to the UK and put them in prison they agreed to give back what they had left. So in order to keep their freedom I agreed to have the case against them dropped. That's it, it's all yours. Do with it as you will and enjoy it after all you really deserve it." Glen explained.

"Wow Glen, seriously I don't know what to say. The last two years has been such a struggle, what with being separated from Jenny and the kids, the secret meetings with them. We have barely got by some months. This is going to make such a difference, thank you." Squid replied.

"That's ok, what are mates for? Anyway on a down side my bosses have given me six months to sort this case or it's getting shelved again." replied Glen.

"I see." said Squid.

"Sorry, I have done my best. Let's hope this little windfall will help you out for now. So what are you going to spend it on?" Glen asks.

"Well the first thing I am going to do is to buy you a pint. Grab your coat." Squid replied.

"I won't argue with that." replied Glen.

"I haven't had the funds to re-new my pilot's licence this year and the Jag desperately needs a service and sorting out and so does Jenny's car. Sophie's car has had it so I really want to surprise her with a new car." Squid explained.

"Sounds a great idea." replied Glen.

"But, most importantly I can build a new house where the old one used to be and sell the one I'm in now. Hopefully still have some money left in the pot and be mortgage free. This really is incredible Glen and I really mean it, this is amazing." Squid expressed his gratitude, as they enjoy a drink together.

"Cheers, to you and your family, happier times and hopefully golden horizons." Glen jested.

"I will drink to that, cheers. I tell you I can't wait to see their faces." Squid replied.

"I can't help but think we're missing something. How many bullets did you actually have in the house? I mean your dad said a 303, not the bullet's or in the 303's, he was isolating them individually. A 303 which must have been pointing to one in particular, one that was different to the others. Can you recall anything about them?" asked Glen.

"Well now you mention it yes. I had three of them but one of them was a live one, unfired, and the other two were cases that were fired. But, this is no help anyway as I don't have the bullets and we don't know where they went. As you know the police tried to find them years ago and just hit a brick wall." Squid explained.

"True, I'm just clutching at straws. Well they only ever found one of the Brinks Mat vans and it's not the one your father was driving, we've proven that. So, wherever it is, my guess is the gold is still in it. So where could you hide a van for so long without it being discovered?" Glen asked scratching his head.

"Well, we asked this question years ago when we started this remember? We decided it was somewhere temporary as they were going to go back for it. Personally, I would have crushed it into a block and buried it, but the old man didn't have time to organise that. Remember they didn't know the gold was going to be part of the heist. So everything was on the spur of the moment." Squid explained.

"No, but they could have had the time to bury it, just drive the van into a hole and fill it in. That's if he had the contacts and my guess is he did." Glen replied.

"It would explain why no trace of the van or the gold has ever been found." Squid replied.

"Well he couldn't have gone far surely? Otherwise the police would have seen them." said Glen.

"You have to remember he was back home that evening as if nothing had happened and he was always in bed or watching TV. One thing I do remember though is he had white paint on his hands and he stank of white spirits. He used to do a bit of painting and decorating for Mad Mickey, but he never before stank like that." explained Squid.

"Probably means he painted something in a hurry, a van maybe?" Glen said raising an eye brow.

"He had a white van of his own. If he painted the Brinks Mat van and put his tax disc in the window with his vans number plates then no-one would have thought any different would they?" Squid replied.

"True, but this is just guessing here, we're just clutching at straws." replied Glen.

"We need to speak to any of his mates who are still alive and knew him back then. Find out if any of them saw him that day. If it was just a white van with him in it, from a distance no one would have thought any different." explained Squid.

"The problem is, that would have taken planning and you have to remember, all this gold wasn't planned." replied Glen.

"No, but he would have driven from our house in Croydon to pick up Mad Mickey. Dad and Mickey were as thick as thieves, excuse the pun. I know Mickey's father had a hanger up at Denham airfield. I used to go there sometimes, and the Jag someone had to move his Jag as well." Squid explained.

"That's ten minutes' drive from Heathrow." replied Glen.

"Now my old man was doing some painting and decorating at the time for Mickey so the paint and tools would have been in the back of his van anyway." Squid replied.

For the first time in years I felt like we were getting somewhere. All we had to do was keep at it and solve this damned riddle!

Chapter Ten

DAY OF ROBBERY—1983.

Mustafa and Mad Mickey are sat in the van outside a phone box.

"What the fuck are we going to do now? It won't be long before every pig in the country is looking for this van." says Mad Mickey.

"Look my van is at your hanger and it's fucking white. We have all that white paint so let's paint the fucker. What will it take 30 minutes the two of us on it? I can swap plates from mine, no twat will know any different. We have the rollers in there, it's mostly flat panels." Mustafa replied.

"You, my randy fucking friend Mustafa are a bloody genius. Let's do it or just swap the gold into your van." replied Mad Mickey.

"No it will take far longer to move that lot believe me, painting the bugger is the answer." replied Mustafa.

James and Mickey pull up at the hanger at Denham Airfield. With both vans parked next to each other, the two started painting. James changes plates, Mickey rollers the van with paint, James climbs in to his van peels the tax disc from screen and puts it in the Brinks Mat van.

"Can you just imagine doing all this and then being stopped and done for no fucking road tax?" James replied.

"Good thinking, good thinking. It looks a bit cleaner than yours and it's definitely faster." Mickey replied.

"Right come on then let's hit the road before it gets any later. We can head from here straight down the M3 then on to the A303 and we should be with Charlie in just over an hour." replied James.

"So what's the plan, stash the van somewhere it won't be found and then come back in a month or so once we have the contacts to get shot of it?" asks Mickey.

"I think so, don't you? We don't want this stashed at our places, what the fuck would we do with it? We hide it for a few weeks or months depending what the heat is like, then we find a buyer and get the cash and lose it all in one go. Let someone else have the hassle of what to do with it." James explains.

"Doesn't Kenny know something about gold?" Mickey replies.

"What Noye! The fuckers mad Mickey!" James replied.

"No I am Mad Mickey." Mickey replies.

"Fucking way madder than you '*and I mean that in the in the best possible taste*.'" replied James mimicking Kenny Everett!

"What's that all about?" asked Mickey.

"What's what all about?" James replied.

"And I mean that in the in the best possible taste." asked Mickey.

"It's Kenny fucking Everett ain't it." James replied.

"What the fuck has Kenny Everett got to do with Kenneth Noye?" asked Mickey.

"Well, he's mad." replied James.

"Mustafa . . . so was fucking Adolf Hitler, but I wouldn't compare him to Benny bloody Hill." Mickey replied.

"OK so mad is the wrong word, nasty then? Mean fucker, bad ass, badder than bad, he makes me shit myself when he walks in the fucking room. So, nah fuck that, I don't want Kenny anywhere near me or my family." James replied.

"I am sure if we start asking about, there's bound to be someone who can fence a few gold bars." replied Mickey.

"Mickey a few gold bars, ave you looked in the back of this van that's not a few gold bars. The Queen has a few corgis, what we have here, is like Battersea Dogs Home in January Mickey." James explained.

"*Gold, always believe in your soul, you've got the power to know, you're indestructible, always believe in, because you are gold*" Mickey started to sing.

"What the fuck are you doing now?" asked James.

"Spandau Ballet" replied Mickey.

"Fucking what ballet?" James asked.

"Spandau Ballet, they're like brothers you know like the Krays." Mickey explained.

"Mickey to my knowledge Ronnie and Reggie didn't do ballet. I am not saying that Ronnie wasn't partial to dressing up in tutu behind closed doors. But, to compare Spandau Ballet to the Krays will get you nothing other than a pair of concrete boots to swim across the Thames in." James replied.

"True, don't go mentioning it to anyone will you? Some people can be a little touchy." Mickey replied.

"Mum's the word." replied James.

"Right, let's get this load to Charlie," Mickey replied.

2004 — Squid and Glen are talking in the pub.

"Amazing, no one would have been looking for a white van with decorators in it. All the police were searching for was a blue security van. So let's say that's what they did. From Denham where would you head?" asked Glen.

"Me personally I would head for the motorway it's the only route on offer to them really. Let's go back to my place and pull out a map and see where they could have gone." replied Squid.

The two drove back to Squids house. Once there they grab a drink. Squid pulls out a map and the two of them search the area around Denham Airfield looking at road directions.

"Right so they would have gone down here, along here and then straight onto the M25 I suppose. Was the M25 open then or the M3 come to that? Shit we need an old map not a new one. It's a long road Squid I mean they could've turned off anywhere. We don't even know which roads were there then." Glen explained.

"According to this map the M25 on this section wasn't open, so say they didn't turn off here. Where would they have gone then? Where does this road go?" Squid replied.

Squid moves his fingers along the map following the route of several roads.

"Christ, Glen look at this, it was never about bloody bullets. Just look where this leads." Squid replies as he notices something very important to the case.

"The M3 ends here, so they would have gone down here to this road which only joins up to the A303. You're right! Your father wasn't talking about the bloody bullets he was talking about the damned Dual Carriageway. Even if the M3 and M25 were not there the 303 was." It makes sense now to presume he meant the A303." Glen replied.

"The A303, *not a 303.* I don't fucking believe it all this time and it wasn't Squadron he was saying, it was *Squid Ryan* he was calling my name." Squid explained excitedly.

"So you reckon the gold's buried somewhere on the A303. So, we're no closer than we were yesterday. Have you seen how long this road is, it goes from the M3 in Hampshire all the way down to Honiton in Devon. Why the fuck would you burry a van under a road?" replied Glen.

"Because it was temporary, it wasn't supposed to have been left. They were going to go back before the road was finished, but my mother ruined that plan when she grassed him up. Well we're closer than we were ten minutes ago. If we've figured this out there may be something else in the statements that will shine some more light on the situation." Squid explained.

"Look I am heading off to the station. You best talk to the missus and let her know about the little windfall and the breakthrough in the case. We're going to find this Squid, we're going to find it." repeated Glen buzzing with excitement.

"Yes OK, see you soon and if I think of anything else I will let you know. This has got to be our most productive evening so far." replied Squid who was now very excited himself.

It was late, but Squid had to ring Jenny with the good news.

"Hi sweetheart sorry if I woke you, how are you all? Right, we've had a bit of a break through on the case and wait for it-Glen has only gone and got back my inheritance from years ago." Squid announced with excitement.

"Really, what, slow down and explain." Jenny replied struggling to take in what Squid was rabbiting on about.

"We have got some money in the bank again. I have decided to get the old house re-built and put Springfield road on the market." Squid explained.

"Wow! You don't hang around, thanks for discussing it with me." Jenny replied semi sarcastically.

"I know, sorry I didn't discuss it, but it's just I need to do what's best for the family." Squid replied.

"It's OK Squid, it's all such a shock. What is the breakthrough in the case, you mentioned a breakthrough?" Jenny asked.

"Look I can't explain everything over the phone, but can you and Sophie meet me at Dunkeswell next week before they close for Christmas?" Squid asked.

"Sure we can, it will be good to see you. We're missing you." Jenny replied.

"It needs to be fairly early as I will be hiring a plane for the day. I need both of you to help with something, bring some binoculars with you as well." Squid replied.

"Sounds a little mysterious, what's all this about Squid? Exactly how much money did you get?" Jenny asked.

"Not really and let's just say enough to get us by for quite some time." Squid replied.

"Ok, we will be up for 9.00am. At least you've given me enough notice for once in order to give me chance to get a sitter in. You can buy us both lunch now you are rich?" Jenny replied jesting with him a little.

"Cool, no problem, I will fly to Popham and buy us all lunch there. Ok then see you next week. Love you. Give the kids a hug from me." Squid replied.

"I will, love you. Bye." Jenny replied.

"Bye." Squid said putting down the phone.

The next morning Glen Maw is in his office when his mobile phone bleeps, he receives a text from Squid which reads: *'HIRED A PLANE FROM DUNKESWELL, B THERE IF U CAN AT 9:00AM NEXT SATURDAY, JENNY AND SOPHIE WILL B THERE. SQUID*

Glen replies with: 'OK, C U THEN.'

Times had changed a bit since the day my father did the Brinks Mat job with his pals, now everyone has mobile phones. We can all go on this thing called the internet we can do searches for anything on a service called 'Google' and history is there in black and white for all to read, in a service called 'Wikipedia'. So much information about anything. Now people who are nobody, with no experience, can track down whoever they so wished and one's past can come back and bite you on the arse. Before you even know they've their teeth around your arse cheeks. Now I had to be more alert than ever before, I needed to solve this curse and quick.

A car cruises past Squid's house. Inside are three youths, two boys and one girl, all are dressed in hooded sportswear. They look like they're bored teenagers cruising in their lowered little car which has an exhaust sticking out the back that looks as if it was one of the lost funnels off the Titanic.

Squid walks out of his front door to see an A4 piece of paper placed under the windscreen. Picking it up Squid looks at it, there's a picture and in big black words are written 'Nokia Man Connecting People.' Squid looks at the picture, something looked familiar, but he couldn't place it. Screwing up the paper he chucked it in the bin.

Squid nipped out to the shops, returning an hour later only to find two more pieces of A4 posted through his letter box. This time he realises that it's not a flyer and that someone is specifically targeting him. Picking up the two flyers Squid looks at them, the title is the same, but the pictures are different. Squid puts them on the table and looks out of the windows to see if he can see anyone watching the house, but he can't. Making himself a drink Squid walks back to the table and picks up the pictures and looks at them. There is something really familiar about them, they look like a photo copy of some bad 70's porn film the image is not clear and the setting is dated.

"Nokia Man." Squid mumbles under his breath. It made no sense to him. Then using his head he decided to turn on his PC and search it. Typing in 'Nokia Man' the search engine takes him through to YouTube where there are several clips. Squid now intrigued by what had come up, he clicked on the movie.

"Nokia Man connects to Pippa. Yes watch carefully as this phone shop is robbed. See the connection the shop owner has with his staff, see Pippa swallow then ride his staff. 'Nokia Connecting people'" Squid reads aloud as the clip starts to play.

Squid nearly spits his coffee out all over the kitchen floor as he realises what it is he is watching. It was in fact the very clip of Squid's mobile phone shop being robbed all those years ago. Somehow it had found its way onto the net. Now it all made sense and someone had obviously recognised him as the man in the clip. Squid sat there watching it, laughing to himself as Pippa appears from under his desk topless.

"Well I'll be fucked, well I was." Squid mumbled under his breath to himself as he watched himself bend both girls over the desk and shag the pair from behind. Whilst on line he put in a search "Brinks Mat." To his amazement three pages of hits came up. Promptly Squid clicked on the first one and there it was all the information anyone could want on the Brinks Mat Bullion Robbery. Everyone, including Squid who was ever involved in the Brinks Mat robbery, was there listed for all to see.

"Come on old man-help me out here and give me a break. We know what happened we just need to know where you stashed the gold." Squid mumbled to himself as he looked at the board he had set up in his house which had everyone listed on it and the possible routes the van may have taken.

Come early evening Squid was exhausted from all the researching and decides to take a bath in the down stairs bathroom. Turning out the lights in the house, he lights a couple of candles around the bath then gets in and relaxes, adding hot water every so often as the bath chills, till eventually he drifts off asleep.

Outside a Vauxhall Corsa with no lights on crawls up outside Squids house staking out the place. After a couple of passes it parks up. Three teenagers, two boys and a girl are inside. The girl pulls on a balaclava. Pete the eldest of the group and the mastermind behind this operation looked around at Tanya who was sat in the back.

"Shit, I didn't think to bring anything to cover my face." Pete explained.

"Me neither." replied Garry, the second lad in the car.

"Well you ain't having my balaclava." states Tanya.

"Well what we going to do now?" asked Garry.

"Tanya, you wearing tights under your trackie bottoms?" asked Pete.

"Yeah why?" she replied,

"Get them off we need a leg each to put over our heads." Pete replied.

"Fuck off!" Tanya replies, unwilling to assist.

"Come on Tan, it's for the greater good, we're a team we need them." Garry explained.

"This had better not be some trick to try to get in my knickers." Tanya replied.

"No Tan honest, we just really need your tights." Garry explains.

"Well, OK, but no looking . . . either of you." Tanya replies as she slips off her trainers and then her track suit bottoms. As she struggles to get off her tights in the back of the car Pete adjusts his mirror so he is able to watch.

"I fucking saw that you pervert." Tanya says looking at him in the mirror.

"Come on Tanya, if anyone comes they will think were dogging or something." Garry replies.

"Here, give them here." says Pete as he snatches the tights from Tanya's hand.

Tanya slips her track suit bottoms back on, along with her trainers and as she looks up she sees Pete sniffing the crutch of her tights.

"Pete you fucking pervert." she shouts.

"Na . . . I was just wiping my nose," Pete replies.

"Yes, caught red handed, no wonder everyone calls you purvey Pete." Garry replies.

"What, who calls me that?" asks Pete as he grabs hold of Garry.

"No one Pete, no one, I was just joking that's all." Garry replies.

"He meant that other Pete, you know the one from Rockwell Green." Tanya replies shrugging her shoulders at Garry.

"That's OK then, it was just a runny nose. I weren't sniffing OK? Why would I want to sniff her snatch when I got a bird of me own?" replies Pete.

"Can I have a leg now?" asked Garry.

"Yeah come on Pete we're on a job here." Tanya replies keen to get on with the raid.

Pete picks up a baseball bat from along the side of his seat, whilst Garry has a replica pistol. Tanya, after reading up about the Brinks Mat bullion robbery on line, chose to be a little different and has a gallon of water in a petrol can and some rope.

"Right are you both ready? I have my skeleton keys and we're all tooled up." Pete asks.

"Yeah we're ready." replies Garry.

"Right here's the plan, I undo the back door and we sneak in, quickly check the downstairs then head upstairs and catch him asleep in his bed. The guy's old. I think he's thirty something so we should be able to overpower him quickly. Once he's out cold, you tie him up and then we douse him in petrol to show him we mean business. Then he tells us where the gold is and we leave him there unharmed OK?" Pete explains.

"Have you remembered to put on your latex gloves? I have a hair net on underneath my balaclava. We can't afford to leave any DNA." Tanya replies.

"Yes, Pete all ready, yes Tan gloves on." Garry replies.

"Yes, Pete. All ready then." Tanya replies.

"No fucking names, remember no names." says Pete in a panic.

"What do we call each other then?" asked Tanya.

"I don't know what about One, Two, and Three?" Pete replies.

"But, who's going to be who?" asked Garry.

"Well I am not being three, I mean why should I be just because I am a girl doesn't mean I have to be last and be three." Tanya explains to the two lads.

"OK, it's not a problem I will be three, Garry you can be two and Tanya you are one, is that all clear?" Pete replies.

"So its Tanya one, Garry two, and Pete three?" asks Tanya trying to confirm they understand one another.

"Yes" reply the boys.

"Ok, cool." Tanya replies.

The three sneak up to Squids back door. Pete takes out his Skeleton keys as he reaches the back door and pushing the keys into the unlocked door. He locks it without realising it. He tries the door handle but it won't move.

"Shit it must have been open you don't suppose he's still up do you?" Pete asked the other two.

"Na, all the lights are out." Tanya replies.

Pete tries again but it takes him longer to unlock the door than it did to lock it. The noise of the three at the back door wakes Squid up. He lies there for a moment listening then slowly and quietly he climbs out the bath. Quickly Squid dries himself and pulls on his jeans and a T shirt then stands behind the bathroom door listening to what's going on. Eventually Pete manages to unlock it and the three sneak into the house, they past the down-stairs bathroom on into the kitchen and then the front room. Squid watch's through the bathroom door which is slightly ajar as Pete, Garry and Tanya walk past. He can barely work out who is who as all three are just shadows, but he could see Tanya's mid-drift, so he knew one was a girl.

"See, look at all this, we're in the right house, YES! I told you both the gold has got to be here somewhere." Pete states as he sees the board with all the info on it.

Slowly they climb the staircase together until they reach the landing. Squid sneaks up behind them without them realising.

"Tanya one to Pete three, did you bring a torch it's really dark?" Tanya asks.

"I said no fucking names you thick bitch, it's just one, two and three. Not, Pete three, Garry two and Tanya one. Christ how many fucking times?" Pete replies.

"Twat Pete, now you have said my name." replied Garry.

"I'm going home dick head. If you are going to disrespect me, no one fucking disrespects me what do you think I am your fucking bitch or sum-in." Tanya replied talking a little louder.

"Sssshhhhhhhh!!" the two boys reply.

"No look, no-one is disrespecting anyone we don't need a torch because as soon as we get in the bedroom we put the light on. It will scare the shit out of him and it will blind him for a few seconds giving Garry and me time to do our bit ok?" Pete replies.

"Now Tanya, you sneak in switch on the light and then stand to one side and Pete and I will deal wiv Squid Ryan." Garry explains.

Tanya walks past Garry and Pete. Slowly she opens the bedroom door switches on the light then stands against the wall. Pete and Garry barge into the bedroom screaming. The light blinds them and Pete stumbles, falling onto Squids bed. Quickly he jumps up and hits the duvet with his baseball bat but they all soon discover the room is empty. They all stand looking at the bed, Squid enters room unseen and in his hand is his beloved Mary.

"Fuck where the hell is he?" Pete asks.

"Maybe he ain't home? We shouldn't ave gone to Taunton and got that McDonalds we should have stayed and cased the joint for longer." Tanya replies.

"We best be getting the fuck out of here before he turns up." Garry replies.

Squid swings the bedroom door shut, as it slams they all turn round and their eyes nearly pop out of their heads as they see how big Squid is.

"Oh fuck, I think it's too late for that." Pete says hiding behind the other two.

"You three are you looking for me?" asked Squid.

Garry see's "Mary" the bat, whimpers, wets himself and then faints. Pete Screams at Squid and runs at him with his bat.

"Argghh fuck you, arse hole." Pete screams as he charges towards Squid.

Squid stops the bat in one hand, twists it and flips Pete over on his back and then punches him knocking him out cold.

"Damn fool! What is this some sort of comedy act, whose the ring leader you?" Asked Squid looking at the only member of the trio still standing.

"Stay back man, I got petrol in here, I'll blow you to hell if you take one more step." Tanya shouts.

"Go on then, blow me to hell." Squid replies tucking his bat under his arm and then folding them.

"What?" asked Tanya.

"I said go on then, excuse me for mentioning it and I am not trying to disrespect you, but if I go up, don't you and your pals go up too? And I don't see any lighter or matches. Now unless you are planning to rub the rope together and light the petrol with friction burns I don't see the need to worry. If that is the case then we could be here for some time, this is just an observation mind." explained Squid.

"What-what, like what you saying man, look Nokia Man, I am sorry just let me go and I won't tell another soul about the gold you got stashed here, promise." Tanya replied.

"Ah *Nokia Man*, so you are the ones behind the leaflets. Fucking kids today got no fucking idea at all." Squid replies.

"Nah, don't know any fing about no leaflets, we're just here for the gold." Tanya replied.

Squid walks over to the boys removing their disguises and hair nets. Then he walks over to Tanya and removes her balaclava and hair net revealing a beautiful head of wavy long red hair. All three still have rubber gloves on their hands. Pete and Garry are still out cold on the floor. Tanya is now stood by the bed on her own crapping herself.

"I thought you wanted to make another movie with me after all the last one seems to be doing quite well." Squid replied.

"I don't know nuffin about no movie I am just here for the gold." Tanya replied.

"How old are you?" asked Squid

"Eighteen, please don't hurt me, I just want to leave, please let me go I promise I won't tell" Tanya replies.

"Eighteen! You know if I thought for one minute my daughters were doing stuff like this, this is what I would do to them." Squid replied as he grabs Tanya's arm and pulls her over to the bed where he sits and then pulls Tanya across his knee.

"I am guessing your father has never given you what you deserve which obviously a damn good spanking." Squid explains.

"No, please no, you can't its illegal." she screams.

"So is breaking into someone's home." replied Squid as he slapped his huge hand down over Tanya's bottom.

"Ow, ooowww, no stop please stop, it hurts owwww ooooooo, owwww!" Tanya sobbed and she kicked and screamed, but Squids huge frame kept her in place firmly and Tanya was unable to do anything other than except her punishment.

"Tanya is it? Or should I say Number One? Maybe you will think twice about ever doing something like this ever again? I am sorry, but it's for your own good." Squid stated as he slapped her arse even harder.

"I promise never again, ouch, I am sorry, really sorry, ouch!" she sobbed.

Squid finishes with Tanya and stands her back up. Tanya immediately puts her hands down her pants and starts rubbing her bottom. Pete then comes around and Squid picks up the two boys and makes all three of them stand up against wall.

"Come on Garry stop pretending, no-one faints for that amount of time." Squid replies as he takes his phone out of his jeans pocket. Finding the camera mode he makes all three face him and he takes their photos. Squid then goes into his contacts, finds Glen's number and calls him asking him to come over. Glen arrives thirty minutes later to find Squid interrogating the trio.

"We were just after the gold. We didn't want to hurt anyone." Tanya sobbed still rubbing her arse.

"Really, so why, the rope, petrol, replica gun and baseball bat?" Squid replied.

"So you think there is gold here?" asked Glen.

"Yes." the trio reply.

"Please can I go now? I don't feel well and it was all Pete's idea." Tanya explains.

"Yes Tanya and I didn't want to do it. As for the gold, well there is supposed to be loads of it, two hundred million pounds worth of gold bars, so they say." Garry replies.

"Where and how did you ever come up with such a stupid and ridiculous amount like that? Do I look like I have a house full of Gold bars?" replied Squid holding his arm out and circling the room with it, till he's facing Glen, at which point he shakes his hand.

"Hi Glen, thanks for coming over." Squid said.

"So what's all this, having a party or something. Why don't you introduce me to your new friends?" Glen replied.

"Glen, meet Tanya, she's the one who's got a sore arse. Garry there has pissed himself and keeps fainting and Pete here is the ring leader who seems to think the house is full of gold. Kids meet Glen he's CID." Squid explained as Garry briefly faints again.

"What shall we do with them, the same as we did the last lot?" asked Glen as he winked at Squid.

"Just as well, I mean we're here in the bedroom and they are the one breaking and entering and we're the innocent party. Who will believe anything they have to say? You kids ever seen the clip with Zed and Maynard in Pulp Fiction, if so then you know what happens to Marsellus? Squid replies with a huge smile, as he watches Garry wet himself again.

"Please no, we're sorry." Pete replies.

"Glen, go to the cupboard and get out the Gimp suit? We'll save one for later." Squid replies.

"They need preparing anyway Squid. I mean when they go to prison they will all be analysed, so just as well break them in here nice and slow." Glen explains as Garry faints again and Pete unable to piss anymore starts shaking and mumbling to himself.

"Please no, no! Please not that, we're sorry, all of us, honest, I promise we will never do anything like this again." Pete starts to cry.

"Which one shall we do first? Let's see. Eeany, Meany, Miney, Moe!" counts Squid as he counts across them with his finger.

"Please, I can't take it my arse is already on fire. Please just let us go we won't tell honest." Tanya begged.

Glen hands them his note pad and pen.

"Right, here I want each of you to write down your names and addresses. What on earth made you attempt such a stupid break in and what the hell are these?" asked Glen as he holds up Pete's skeleton keys and fake pistol.

"Pete bought them off e-bay." Tanya explains, grassing up Pete once more.

"It's Pete's idea, he googled you. It said that Squid Ryan lives here and that he has the Brinks Mat missing gold or knows where it is or something like that...I think." Garry replied.

"How were you going to move all this gold?" asked Squid.

"Pete's got a Vauxhall Corsa." Tanya replied.

"A Corsa eh! Wow! Guess Pete here is one cool dude." Glen said laughing to himself.

"Do you actually know how much a single Gold bar weighs, let alone two hundred million pounds worth of them? Right, I will say this once and once only. There is no hidden gold it's just a stupid story going around the internet." Squid explained.

"If Mr Ryan here wants to press charges you three will spend the next twenty five years inside being arse fucked and raped. You Tanya, well I hope you like pussy and dildos because as soon as you enter a woman's prison the lesbians in there will have a hay day with you. Now, I know what you look like and I have your addresses. You three are pathetic. Now get the hell out of here and if I see you ever again doing the slightest thing wrong, I will bang you up for a long, long time. Do you under-stand me?" Glen lectures as he snatches back his address book from Pete. As the two boys walk past Squid he growls at them and as Tanya walks past he slaps her arse one more time. All three leave, squabbling at one another. Tanya is rubbing her arse with both hands. Squid and Glen are laughing at them as they go.

"Can you fucking believe that they Googled me?" Squid replied as he shut the front door behind the three.

"I can't believe their getaway car was a bloody Vauxhall Corsa. There was three of them in it, where the fuck were they going to put the gold on the fucking roof rack?" Glen replied laughing.

"I know crazy, but on a serious note, we need to find this damned gold and put this to rest. With the internet like it is, I am going to end up with idiots like this around here every night of the week. Googled me! I can't believe they actually Googled me!" Squid moaned.

"So you really got a Gimp suit in your cupboard?" asked Glen.

"No! Tell me Glen I have been meaning to ask for a while, has the name Yoda ever cropped up before? Do you know a Yoda? Squid asked.

"Can't say I have what makes you ask this now?" replied Glen.

"It's just come up over the years. Morris asked me once if I knew anyone called Yoda and this girl I used to know said some guy called Yoda in a blue Rolls approached her once. It's just been playing on my mind. It could be a missing link." replied Squid.

"I wouldn't worry about it. I've never heard the name and Morris never mentioned it whilst I worked with him. If it was important I am sure we'd have had it come up a few more times by now." explained Glen.

"You know, I still got that old video at home of Nokia Man screwing those bird's in that mobile phone shop. Maybe we could black mail him instead?" Pete said as they walked to Pete's Corsa.

"Just fuck off Pete. You heard what he said about that Gimp suit. If it is the same guy, fuck knows what he will do to me next time." Tanya sobbed, as Garry puts his arm around her.

"Yes fuck you! Pete this was all your fault and Tanya got spanked as well." Garry replied.

"Ok, OK. It was only a thought and Garry you're only being nice to Tanya because you want to rub her arse better." Pete replied.

"No, no, Tanya knows I care about her don't you Tan?" Garry replied.

"Yes." Said Tanya nodding her head as her and Garry walked together.

"I can rub your bum better if you want me too?" Garry whisper's in her ear as they reach the car.

"Fuck off the pair of you. I am walking home." Tanya announces as she pushes Garry away and walks off up the road.

Chapter Eleven

Saturday came around quickly, Squid was first to arrive and proceeded to check over the plane for flight.

"Morning my darling, so how's the most beautiful woman in the world?" Squid asked as Jenny approached.

"Maybe you should ask your daughter that question. She's looking far better than me these days." Jenny replied feeling a little down. Squid embraced her, he had missed her so much.

"Not possible my sweetheart. What's wrong? It's not like you to say something like that?" Squid replied.

"Just all this living apart business, it's getting me down a bit I suppose, anyway, Sophie has only gone and got herself a good job at the council. She starts next week. Reckons in three years she will have enough money for a deposit on a house. You should be real proud of her she's doing so well, and she's started flying lessons." Jenny replied.

"I am proud of her and you look great babes, you really do. Got a treat for Sophie this week, I'm going to take her to buy a new car, nothing big just a little Fiesta or something. Don't say anything though, as I want to surprise her." Squid replied just as Sophie came running over.

"Daddy, guess what I got a job." she shouted.

"Don't tell me, it's with the council and the money's really good and you will probably have a deposit for a house within three years." Squid replied with a huge smile on his face.

"Mum you can be a real cow at times. I told you I wanted to tell him." Sophie replied.

"It's ok, sweetheart I am only pulling your leg. Come here and give me a hug. You should know your mother can't keep a secret. Now if my old man had told her where the gold was hidden this whole ordeal would have been over years ago." Squid replied jesting with Jenny.

"Morning all, you recovered from the other night then Squid?" asked Glen as he walked towards them.

"Good morning Glen. Yes, bit of a laugh wasn't it?" replied Squid.

"What's that all about then?" asked Jenny.

"I had a couple of teenage visitors the other night, they thought the house was full of gold. It's a long story, will tell you later." Squid replied.

"Morning Glen, you'll be saying 'allo, 'allo, 'allo, next." giggled Sophie as she said hello to him.

"How are you, it's been a while? Squid tells me you two have had a breakthrough in the case." asked Jenny.

"Well we hope so, too early to celebrate yet though and it's only taken two years to get this far." Glen replied.

"How are you? Thanks for coming." Squid replied shaking his hand.

"Fine, thank you for asking, so what's all this about?" asked Glen.

"I will explain everything over breakfast at Popham. Come on everyone in you get." Squid replied getting them all into the aircraft.

It isn't long before the Cessna leaves Dunkeswell and heads east. Squid points out Stonehenge to them as they fly past. It isn't long before Squid's putting the plane down on the grass strip at Popham. They all sit around a table drinking coffee and filling their stomachs with a Full English breakfast.

"I know you're all wondering what this is about, so here it is. Glen and I have worked out that my father buried the van and its contents somewhere along the A303. Well it's been years now and I am hoping with subsidence something might show up from the air. Four sets of eyes are better than one and we have a few pairs of binoculars for close up inspection." Squid explained.

"Are you serious?" replied Sophie.

"This road here is the start of the A303, so we are going to fly its full length and see if we can see anything that might be of interest. If we see anything worth looking at, I will mark it on my flight map and then drive up and take a look another day." Squid explained pointing to the road that ran alongside the airfield.

"What are we looking for?" asked Sophie.

"Anything that could hide a van long term. Small sunken patches in the ground, old barns close to the road and old garages. Anything that could hide a Transit van, we don't know for sure it's buried. We're just guessing it might be." Squid explained.

"It's going to be like looking for a needle in a hay stack." Glen replied.

"It could save weeks or even months of searching on the ground, so do you all understand what to look for?" Squid asked.

"Yes, all clear here." replied Jenny, whilst the others nodded as they looked at the map.

"Well let's hope something jumps out at us." Glen replied.

Forty five minutes after landing Squid has the Cessna lined up on the runway ready for take-off. As they leave Popham they all look down onto the A303, each in turn point out something they think is of importance.

"Well there's Thruxton Circuit. Glen, we need to get a map on a pin board for when we get back and work out all the areas where work has been carried out since the robbery." Squid explained.

"Good idea. Like you, I know this stretch of road and it's been getting improvements on it all the time." Glen explained.

"We can then remove that area from the search, as something would have been dug up when the work was being done. We also need to check what sections were being built at the time of the robbery and see if any of the construction workers knew my father." Squid replied.

"Good thinking. I will get on it as soon as we land." Glen replied.

"Well the same goes for some of these old petrol stations and workshops. Many became derelict after the new road went in even some of the old cafes closed down. They could all hide a van." Jenny explained.

"Dad don't you think this is getting a bit pointless? You're wasting your life on trying to solve a mystery that probably died with your father. Just look what it's done to our lives. Are you sure you want to spend your time looking for something you may never find?" said Sophie, now getting bored with the flight.

"Sophie your parents have had to do what they've done in order to keep you safe. Dad's only doing this to protect your future otherwise once he dies it will be you these thugs and no hopers will be coming after you, thinking you know where the hiddengold is. This way we'll end it once and for all." replied Glen.

"I suppose, I just hope you find it then." Sophie replied.

"Never doubt your father sweetheart. He always comes through and delivers." replied Jenny giving Sophie a hug.

By late morning the Cessna lands back at Dunkeswell.

"Oh Sophie, Friday get mum to bring you into Taunton. I thought I'd take you shopping for a Christmas present." Squid announced as they all got in their cars to leave.

"Really, thanks Daddy, love you." Sophie replied.

"Love you too, see you both Friday and I'm really proud of you getting that job." replied Squid.

They all go to their homes with tasks on their minds. Squid pours a drink puts on some classical music and sits in his favourite chair with a photo of his family.

I now felt like something was going to happen. The riddle was being solved and life felt like it was going really well for a change. I had to get my relationship with Jenny back on track though.

Hours went by and Squid and Glen did as much research as they could, but it was in the days that followed after their meeting that would give them an unexpected, but exciting break though. Squid drives into Taunton as planned to meet up with Jenny and Sophie.

"Don't you think it's about time you got rid of this old thing dad? I mean it's a bit Inspector Morse isn't it?" said Sophie as Squid climbed out of the Jag.

"Don't go upsetting him Sophie or at least not until he's spent some money on us both." replied Jenny.

"He knows I am only playing with him mum. I wouldn't let him sell that Jag for anything. Anyway I want it when he snuffs it." Sophie replied jesting.

"Thanks for that Sophie." laughed Squid.

"You know what I mean. It's the car you had when I first met you. It's got real sentimental value to me. It's my dad's car and always will be." Sophie replied taking her dad's arm and giving him a hug.

"OK, you dug yourself out of that quite well!" Squid replied.

"So where are you taking us old man?" Sophie asked.

"Depends how much you love your old dad, doesn't it?" replied Squid.

"I love you loads and you know it, so what are we doing? Come on tell me, I want to know." asked Sophie.

"Well dad and I thought we would buy you a new car." Jenny announced as she took Squids other arm.

"Yeah right, as if that's going to happen. Come on stop mucking about, where we going Dad?" Sophie begged feeling excited and wanting to know what was planned for the day.

"Your mother is not joking sweetheart. We've come into a bit of inheritance and we want to treat you, let you know how much we appreciate you looking after your brothers and sister." Squid explained.

"Really?" asked Sophie looking shocked.

"You have seen and been through too much, so we wanted to let you know we love you." Jenny explained.

"Straight up, you're not taking the piss. You're joking with me, aren't you?" Sophie said getting excited.

The girls and Squid walk into the Ford garage. Sitting outside on the forecourt is a brand new silver Ford Fiesta with balloons, a big red ribbon and a bow wrapped around it. Across the windscreen is a banner saying 'Sophie'.

"Well aren't you going to say something? I mean, thank you would be nice." Jenny said as she opened the door to the car.

"Here's the keys, go on sit in it. It's all insured, taxed and ready to go. Its diesel so should be cheap to run." said Squid handing Sophie the keys to the ignition.

Sophie is gob smacked and starts to cry. Squid and Jenny both give her a hug.

"I don't know what to say, Mum & Dad, I am gob smacked. I feel like I did that day when you told me dad was my dad." Sophie sobbed feeling really overwhelmed.

"Good, you deserve it sweetheart." Jenny replied.

"Thank you so much, I love you both more than I can ever say. Can I drive it home? Is it ready to go?" Sophie asked.

"Yes, I just said it was. Wait here while I just get the rest of the paper work and the spare keys. Then you can go sweetheart." Squid explained as he wandered off inside to see the salesman. Jenny and Sophie continued to look around the car, opening the boot, lifting the bonnet, Sophie really liked it.

"Have fun but don't do anything me and your father wouldn't do." Jenny replied.

"I am going to take your mother out and spoil her a little. Then pick up some presents for your brothers and sister. Drive carefully, I'll catch you later." replied Squid as he returned with the paperwork and spare keys.

The three have a big hug and then Sophie jumps in her new car and drives off leaving Squid and Jenny walking off towards the town. As they stroll through the Old Pig Market in the town centre, Squid enjoys being able to spend time with his wife and holding Jenny's hand. After some lunch Squid takes Jenny into a jewellers shop.

"Here we are Mr Carr, as requested a perfect match. And here's the bracelet you brought in for us to match." replied the shop assistant.

"My bracelet, how did you get that?" asked Jenny.

"Daughter number one." he replied.

"It's all cleaned and looking like new. They certainly complement one another." He declared.

"Oh Squid it's beautiful, you shouldn't have. What a lovely surprise. I didn't even notice the bracelet was missing." Jenny replied.

"That was lucky then." he said smiling at her and feeling happy that he had been able to cheer her up.

"Very crafty aren't you Squid Ryan, but thank you, it is lovely." Jenny expressed.

"I got Sophie to get it for me. Told her I wanted to surprise you." Squid replied.

"Squid, that's an unusual name. Not heard a name like that for many years, you are not related to a James Ryan are you?" asked the shopkeeper.

"Yes, he was my father." Squid replied a little surprised that someone so far away from Croydon should know his father. Alarm bells started to ring, what if someone had tracked him down from the bracelet. The shop had hold of the bracelet for around two weeks and they probably had Squid on camera from when he came in last. His protective side came into force and Jenny felt his grip tighten around her waist as he pulled her in close to himself. Constantly looking around the shop Squid looked for signs of an ambush, but there was nothing.

"Really what a small world, years ago I worked with chap called Mickey, *"Mad Mickey"* I think they called him. Did some decorating for him, he introduced me to a mate of your fathers called Charlie, worked on the roads, a construction worker and I joined his team. I spent six months working with Charlie. We were working on the A303 at Andover the time of the robbery . . . You know the Brinks Mat thing, boy did the shit hit the fan for them back then." the man explained.

"Guess you have been on the internet too being a jeweller. It seems everyone is still obsessed this this story of lost treasure." replied Squid as he tried to dig at the man for some info, he needed to work out whether this was a fluke meeting or if he had been tracked down and whether he and Jenny were in danger.

"No not at all. I was a young man then working hard to feed my family, but had no idea all that Gold stuff was going on under my nose. As they say, it was 'Fools Gold' I don't think anyone connected with it has done very well. So, me personally, I am glad I never got caught up in it." replied the shopkeeper.

"Mickey, Charlie or my father, did they never hint that they were involved?" Squid asked.

"No, none at all, of course he died not long after. That was quite a shock back then, scared the hell out of me all these gangsters around. So I got out and did my apprenticeship in the jewellery business." explained the shopkeeper.

"Tell me about it. Everyone I know is either dead or banged up due to that damned Brinks Mat curse. Some committed suicide, others blasted away, a few months after you got out you know my father and mother died. Well I probably don't need to tell you, I expect you've read the papers over the years." Squid replied.

"No I didn't. You know if you bought that chain back in the 80's it is probably made of the Brinks Mat gold." the man replied.

"Really!" Jenny said, looking surprised.

"They say 75% of all the gold in the shops at that time came from the robbery." explained the shop keeper.

"Wow, probably explains all the bad luck we have had over the years if that's the case." Jenny replied

"One of those stories passed down through the trade when you are an apprentice." he replied smiling at them both.

"Wouldn't surprise me, you didn't know my father very well then?" asked Squid.

"No, he would come and go, just an acquaintance really. I did see him one morning in fact, it was the day of the robbery. Drove an old Transit, decorator's van, at least that's what Mickey told me at the time." the shopkeeper explained.

"Amongst other things." Squid replied with a smile.

"Can't believe he was involved to tell the truth. He was as cool as an ice cube that day. You would never have guessed they had just pulled off the biggest heist in history." replied the man.

"Crazy times, for me anyway." Squid replied.

"Me too!" replied Jenny.

"Mickey would talk about you, *'Squid Ryan.'* He said you'd work for whoever you could in your holidays. You'd do anything to earn some cash, said you were going to make something of yourself. Even Charlie would talk about you, just one of those names you remember." explained the shopkeeper.

"Really, where was this? At Andover you say, are you sure . . . you know when you saw my dad on the day of the robbery?" asked Squid.

"No further on by then." replied the man.

"I thought he was at Denham on the day of the robbery. Well that's what his alibi was anyway, said he was painting a flat for Mickey. Bet that's what they were discussing, getting their stories right." Squid replied

"No, no this was past Andover heading towards Middle Wallop. I remember because there's an Army airfield at Middle Wallop. I used to nip down and look at the planes." explained the shop keeper.

"Really that far up!" Squid replied.

"Yes for sure, *'Squid Ryan'* you'd never forget a name like that." replied the man as he repeated Squid's name under his breath.

"Amazing, what a small world it is. I'm into planes myself. I got my PPL when I was 19. After what happened to everyone back then I wanted something totally different. Well nice meeting you and thanks for the lovely job on the necklace." Squid replied, this had all been very interesting but he didn't want to hang around too long, just in case.

"Ironic really, if things had been a little different it might have been me buying my gold from you. Not vice versa." the shopkeeper replied as Squid and Jenny turned to leave.

Squid and Jenny leave the shop and head back to their cars in the car-park. As they walked they discussed things. Jenny followed Squid to the castle hotel. Squid had booked them in for a couple of nights to spend some time together. It didn't take them two long to get undressed and get into bed.

After a couple of hours of love making Squid and Jenny lay in bed together cuddling.

"I guess we should go get something to eat, I've booked a table for seven thirty." Squid explained.

"I wish it could be like this all the time. It's like the night we were in your house and Sophie was conceived, although we didn't know it at the time, but it was a nice moment like this." replied Jenny.

"Well let's hope we haven't just made another little one, don't think we could cope with anymore." replied Squid.

In the restaurant the two talked about Squid's encounter with the three teenagers Pete, Garry and Tanya.

"So...The other two are out cold on the floor, so I grabs Tanya and before the kid knows what time of day it is I've pulled her over my knee and spanked her arse so hard. I bet she couldn't sit down the rest of the week." Squid explained.

"Oh the poor girl bet she hadn't planned that into her evening." Jenny replied.

"Sweetheart you should have seen it. It was like some Laurel and Hardy sketch." Squid explained.

"I am a little jealous." Jenny replied winking at Squid.

"What of?" asked Squid.

"You spanking a younger woman." Jenny replied as she slipped off her shoe then lifting her foot she massages her toes into Squid's groin.

"I see going to be like that is it." Squid replied as he did the same to her.

The evening seemed to end up a teasing contest, to which Jenny was going to lose or win whichever way you want to look at it. But, no sooner did the two get back to their hotel room Jenny found herself promptly bent over her husband's knee, being dealt exactly the same as Tanya had. He fulfilled her with the deepest pleasure as each seductive slap of Squid's hand sent a vibration of lust and wanting tingling through her body. The two had a lot of catching up to do, they had been deprived of intimacy together for far too long and both knew that come the following morning they would be parted for a while again.

By eleven o'clock the next day Squid is back at home and he and Glen are looking at the map of the A303. They are pointing to places and have stuck pins into the areas covered and now a new pin the one that Squid thinks marks where the gold is.

"So, according to the chap in the shop, he saw my father driving a white van here," explained Squid as he marked the map.

"So I think the van has to be buried between here and here." Squid announces as he pushes in the pin.

"It's too much of a coincidence for my father to be in this place on the same day of the robbery and in a white van." Squid explained further.

"Yes I agree." replied Glen.

"It has to be here. I can feel it in my bones we're close now." Squid says as he stares at the map.

"Let's just take a look ourselves first before I involve the rest of the force. It's a busy section of road that stretch of the A303. I hope it's not under the tarmac because if it is, then it will be a major job to recover it." Glen replied.

"Busy and dangerous, the luck this gold has brought everyone over the years, it would be just my luck to get hit by a truck. But, seriously, let's think about this. If you had done that robbery and got a mate to bury it knowing you'd be coming back to get it at a later date wouldn't you have buried it on the side of the road not under the tarmac." Squid replied.

The next few days flew by, each one bringing them closer to the gold. Squid was finally on the brink of freedom. Glen talked to the highways people, but then as if by fate things seemed to fall into place at 6:33 pm on the sixth day a call comes in.

"Hello," Squid said answering his phone.

"Hi Squid, its Glen, look I've just got word that the section of road we want to look at is coned off for overnight road works. They're going to re-open that section at 6.30am in the morning so if you are up to it, tonight's the ideal opportunity to see what's there?" Glen explained.

"Really, great news, I'll head on up." Squid replied.

"How long will it take you to get up there?" asked Glen.

"About two hours. I'll put a couple of shovels in the boot just in case, you never know." replied Squid.

"I think I can get there in about two hours as well. Right, I'll grab a couple of metal detectors from the yard and meet you under the bridge at the Middle Wallop Junction. It should be all coned off so pull off into the coned area on the hard shoulder and wait for me or if I'm there first pull up in front of me." Glen explained.

"OK, see you there." Squid replied.

"Let's hope we find something. If we have no luck, then it means we go to the boys at the top and that means digging up the tarmac." Glen replied.

"Will they do that?" asked Squid.

For sure, they will bring in some fancy searching equipment I would have thought, then once found dig a big hole and recover it. Then fill it in and resurface, can you imagine the cost of that?" Glen explained.

"Yes, but imagine what the haul is worth now." Squid replied.

"OK bye for now, see you up there later." Glen replied.

Squid goes out to the garage and stuffs some tools into the boot of the MK2 Jag, a crow bar, a sledge hammer and two shovels. He then jumps in the Jag and heads off down the M5 towards Taunton, then taking the rat run went through Langport and out onto the A303.

Glen arrives first at 9:30 pm and Squid at 9:45pm. Squid parks his car behind the Police car in the coned off area. Taking a metal detector each they set them for 'Gold' and then start checking the road. The night is dark and there is a mist, by the early hours of the morning the wet is clinging to their florescent waterproof jackets. Stood by his Police Range Rover Glen looks at the tarmac in front of him and sighs.

"Apparently I've heard construction workers are known for sticking all sorts in the ground. Even their old motors, I bet there are a few cars and vans underneath here." Glen announced looking at Squid.

"Exactly then you've copper wire running underneath as well as whatever reinforcement they used at the time. Bloody good these things can be set for Gold only." Squid replied.

Squid walks over to the Jag and pulls out a flask with two cups.

"Here, stop, have a break. We need to think about this a bit better because where getting nowhere fast." Squid explained, pouring them both a drink.

"There's a lot of Tarmac to cover." Glen replies taking the cup. Squid checks his watch, four hours had passed and nothing, not even a single bleep.

"I've been thinking we know at some point they were going to come back and collected the gold. It's not going to be under the tarmac. No-one in their right mind would stick a van under the road. Even they would not have been able to dig a hole in the middle of the dual carriage way. Also they were heading from Heathrow so it's got to be here on my side." Squid replied.

"We're running out of time so let's both concentrate our efforts on the edge of the west bound carriage way." Glen replied.

"I think we should do a sweep from the edge of the Tarmac, over the stones and across the verge. It makes more sense." Squid suggested.

"Sounds like a sensible move to me. Tell me Squid, why do they call you Squid, I mean it can't be your real name so where did it come from? Glen asked as the two leant against the patrol car chatting.

"No my real name's Stuart, Stuart Ryan." Squid announced.

"Stuart, you don't look like a Stuart." Glen replied.

"Something to do with having a furry bright orange Squid as a child, I'd take it everywhere with me, so I was told. Somewhere along the line people started to call me Squid Ryan the name stuck." Squid explained.

Squid puts the flask back in the Jag and the two men continue with their search. Glen looks at his watch another hour has past, still not a bleep. Glen continues to work one side of the bridge whilst Squid works the other. At 3.30am Squid gets one small quick bleep, it's dark where he stood so he taps the torch a couple of times but won't come on. Squid looks at watch 3.33am.

"Glen, come here, I just got one single bleep and now my damned torch has died and I can't see if the metal detector is working or not." Squid shouts over to Glen.

"OK, I've got another torch in the patrol car, I'll go get it." Glen replied.

"Fucking torch, for fuck sake old man you could've given me a bit more fucking help than this." Squid mumbles to himself as he fumbles forward in the dark. Suddenly he feels the ground beneath his feet fall away, slipping backwards Squid lets out a cry as he falls. He lands hitting his head on something hard.

"Squid, what is it, are you all right........... Squid?" called Glen.

Glen shines the torch up to where Squid was stood but he's not there. Slowly he walks towards where Squid was last seen but still there's no sign of him.

"Squid! Where the fuck are you?" Glen called.

"Down here." moaned Squid as he came too after being knocked out for a few seconds. "I have fallen in a bloody hole, can't see a damned thing. Watch where you are walking don't want you in here too." Squid replied.

"Where, keep shouting I can't see you." Glen replied as he walked towards Squid's voice.

"Here, watch your footing you sound close, follow my voice..." Squid replied.

Glen walks closer to Squid he can hear stones falling into a hole. Glen shines the torch in the hole. Squid sees a plastic road marker lying across his legs, it reads 63.3. Squid picks it up, looks at it.

"I don't fucking believe this, out of all the fucking holes I should fall in, it has to be one by the marker 63.3." Squid moans.

"That ain't no hole. I think you have fallen through the roof of the van. It must have corroded through." Glen explained.

"Throw me the torch." Squid replied.

"Here, catch." said Glen throwing the torch in the hole.

There was a stench of dampness, and death down in the whole, Squid grabbed the torch mumbling to himself.

"Mark, it wasn't Mark it was Marker! Marker 63.3." Squid replies.

Squid tries to stand as he turns and shines the torch the other way the beam hits the face of a skeleton looking straight at him. Squid nearly has a heart attack!

"Aaaaarrrrrrr, fuck, fuck fuck!" Squid screams.

"What the fuck is it Squid?" cries Glen.

"A skeleton, there's a fucking skeleton here." Squid screams.

"There can't be, there are no other victims." Glen replies as shines in his torch whilst he manoeuvres around the edge of the hole.

"Well I think the Mummies cousin here would disagree." Squid replies calming himself down.

"That's better, now I can see. Oh my fucking god, I wonder who he is?" Glen replies.

"Some poor bastard." Squid replied.

"Well on the bright side, we've done it, we've done it, we've only fucking done it. You're sitting on the lost Brinks Mat gold." Glen replies smiling.

Yes, yes, yes, yes, finally!" Squid replies through gritted teeth as Glens torch catch's some gold bars and they sparkle.

Squid looks around shining his torch he finds two holdalls filled with cash, three suitcases of diamonds, loads of gold ingots all are damp or wet where the roof must have been leaking for quite some time. Then Squid sees something that explains everything especially the curse. Scratched in the side of the van is some writing, it was very rusty and hard to read.

"Glen there's some writing on the side of the van." Squid replies.

'My name is Paddy O'Brian. I am twenty three and Charlie locked me in here after I stumbled across him burying the van. The airs running out fast, to whoever finds me, please take me back to Ireland, and tell my family I love them. May everyone involved with this gold be cursed till the day I'm found.'

"Well I guess that does explain everything. There really was a curse on the gold." replies Glen.

"Poor bastard, looks like Charlie buried him alive no wonder he was pissed off. Don't worry Paddy, I will do the right thing, you'll soon be on your way home." Squid replied.

Squid throws the two bags of cash up to Glen.

"Look, I need you to take my cut back in your car. I'll meet you later, I have to call this in technically this is a murder scene." Glen explained.

"OK but you sure you want it? Give me chance to get away from here first. I don't want to be getting stopped with all this cash in the back." Squid replied.

"Take the two holdalls of cash as that's not supposed to be here. There is only supposed to be two cases of diamonds so take the third with you as well and I want to take just a couple of gold bars as well." Glen announced.

"You sure, I don't want us getting greedy at this stage and I am not touching the gold, it's cursed, I don't even want it in my car. Let's just stick to the plan." Squid replied.

"Please yourself, but you read his last words "Cursed till the day I am found" so take it, leave now and call me once you are home. I will guard this till I get a call from you. That way I know you are back safe before I call it in." Glen replied.

"No problem." Squid replied.

"The force and the insurance company have already agreed a deal for you should we find this. So tomorrow you need to go into the police station when I am on duty, so that I can register for the reward, once you get the reward, we split it as agree OK?" Glen confirmed.

"Except the plan has changed a little." replied a voice that wasn't Glen's.

"Ok no problem, a deal's, a deal but no gold, don't touch the gold. We have more than we were expecting anyway, who's that, who's up there with you Glen?" Squid asked suddenly feeling a little concerned.

"There's a lot of gold here, I am sure they won't miss a bar or two." replied the voice.

Squid looked up to see Ox standing at the top of the hole.

"Ox seriously. Where the hell do you fit into all this?" asked Squid surprised.

"We have mutual a friend, have you heard the name Yoda, I'm sure you have, it must have been mentioned any amount of time over the years, well he's our boss." Ox explains.

"He may be yours, but he ain't mine, so what, now you take the gold and kill me? Where does Glen fit into all this?" Squid asked now feeling completely pissed off. There is a few seconds silence and Squid realises this is it, there is nowhere to hide, he sighs excepting his fate.

"So this is it, this is how it ends. Promise me you will make sure Jenny is OK, please don't let anything happen to my family, this has nothing to do with them." Squid explained feeling defeated.

"You have it all wrong, Yoda is your guardian angel. You would have been dead years ago if it wasn't for the boss. Here climb up this ladder, its time you understood." replied Glen as he appeared next to Ox with a small telescopic ladder.

Squid was confused nothing was making sense any more, he was however grateful to still be alive, he had gone through too much to fall at the last hurdle.

As Squid climbed out Ox took his hand, he noticed a tattoo on the back of Ox's hand it read 'Death before dishonour'. Squid could hear the sound of a helicopter flying in.

"Don't worry, all will be explained." replied Ox patting Squid on the back.

The noise of the helicopter became louder. A light shone over them and around as it flew overhead checking the area. It turned once, came in low and settled fifty yards from them. As the helicopter shut down to an idle, a figure got out and walked towards them. As the person got closer Squids mouth fell open, this he didn't expect. There in front of him was an extremely well dressed man, clean shaven, no glasses, hair looking like he had just left the barbers.

"Hello Squid my boy. I guess this is all a little hard to take in at the moment. Don't worry, you're safe, you always have been. Come sit with me in your Jag let me explain." said Duke Smith

"Duke, Duke Smith . . . or should I call you Yoda?" asked Squid.

"Either, although for you and I, Duke is who I am so let's stick to that." Duke replied.

"So I am guessing the reward money is down the pan?" asked Squid. As Ox opened up the boot of Squid's Jag and removed the holdalls of cash.

"It was never on the table Squid. You are the son of one of the original bank robbers. For that you can't have any claim on the reward. That is why Ox is here, his car broke down and he was walking along the edge of the road when he falls through the roof. At the same time as an off duty police officer happened to be driving passed and bam the rest will soon be history." Duke explains.

Squid looks out of his car window to see two vans pull up and the haul get transferred into them.

"So that's why you always wore the gloves, to hide the tattoo. I still don't get it, where the hell do Jenny and I fit into all this?" asked Squid looking at the back of Dukes hand which had the same tattoo as Ox's '*Death before Dishonour*'.

"Ah yes the tattoo, would have been a bit of a giveaway. As for Jenny, well you see that girl fell in love with you and wouldn't let things drop. Despite what her father said she went looking for you, she put herself in real danger. She started to ruffle the wrong feathers on some pretty nasty people. Let's go back to 1984 someone was poking about and I didn't know who so I put a hit on them, thinking I was protecting you . . . " Duke said in a fatherly way.

Flashback 1984

YODA showers with a young blonde woman, as she suds up his back with a sponge she runs a finger over a scar on his back.

"You are so brave, what you did for Ox." says the girl rinsing off his back with the shower head.

"It was the honourable thing to do, he saved my life on more than one occasion." Yoda explained.

"But it wasn't even for Ox." the girl replied.

"You still have much to learn my dear." replied Yoda as he gets out of the shower. He goes down stairs where a maid has prepared two boiled eggs for him for his breakfast. He sits at the table in his silk dressing gown and looks at his cutlery. Yoda takes a quick glimpse at the paper before turning to the maid.

"Now do I chop off his head Bridget or smash it in?" asked Yoda smiling.

Bridget approaches the table with toast sliced up into soldiers.

"What do you think his fate should be Bridget my lovely young sweetheart, a swift slice and off with the head or a beating and smashing in of the skull Bridget?" Yoda said while tapping the egg with his spoon.

"Personally a beating and smashing of the skull and you do that so well." Bridget replied.

"You know me far too well my little Honey-bun, why don't you go up stair's and make yourself comfortable. I'll be up after I have dealt with my none chicken friends." Yoda explains.

Yoda picks up a spoon on the back of his hand is a tattoo which reads 'DEATH BEFORE DISHONOUR' in a scroll. He spanks Bridget on the bottom as she turns and leaves.

"Go, I will be up shortly." he mumbles at her as he dips a piece of toast into the egg.

The maid smiles as she turns and walks away. As she exits the room she is passed by Ox heading towards the table.

"You look troubled I do hope it is not bad news?" asks Yoda.

"Sorry YODA, I have a problem." Ox explains with a look of shame on his face.

"A problem, I don't like problems, where is he?" asked Yoda.

"In the boot of the Jaguar, but that's not the problem, he's a she." Ox explains

Yoda hit's his egg hard over the head smashing the egg completely. He stands up and walks to a draw there he takes out a gun.

"It's a Sunday today isn't it?" Yoda asks.

"Yes Yoda." Ox replies.

"Best not worry the neighbours, then." replies Yoda.

Yoda reaches in the draw and screws a silencer to the end of the pistol. The two then walk out to the Jaguar which is parked out the front of the big house next to Yoda's blue Rolls Royce.

"Nice morning, has she told you what she knows?" asks Yoda.

"She says nothing, she just hits a lot." Ox replied.

Ox opens the boot, Death before dishonour tattoo is also seen on back of his hand. Jenny's struggling to get free she is screaming at them through the gag around her mouth and she's blindfolded as well as having a bag over her head.

"Fiery one, put up a struggle did she?" asks Yoda

Noticing Ox has a red mark on the side of his face.

"She's got spunk boss she fought me like a Jack Russell, bites too." Ox explains showing the teeth marks on his arm. Yoda brings up the pistol to aim at Jenny, but Ox stands in the way.

"Sorry boss, I can't let you it's not just her. You see she is pregnant there's an innocent life inside her." Ox explains.

"My we do have a problem don't we? I thought you and I had an understanding, your daughter has a wonderful career now. It could have been different, organ failure would have been a very unpleasant way to go." Yoda replies.

Jenny's blind fold comes off a little and she can hear the man talking to Ox in a very posh voice but she can't see Yoda just a dark outline of the gun. Her eyes fill with tears and her pupils widen as Yoda points it at her head.

"Please boss I beg you, please. If you have to take a life this day then let it be mine, I beg you boss kill me not her." Ox replies falling to his knees in front of Yoda offering himself as sacrifice. Yoda lowers his gun a little to Ox's head.

"This one means that much to you that you would give your life for her. We've been through so much together you're like a brother to me." Yoda replies.

"YES!" Ox replies.

"So this is how it ends." Yoda says as he looks at the two of them.

"I owe you everything boss, I know that, everything. But, this is wrong she's just an innocent child herself, only fifteen." Ox explains.

Yoda lifts the gun and points it at Ox's chest, a few seconds pass then he swiftly turns and fires off several rounds into a Guiney fowl that is stood nearby and an explosion of feathers goes everywhere.

"I knew I was going to have problems with you ever since you started this 'Born again Christian' stuff and you're sure she's with child, what is her name?" Yoda asks.

"We've never exchanged names." Ox replied.

Yoda walks up to her leans in the boot and removes her gag.

"If you want to live girl tell me your name." Yoda tells her.

"Jenny . . . Jenny Davison." Jenny replied.

"Damn you man, we're of the same blood you and I as if I would ever want to hurt you. You deal with her, Jenny works for us now. She's your responsibility as well. She's the boys ex-girlfriend you idiot, no wonder she was asking questions." Yoda replies in an angry voice.

Yoda puts the pistol away and holds out his hand which Ox takes, he pulls him up and the two hug. Yoda turns and walks back inside, Ox then unties Jenny.

"You heard what he said, if you want to live you work for us now, understood?" Ox explains.

"Yes, I understand and thank you for what you did back there, I won't forget it." Jenny replied.

Ox opens the passenger door for her, he unties her hands and Jenny climbs in the car.

"So you see Squid that's how Jenny ended up working for me and like you she doesn't even know, she only knows Duke Smith." Duke explains.

"What do you mean like me, explain?" replied Squid.

"Squid I have had your back ever since this began back in 1983. I knew you were a good person. You paid me back the money your father owed me and I have and always will think of you as a son. But, that meant looking after you and when you and Jenny got back together, well that meant looking after you both." explained Duke as he pulled out a white cotton hanky and wiped his brow.

"Explain looking after?" Squid replied still confused as to what was happening.

"For instance Glen tracking down your foster parents or further back the Asil Nadir flight." explained Duke.

"You know about the Asil Nadir flight from Compton Abbas?" Squid replied a little shocked.

"Who do you think Reginald worked for back then? All those jobs were put your way, when it came to finding that rat bag Dominic, who helped, me. You see I have always been there for you lad. And I know what you did, and how you disposed of Morris." Duke explained.

"I feel like your puppet. It's like nothing has been real. What about the house fire and Morris? Was he also working for you in the beginning? Where does all the shit fit together? Do you know what happened to my mother or my father?" Squid asked.

"The shit is just life's shit, we all get shit Squid. You were in control your life has been your life, I have simply been here in the back ground helping out. The fire was just a fire and Morris simply a dirty police man. I wish I could have prevented the shop fire, and your mother and fathers deaths, but even my eyes and ears are limited. Bloody Morris was just a thorn in my side for many years. When you took the car to the breakers yard, who do you think made sure it disappeared fast? And who do you think asked me?" Duke replied.

Squid took a deep breath, ran his fingers through his hair, the two sat there for a few seconds in silence.

"So Jenny, does she know all this, is what I have real or have you been manipulating our marriage as well?" asked Squid.

"Dear sweet Jenny, she worked for me for many years not as Duke but as Yoda, she still, to this day, only knows me as Duke, but under the mask of Yoda she helped me out several times. In exchange I helped her out. She was doing a job for me the day you met. You turning up and doing the hero thing changed everything. Her job was to get into debt with a loan shark he was trying to muscle in on an area I have controlled for many years. Sorry about the house boat, I didn't see that coming. Anyway once Jenny had found you she made a call, she wanted out and I obliged. Squid don't question that girl's love for you, from the day you met it's all been real." Duke explained.

"I am so pissed off with you right now Duke but thanks for that at least. If what I have with Jenny wasn't real then, my whole life would be a joke." Squid replied.

"It's real Squid, I stepped back completely, but where you were concerned I knew I would always need to have your back. There are still people, Squid, looking for this and that's how I knew that unless we make this all disappear you will never be free from the curse." Duke explained.

"So where do we go from here?" asked Squid.

"Well there are going to be some big changes for you. I am not a bad man Squid. Yoda does a lot of good so when this is over I want you to visit me. I want you to see and understand. I think it is better if you don't mention this chat to Jenny, no sense in making her feel guilty. What I want you to do is go home forget all about tonight and just watch and listen. Someone will be in touch in a couple of months." Duke explained.

"Duke, promise me something? This chap Paddy O'Brian, can you make sure he gets home to his family and make sure he gets a decent burial? We all owe him that much. I don't want this curse biting us on the arse again. It needs to end here tonight." Squid replied.

"Not a problem, I will make sure Glen informs me of what is happening with the remains and once released I will make sure the family incur no expense." replied Duke.

"Thank you." Squid replied.

Climbing out of the car Duke smiled at Squid.

"Please don't be too mad at me." he said as he walked back to the helicopter. Moments later he was gone. Squid got out of the back of the car and watched the two vans drive off with the gold. Glen walks up to him.

"I am sorry Squid but you have to understand I had a good reason to keep the truth from you." Glen explained.

"What that my old friend and father figure is really called Yoda a gangland overlord manipulating all our lives." replied Squid still very angry.

"No Squid you have it all wrong, it's not like that. Give the guy a break, give it time, let him explain." Glen replied.

"Glen you're a copper, a fucking bent copper! You're no better than Morris!" replied Squid.

"I'm sorry you feel like that. Just do as Duke has asked, please, maybe then you'll understand." Glen explained.

"Right I will go then, piss off back to my stage ready for the puppet master to pull my strings again." Squid replied angry.

"Ok, go then. Call me as soon as you get back please?" said Glen.

"OK, don't want you all losing tabs on me do we?" Squid replied as he climbed in the Jag and headed back to Wellington.

Squid drives off west on the A303, he feels like a weight has been placed on his shoulders. As he settles back in the seat enjoying the drive he puts on the radio, ABBA are playing (Money-money-money.) Squid frowns as if someone was trying to tell him something and take the piss.

Twenty four hours later and the Ryan family are all sat around the TV together watching a special news broadcast about the robbery.

"This is it sweetheart hopefully it will all be over soon." Squid said as he turned to Jenny and gave her a hug.

"I am joined here as you can see by two security guards who are here to watch over the gold, making sure I don't slip the odd bar into my jacket pocket. Also with me is Detective Glen Maw who has been working on the missing Brinks Mat gold case for the last few years. With him is Oliver Ramsbottom who discovered the gold by accident I believe. Can I ask you Oliver, how did you feel when you discovered the missing gold it must have been quite a shock?" asked the News reader.

"Well yes it was. There's all this gold, it was weird. My car had broken down close by and I was walking to the petrol station further back along the road when I fell upon it." Oliver explains.

"And you Glen, you must be so pleased this case is solved" asked the news reader.

"As you correctly said, I had been working on the case for quite some time and then we got a fresh lead, so we knew it was somewhere on the A303. Then Oliver here broke down and everything seemed to fall into place very quickly." Glen explained.

"And there is a pun in the word fall there because am I right in thinking Oliver you actually fell through the roof of the van onto the gold?" asked the News reader.

"Yes that is correct. The roof which had obviously corroded over the years collapsed, taking me with it was a bit scary to be honest. There was a dead body in there, I am glad it's over." Oliver explained.

"It was then that the gruesome remains of Paddy O'Brian were discovered, a construction worker who was innocently caught up in the aftermath of the robbery. I also read in the papers, that Stuart Ryan the son of one of the original robbers has been working with you on this and that an undisclosed amount of money has been paid to Oliver here as a reward." said the News reader.

"I can't comment on what's written in the papers, but it is no secret there's always been a reward on the missing gold. I can confirm we had been getting very close to this hidden haul. This was down to several individuals who came forward with information. Oliver falling through the roof has just brought forward the closure of this case. I would also like to state that the full amount of missing gold has been recovered and the two cases of diamonds that were also stolen in the robbery were found alongside the bullion. Over the years this gold has been referred to as cursed and 'Fools Gold,' many people have had their lives ruined, family's torn apart and murdered. This case is now closed let this be an end to it all. When will people learn crime does not pay." Glen replied.

"Well there you have it. Finally after all these years the Brinks Mat bullion robbery case is closed. This is Mike Bussell for the BBC here outside Taunton Police Station in Somerset." said the news reader with his closing statement.

"Well this is weird, Jenny sweetheart did you know Ox's real name was Oliver Ramsbottom and how about this . . . he just happened to break down close to where the van was buried and fell through the roof." Squid announced.

A look of shock came across Jenny's face, she fidgeted nervously.

"Kids, upstairs with Sophie and sort out your rooms I need to talk to your father." Said Jenny. Sophie poked Penny in the ribs tickling her "Come on last one upstairs is a sissy!" She said as she made a head start on them.

"I need to tell you something it may explain some of this. I don't think it is coincidence that Ox was there." She said quietly.

"Really how's that?" asked Squid intrigued at what Jenny was going to come up with, however he wanted to stop her. Depending on what story she tells him it could make or break their marriage.

"Please don't be mad at me." but before she could finish Jenny started to cry.

"I am so sorry Squid, I should have told you long ago but I didn't want to lose you again." Jenny sobbed.

Squid took her in his arms. He knew what Duke had said was now the truth. She didn't need to explain, if it wasn't she would have lied by now and just shrugged it all off. But, she was clearly distressed about it all.

"Ssshhhhh, it doesn't matter. You and I live in each other's hearts remember?" Squid reassured her.

"Barbra Streisand woman in love, it took me ages to find out where you got that from. It matters Squid it really does, it matters for that very reason we do live in each other's hearts. There are things you should know, about my past, about Duke. Fuck, why now, everything was so good. Damn it!" Jenny sobbed holding on to Squid.

"I would like to think everything is still good. It's a right I defend right to the end . . . and Jen I know. There are some things I need to tell you also so stop beating yourself up, we're good. I am not mad at you." Squid replied.

"Stop quoting Barbra Streisand woman in love and making me cry you soppy git." Jenny sobbed.

"Listen to me sweetheart, I said I know." Squid repeated.

"I don't understand you know what? That I've lied to you all these years that Duke isn't just a scrap metal dealer? What do you know?" she asked trying to dry her eyes.

Squid steps back takes out a tissue and wipes her eyes he then kisses her on the forehead.

"It was me that fell through the roof of the van. Glen and I found it, but there is no reward money sweetheart, there never was. I discovered that night that my old friend Duke Smith has been manipulating my whole life. He told me about you and his boss Yoda, I don't know too much about what you were up to before we met and to be honest I don't want to. What he did do was explain to me that our meeting was down to fate and that ever since that day he hasn't been involved with you and that you wanted out right from the start. So stop fretting sweetheart we are ok." Squid explained.

"I see, this is real Squid, I do love you and give Duke a break he's a good man as are the other two Ox and Glen. I don't know much about what is going on with them with the Yoda thing but I feel even Yoda is a good man. It's just a gut feeling I have." Jenny explained.

Three weeks passed and Squid and Jenny did a lot of talking. They discussed their pasts both wanting to understand what the other had been through, and clear the path so that they could become even closer. But, neither were prepared for what was about to happen next. There was a knock on the door when Squid answered it he was asked to sign a recorded delivery letter from the post man.

"What is it?" asked Jenny

Squid tore open the large envelope, he stood there reading then he put his hand over his mouth and sat down.

"Well tell me, you look terrified!" Jenny said concerned at what was in the letter.

"Not terrified, shocked and a little confused. It's from Dukes solicitor it's his last will and testament. Apparently Duke passed away two weeks ago and has left everything to me, here look read for yourself." said Squid handing her the paperwork.

"It says we have to go for a meeting next week to sign things over, they're requesting I be there too and Sophie." Jenny replied.

"Ok well I don't care what this says but Dukes not dead. We would've been the first to know, Ox or Glen would have informed us. This is his way of saying don't be upset." Jenny explained.

"I agree, just more of him pulling our strings." Squid replied.

"Or cutting them sweetheart." Jenny said.

"So instead of a million quid reward money, it looks like we're getting a scrap yard." Squid said laughing to himself.

The two weeks flew by and Squid, Jenny and Sophie made the trip to London for the reading of Dukes will. As they sat on the A303 Squid pointed to where the security van was buried.

"So you are saying Uncle Duke is not really dead then Dad and this is all some sort of game." Sophie asked.

"We think Uncle Duke wanted a fresh start or uncomplicated retirement. We're just guessing at the moment, until the reading is done we're a little in the dark." Jenny replied.

"So he could be dead?" she replied.

"No, if that old bugger had died believe me we would know." Squid replied.

The drive took a little over three hours to reach the offices of Dean Bishop and French the solicitors dealing with Dukes estate. On arrival they were shown to a large room where a funny little thin balding man with glasses sat behind a desk.

"Henry French" he said introducing himself. They all shook hands and sat back down around a large desk.

"I am sure you want to get home, it is quite a drive from Somerset. You must be quite tired after your journey so shall we get straight on with the reading?" asked the little man.

"By all means, please do." replied Squid.

"Right, it seems Duke had a soft spot for your family Mr Ryan. I have trust funds here to the amount of four hundred thousand pounds to each of your children including you Sophie. None of which can be touched until they reach thirty." explained Henry whose reading was interrupted by sharp intakes of breath.

"If I may continue, Duke also had a collection of classic cars and to you Miss Sophie he leaves his 1976 XJ12 Coupe. If you could just sign here I can hand you the keys and relevant documents." Henry explained leaning over the desk with a pen and the paperwork. Sophie signed them and then sat back down with a beaming smile on her face.

"To you Mr & Mrs Ryan, Duke leaves the whole of his estate. A house in Loxwood which has a canal boat moored at the rear of the property and the remainder of his classic car collection. There's another property in Croydon and a scrap metal recycling plant which is an ongoing business in Croydon. There's three million pounds sterling which was in several different accounts found by my assistants. Oh yes a Sunseeker boat which is moored at Portland." Henry explained lifting his glasses to look at Squid.

"What!" replied Squid nearly falling of his chair.

"If you could just sign these relevant documents I will have the funds transferred into your account this afternoon." explained Henry.

"As for you Mrs Ryan, Duke asked me to pass you this." said Henry as he handed over a letter to her.

"That concludes our business here today, I'm sorry for your loss, but it seems Mr Smith thought very highly of you all." Henry explained as he shook their hands and escorted them to the door.

"Sorry I need to find a pub." Squid explained as the three entered the London street below the offices.

"Me too!" Jenny replied.

"Can we go get my car I really want to see it?" asked Sophie.

"So what do you think dead or alive?" asked Jenny as the three of them entered a Wetherspoons pub in Shepherds Bush for some food and a well needed drink.

"Alive for sure, open the letter see what it says?" replied Squid.

Jenny opened up the letter and sat there reading it. Inside was a card she handed it to Squid who showed it to Sophie.

"It's an invite to Dukes wake, a celebration of his life it says being put on by some Lord Lucas." Sophie replied.

Squid and Jenny look at each other and both reply with the same name.

"Yoda!" replied Squid and Jenny.

"Yoda, who the fuck's Yoda, you two have some really weird friends you know." Sophie replied.

"I think we should all drive to Loxwood and check out the house. Bet the canal boats my old one, and the fucking Sunseeker." says Squid smiling.

"I like the boat idea. Let's see if it is your old Sunseeker dad, let's go to Portland in stead." Sophie replied excitedly.

"Wouldn't surprise me in the slightest, but Loxwood is closer." Squid explained.

"Well mum and dad will be more than happy to look after the others tonight if we want to stay there the night. Come on I want to see what's there?" an excited Jenny replied.

Deciding it was a good idea the three headed off to Dukes old house in Loxwood. The drive took a little over an hour, turning into the drive they were confronted by a pair of large electric gates.

"I guess that is what this is for." said Jenny as she picked up the bunch of keys and pressed the large button on the plastic fob that was attached to them. Slowly the gates opened revealing another drive which went on for about quarter of a mile. At the end was a sharp left bend and as they drove round it they were faced with a rather large Tudor styled house. The courtyard to the house was large and had three other tracks going off to a number of other buildings.

"I hope it has a pool." said Sophie looking very excited.

"A gym would be nice too." Squid replied.

"Wow, just look at the size of the place Squid? Who'd of thought there was so much money in scrap metal." Jenny said as she opened the car door and stepped out onto the tarmacked surface.

"Well were not sure at this moment in time exactly how Duke made his money but I am sure all will be revealed soon." Squid replied.

Chapter Twelve

Yoda lowers his head as he walks into the charming old cottage called the Granary, Ox was close behind. It was in the isolated hamlet of Donadea near Clane in County Kildare. There was a small stone plaque to one side of the porch saying built 1752. It was the family home to the O'Brian family, Paddy O'Brian's sister and two brothers were the only members of the family still alive, their parents having passed away ten years ago. Yoda and Ox mingled amongst the other guests. There was a photo of Paddy O'Brian sat on an old oak table.

"Well you did it boss just like you promised, you brought him home to his family." Ox said patting Yoda on the back.

"I would have done it anyway, Squid didn't need to ask." Yoda replied.

"You have to understand he doesn't know you like the rest of us. You're a good man he will find this out. Do you think you have done right where Duke is concerned?" Ox asked.

"It was all going to Squid anyway, apart from you he's the only family I have. He's been like a son to me and it's time to retire, putting on that persona day in day out was becoming tiring. Duke has served his purpose over the years. Between us Ox we have achieved quite a lot. You should think about it yourself." Yoda replied.

"What retiring, then who'd have your back? Nah I am ok thank you. You've always made sure I have what I need and like you I am happy. I still worry for Jenny a little, she's come a long way. Do you think her and Squid will be ok with all that money?" Ox asked.

"They'll be fine, stop worrying. It's the right time for all this, none of us are getting any younger." Yoda replied.

A man and a woman walk up to the pair.

"I believe you are Lord Lucas, they say my brother was caught up in some bank job and that he was a bad un. Is it true, I need to know?" asked Mary who was Paddy's sister.

"He was never a violent person, Paddy, I don't understand why someone would have killed him like that." explained Peter who was one of Paddy's brothers.

"No . . . from what we've found out he was in the wrong place at the wrong time. He was just working on the road earning an honest wage. I have put a few words in the papers to explain don't worry he can rest in peace now. He's been totally vindicated from the Brinks Mat robbery and his killer is already dead." explained Yoda.

"He was a good man. Look out for the news reports coming out over the next week. They will be explaining what we know went on. I have been told by a police friend that Paddy's name will be totally cleared." Ox replied.

"Good, for years' people said he had run off with the gold and that he was the secret missing link. We always knew it was lies. If Paddy had ever come into that sort of money he would have shared it with his family. He was a hard worker and a simple man . . . that was Paddy." Mary explained.

"I have been told you have paid for all this, the funeral, the wake and a head stone. That's very generous of you but can I ask why?" Peter asked.

"I've followed the case for many years and have seen the devastation it has caused. Families torn apart. I suppose I just felt Paddy deserved something better. It's not much, but I just felt I could help that was all. You see I have a cousin in the force and he would often talk about the case. I do hope I haven't offended anyone? Yoda replied.

"No, it was very nice of you." replied Mary.

"A gentleman." replied Peter.

"Well we should be heading back boss." Ox suggested.

"Yes we've a long trip. It was nice to meet you all, a lovely service." Yoda replied as they shook hands with Paddy's family and left to head back to the mainland.

Yoda looked at the countryside as they drove back to the ferry.

"You know I don't understand why I've never been here before it is such a beautiful place. Remind me to look up properties when we get back. If I could get a place with a nice bit of land, dear old Squid could fly us over Ox." Yoda suggested.

"Now there's a plan." Ox replied.

A week went by and Squid was relaxing after a good workout in the gym when Jenny came in with a paper.

"Thought you might like to read this? It's all about that 'Paddy O'Brian' his funeral was last week and it just goes on to say how he had no involvement in the Brinks Mat thing. Nice for his family to have it all cleared up." Jenny said as she handed Squid the paper.

"I'm glad Yoda . . . Duke or Lord bloody Lucas or whatever else he wants to call himself has kept his word and made sure he was laid to rest properly." replied Squid.

"I've decided to sell the lingerie shop." Jenny announced as she sat down beside Squid on one of the exercise benches.

"Really, you loved that shop, why?" asked Squid.

"Well, mainly because we have enough money and I don't want to work anymore. Secondly the kids, I want to have fun enjoy them . . . maybe have another?" She suggested giving Squid a shove with her elbow.

"I must say this 'Inheritance!' Has changed everything it is quite hard coming to terms with the fact we don't need to work anymore." Squid replied throwing the paper down on the floor.

"So what now?" asked Jenny.

"I don't know but these last few nights I have been thinking. In fact it has been keeping me awake trying to work it all out but it all comes down to fate and what we want. So, I was thinking, remember that night we spent together back in 84, our last night together when you fell pregnant with Sophie?" Squid asked.

"Of cause, we had so many plans." Jenny replied thinking back to that night.

"Exactly, I wanted to be a pilot, you wanted the big house and six kids from what I can remember." said Squid as he moved and sat behind Jenny cuddling her in his arms.

"Cars, you wanted cars." Jenny replied.

"And you wanted to see the world." Squid said kissing her neck.

"Money, we both wanted money, to be comfortable and not have to worry." replied Jenny.

"And we both decide we didn't want our kids growing up to be criminals and follow in my father's footsteps. We wanted the best for them, I guess I failed that part where Sophie is concerned, she's seen too much that one." said Squid.

"That's not your fault or mine. We did what we had to do but we got through it Squid as a family and that was one of the things we wanted to be, a good strong family." Jenny explained.

"True, so I was thinking, when it's all put in black and white like this where do we go from here? Most of what we wanted we now have although we had to go the long way round to get it. So like I was saying, I think we should get this party thing come wake out of the way of Duke's and see what that throws up. Then let's take some time out and travel as a family, I can buy a plane and we can just fly from place to place, country to country. If we like a place we buy a house there so we can visit again and what better way to educate the kids than to let them see places instead of reading about them in some boring text book. What do you think? Squid asked excitedly.

"What like travel the world, America, Europe? We could go to Australia I always wanted to go there." Jenny said as she leant back and smiled at him.

"Well I think we should do it. There's been enough shit and we know more than most that life is just too short. And maybe somewhere along the line a couple more kids like you wanted." Squid said as he started to tickle her.

"Really, you don't mind?" replied Jenny as the two of them fell in a pile on the gym floor.

"Not at all Mrs Ryan, in fact I think I just might start practising now." he replied pulling off Jenny's top.

Chapter Thirteen

It was a warm summers evening in June of 2008 when Squid, Jenny and Sophie headed off to Yoda's house. As they drove they listened to the radio singing to the songs as they travelled, but they all fell silent when a song none of them had heard before started to play called Gold Bars and Jaguars, it was by a musician called Jules Winchester on the south coast of the UK.

"Shit dad, are you listening to the lyrics of this song it's weird like the writer knew about our past." Said Sophie singing the chorus. Jenny and Squid listened he raised an eyebrow as he drove and smiled at Jenny.

"Maybe it is some sort of Karma shit letting us know tonight is the end of the curse and our life's become ours." Jenny replied.

"I know one thing it's going to be strange knowing no one is pulling our strings anymore and whatever happens, happens and it's just fate. Explained Squid as the song finished and he pulled up outside the big mansion house. Jenny got out of the car she looked around.

"I recognise this place I've been here before years ago back in 84 after you had left." she said as she turned to face Squid. Looking around she sees the Blue Rolls Royce.

"That car it's Yoda's, I remember it being here I thought I was going to die that day." said Jenny as she took a firm grip of Squids arm.

"What, how?" asked Sophie stepping in front of her parents.

"We are safe to go in here aren't we? What happened here Mum?" Sophie asked looking nervous.

"Knowing what I know now it's not what I thought was happening. Some sort of charade to keep me in line I suspect." Jenny explained as she re-assured Sophie things were ok.

The three walked into the house where they were met by a young blonde woman, they were escorted to a large room full of people.

Squid noticed a picture of Duke sat on the table then he saw Ox walking towards them He was dressed as a vicar in a white collar and all the trimmings.

"What's this fancy dress Ox, nobody told me." Sophie said pulling his leg.

"So you're a vicar? That's weird!" Squid said looking him up and down.

"Seriously, don't tell me Yoda's the bloody Pope." Jenny replied.

"I told you all would be explained. Come and meet Lord Lucas. Your Lordship, our guests are all here now." Ox replied as he turned to the man standing behind him.

The smart dressed man turned around revealing himself as the person they had all known as Duke Smith, except instead of looking like Steptoe he look all of the eccentric British gentleman. Squid looked him up and down it felt really strange seeing Duke like this. He was wearing a waistcoat with a gold watch and held a dark cane in his hand which had silver top to it. The man's shoes were handmade Italian, he stank of wealth.

"Hello Squid, Jenny and of course my lovely Sophie, I am so glad you could come. I am guessing you have many questions, but first let Ox take you round and introduce you to some of the other guests. We will meet in the study after and then I will answer whatever questions you might have. For now mingle, Sophie why don't you walk with me there are some things I would like to discuss this you." Lord Lucas said in a very posh British accent, he held his hand out to Sophie.

"I am not sure I want you going anywhere with my daughter until I know more." Squid replied.

"It's ok Dad I am a big girl I can look after myself. Go I'll see you in a bit." Sophie replied.

Sophie and Lord Lucas walked off together leaving Jenny and Squid with Ox.

"Please don't worry she is very safe. In fact you're probably in the safest place you've both ever been in your lives." Ox explained.

"This is where you brought me in the boot of that Jag all those years ago isn't it?" asked Jenny.

"It is and even then you were safe. Come walk with me let me explain as we meet some of his Lordships friends." Ox said leading them off to another side of the room.

Sophie walked with Lord Lucas down a corridor into another large room. There were a few people in the room all around Sophie's age. To her left were some young men working on gym equipment and to her right some girls learning martial arts.

"I am confused Uncle Duke who are all these people? I don't even know what I should call you anymore, my whole life you've been there as Uncle Duke? Now Dad tells me people know you as "Yoda" and here you are in front of me as 'Lord Lucas.' Who are you? Sophie asked.

"My full, real name is Lord Humphrey James Lucas. I am as you can see a multimillionaire. Duke was a character I set up many years ago to make contact with a different class of people. It allowed me to deal with a different level of cliental and he was my eyes and ears to the criminal underworld. There's not much a scrap man doesn't know." Humphrey explained.

"So what do I call you now?" Sophie asked.

"Humphrey is fine my dear you will get used to it." he explained.

They wandered around the room. He smiled and acknowledged the people working in there.

"See that girl there her name is Christine. Twelve weeks ago she was on the streets of London, homeless, on drugs and selling her body to feed her habit. Now she lives here she's off drugs and is doing extremely well in turning her life around. She works for me now." Humphrey explained

"Works for you?" Sophie questioned.

"Yes as does Tom over there he's done wonders with his life in the last few months. He came to me in March. Ox brought him in close to deaths door the poor boy had tried to commit suicide, I'm sure he would have succeeded if it wasn't for Ox. He is now on his way to become one of my brightest students. He's an absolute whizz with computers it would have been such a waste." explained Humphrey.

"So what you run some sort of a refuge here?" replied Sophie.

"A refuge, I suppose we do to start with then we give them the choice of either leaving or staying on and working for us." Humphrey replied.

"So what is it you do here Humphrey? I mean it all looks a little weird. What is this some sort of secret society that goes around doing bank jobs and stuff? I know about the Brinks Mat haul dad told me." Sophie explains.

"There is a lot of corruption in the world Sophie it's a very unfair place. There is also a lot of bad money around, gold, diamonds even property these days, you would be amazed at what an office block in London is worth these days. Then you have the companies running those businesses and how they deal in the worlds markets, what commodities they are into. Then of course once you know what they are dealing with, whether it is stocks and shares, Gold, Diamonds or cash, it has to be moved. It is in this moving process where companies are most vulnerable, whether it's a click on a computer or a raid on a warehouse full of Gold bullion." Humphrey explains as he and Sophie wander around the house moving into another room.

The room was full of the very latest computer equipment and there was a bunch of mixed age and race people sat at desks working them.

"You see my dear what looks like a very legit business is very often very corrupt. The same as people, just look at Tony Blair." Humphrey said as they moved on to the next room.

"You see Sophie we steal from the scum of this world and when I say scum I mean dodgy governments, companies and people. We do something good with the money and we take some of cause for ourselves to cover our running costs, wages and investment. After all we all want nice things don't we?" he said leading Sophie up a flight of stairs.

As they walk along another corridor a young lady comes out of the room she is dressed very sexily.

"Hi Humphrey, I'll see you later I hope?" said the woman as she walked passed the two, she winked at Humphrey who turned slightly slapping her on the bottom as she walked past.

"Uncle Duke . . . I mean Humphrey really, she's old enough to be your granddaughter." Sophie said a little disgusted.

"Like I said we all like nice things Sophie, I like beautiful women." Humphrey explained.

"Young beautiful women I see." Sophie replied.

"No one here Sophie does anything they don't want to do, the doors are always open. It hasn't done Heff any harm." Humphrey replied smiling to himself.

"So what you are telling me that you're some sort of Robin Hood, stealing from the bad guys and doing good with it, whilst you live some playboy life style?" Sophie asked.

"Exactly, I couldn't have put it better myself." Humphrey replied giving Sophie a hug.

"So why are you showing me all this?" she asked.

"Because Sophie you are young and I am not getting any younger. You are a good person, your father and mother have brought you up well. I know you have seen the other side of people, the greed and corruption that infects every country on the planet." Humphrey explained.

"Good, even I have done bad things Uncle you don't know what I am capable of." Sophie replied.

"Ah but I do, I know about Morris Sophie, but you can't say that makes you a bad person. You did what had to be done, as have I and Ox. That's why we need fresh young blood in our organisation someone who can see things for what they are.

Death is just part of the cycle of life. Take Christine, it seems the man who was dealing her drugs was a drug addict himself. He was supplied by another drug addict who was supplied by a very wealthy man who ran a day care centre for single mums. Whilst they took advantage of his cheap day care rates he took advantage of them, drugs and loans. He wasn't a nice man. Then one day his bank account got hacked and he lost everything, he drove his car over a cliff one night apparently high on drugs himself." Humphrey explained.

"I see, so you are offering me a job?" Sophie replied.

"Not just a job Sophie, a legacy. Like I said I am not getting any younger, your parents have been through enough so I don't want to involve them but you're family. I think you could carry on with this once the likes of me and Ox are long gone." Humphrey replied.

"I see." said Sophie.

"Time to get you back to your mum and dad, you know where I am should you want to discuss thing further, think about my offer. Do you like the Jaguar?" Humphrey asked.

"Love it Uncle Duke . . . I mean Humphrey, thank you." Sophie replied.

"Best not mention our little chat to mum and dad they may not understand. They've been through a lot over the years." Humphrey explained.

Sophie smiled and nodded to Humphrey as they entered the room down stairs where Squid and Jenny were still busy talking to people. Glen Maw walks up behind Squid and pats him on the back.

"Glad to see you could make it, nice to see both of you, where's Sophie?" he asked.

"Hello, nice to see you too . . . she's . . . " Squid replied as he got interrupted by Sophie.

"I'm here Humphrey's been showing me the house, it's massive!" she replied.

"So Squid what do you think?" asked Humphrey.

"I think I owe you an apology and you Glen, we understand now. We have been talking to some of the people you've helped over the years. I'm sorry, I never knew." Squid replied.

"It's been a long journey for you all, that's why Duke wanted you to be able to have some fun now and enjoy life. You're good people, I am certain you won't waste it." Humphrey explained.

"So . . . Humphrey, you never struck me as a Humphrey, kept that quite didn't you." Squid said jokingly.

They all had a chuckle at Dukes new name. Humphrey put his hand in his pocket and pulled out two keys and handed them to Jenny and Sophie.

"I thought you'd like your own rooms. Squid, Jenny you are in the bridal suite it's on the top floor. Sophie I've given you the room with the sunken spar bath, thought you might like to relax come the end of the evening." Humphrey explained handing them the keys.

"Thank you, I just might retire early this evening" said Squid as he pulled Jenny in and kissed her.

Humphrey smiled at them he turned to Squid and said in the voice of Duke Smith "You're still pussy pissed after all these years."

So there you have it my story. Do I still look over my shoulder YES! Just not as often. Has the curse gone YES! But, I still remain vigilant. Are Jenny and I still together? By some miracle YES! We are all doing well, Sophie got her pilots license and spread her wings and flew the nest. I miss her. Out of all the kids our bond is the closest, but then it would be wouldn't it. She calls regularly and pops in when she can. If we're out of the country she will often meet us somewhere and stay for a few days, but she's all grown up now and making her own path in life. Every so often a reminder pops up. Peter Dimond still trying to convince people he flew Asil Nadir out of the country even though the two fell out. Then there was Asil Nadir coming back to the UK and getting banged up, seems he was a crook after all. Compton Abbas Airfield still there for family days out and a lovely meal, just the next generation doing stuff now, it seems I am retired now. Then there is still the story of missing Brinks Mat gold, a story started no doubt by Lord Lucas apparently once in police custody hundreds of bars disappeared, this time without a curse attached to them. Jenny and I now have the six children we always wanted, so things are good, touch wood what could possibly go wrong . . .

Feb 19th 2013

Sophie shuts off the engines on her King Air 350i walking to the back she opens the door. As it opens she tucks a gun into the back of her jeans. She waits patiently as a black car heads towards her on the deserted disused airfield. Her phone rings, she looks at the screen it says 'Dad' she answers it.

"Hi Dad, look I am a little busy at the moment can I call you back later. May be meet up at Compton Abbas next Friday, I have to deliver something for some body." she explained and then hung up placing the phone back in her pocket.

"She hung up on me, said she's busy." Squid said looking across at Jenny.

"Well I expect she is, she'll call you later. You know how busy she is these days. Here read the paper." Jenny replied handing Squid a copy of the Daily Mail.

Squid opens the paper he reads the head line and his eyes widen.

"Have you seen the paper, did you read this?" asked Squid.

"No it's only just come, why?" asked Jenny.

"It says here "*On Feb.18th, 2013, eight gunmen cut a fence around Brussels airport, drove onto the tarmac where an armoured car was transferring the gems worth £32 M onto a Zurich-bound airplane and drove off again with the loot.*" Squid read to her he looked very concerned.

"Brussels. That's where Sophie said she was going." Jenny replied.

THE END . . . ?

www.ingramcontent.com/pod-product-compliance
Lightning Source LLC
Chambersburg PA
CBHW030920120626

46554CB00001B/218